CRYING LAUGHING

ALSO BY LANCE RUBIN

Denton Little's Deathdate

Denton Little's Still Not Dead

CRYING LAUGHING

LANCE RUBIN

EMBER

For Dad, for Mom, and for Katie

Text copyright © 2019 by Lance Rubin
Cover art: emoji copyright © 2019 by Apple, Inc.

All rights reserved. Published in the United States by Ember, an imprint of Random House Children's Books, a division of Penguin Random House LLC, New York. Originally published in hardcover in the United States by Alfred A. Knopf, an imprint of Random House Children's Books, a division of Penguin Random House LLC, New York, in 2019.

Ember and the E colophon are registered trademarks of Penguin Random House LLC.

Visit us on the Web! GetUnderlined.com

Educators and librarians, for a variety of teaching tools, visit us at RHTeachersLibrarians.com

Library of Congress Cataloging-in-Publication Data is available upon request.
ISBN 978-0-525-64467-5 (trade) — ISBN 978-0-525-64468-2 (lib. bdg.) — ISBN 978-0-525-64469-9 (ebook) — ISBN 978-0-525-64470-5 (pbk.)

Printed in the United States of America
10 9 8 7 6 5 4 3 2 1
First Ember Edition 2021

Real humor does not come from sacrificing the reality of a moment in order to crack a cheap joke, but in finding the joke in the reality of the moment.
—*Truth in Comedy, The Manual of Improvisation*
Charna Halpern, Del Close,
and Kim "Howard" Johnson

Laughing and crying, you know it's the same release.
—Joni Mitchell

I am big enough to admit that I am often inspired by myself.
—Leslie Knope

1

No one knows how funny I am.

Well, that's not entirely true. My dad, and sometimes my mom, and my best friends, Leili and Azadeh, know.

And *I* know.

But no one else.

Definitely no one in school, where successful humor tends to involve farts.

I'm not knocking fart humor, but I recognize it is but one color in the comedy rainbow. For many people at my school, however, it is one of just three primary comedy colors, the other two being sex humor (e.g., pretend-humping in the hallway) and mean humor (e.g., pulling away someone's chair as they sit down), which isn't even humor so much as an excuse to be an asshole.

Anyway, if a joke falls in the forest and no one's there to hear it, it does not make a sound, so sometime in the middle of last year, I stopped saying my funny thoughts aloud. It's like giving your finest, most expensive jewelry to your hamster. Guess what? That hamster does not give a flying eff about carats.

(He might, however, care a great deal about carrots.)

(Ha-cha!)

(I'm sorry. I am aware puns are, in many ways, no better than fart jokes, but there's a long tradition of really smart comedy writers appreciating puns in a manner that is half ironic, half sincere—and that is the way I appreciate them.)

So, yeah, when it comes to my sense of humor, most of the people in school are hamsters, which is why it's incredibly surprising that just now, on the second day of my sophomore year, I seem to have made Evan Miller laugh.

"Ha, that's hilarious," he says, standing next to me, our lunch trays balanced on the metal rack of the cafeteria line, as his less sophisticated friend Tim Stabisch looks on like *Wait, seriously? Was it?*

I should mention: Evan Miller is, by many accounts (not mine), the funniest guy in school. He's a junior, and though our interactions have been minimal, I've had quite a bit of time to become familiar with his comedic stylings, as I assistant-directed last year's production of *Arsenic and Old Lace,* in which Evan played the brother who believes he's Teddy Roosevelt and is always maniacally charging up the stairs of the house. And yes, Evan was truly hilarious in that play, mainly because he was so confident and committed to the role. As my dad has said, "The secret to being successful in comedy is confidence. That's, like, ninety percent of it right there." And Evan Miller has that, so I understand why his comedic reputation has soared.

Now, does he possess the other ten percent of the formula, which includes having a smart, interesting perspective on the world around him? Not so much.

Though it's possible I've underestimated him, because he did just laugh at the thing I said moments ago (which was not a pun or a fart joke). I was standing in the lunch line by myself when this happened:

EVAN (next to me in line the whole time, though I hadn't acknowledged him because I assumed he had no idea who I was): Hey, you worked on the play last year, right?

ME: I did.

EVAN: Winnie, right?

ME (surprised he knows my name): Oh. Yeah. And you're . . . (I pretend I don't know his name, I have no idea why.)

EVAN (slightly disappointed): Evan.

ME: Right! Evan, yeah. You were really funny in the play. (I felt bad that I'd pretended not to know his name, which is why I gave him a compliment.)

EVAN (perking up again): Oh, thanks! (inexplicably going into stereotypical California girl voice) That's, like, totally cool of you to say.

ME (unconvincingly): Ha.

PEARL THE LUNCH LADY (to me): Chicken or vegetable?

ME: Wait, what is it?

PEARL: Stir-fry. Chicken or vegetable.

ME: Oh. Chicken, please.

(PEARL slops stir-fry onto my tray.)

ME: Thanks. (looking to Evan) She and I go way back, that's why she hooks me up with the good stuff.

EVAN (laughing): Ha, that's hilarious.

TIM: Huh?

And there you have it. Evan is laughing at something I said. I don't even know why I said it.

Tim, trying his best to keep up, asks, "Wait, did she just give you extra chicken?"

"Yes," I say, even though she obviously gave me the same amount she gives everyone. "But don't feel bad, that's only because we were platoon mates in Vietnam. I saved her life. Twice."

Evan laughs harder, and Tim is more confused. "I want extra chicken too," he says. "They never give enough."

"You're really funny," Evan tells me. "You should join Improv Troupe. We always need new funny people."

This catches me off guard. I mean, he's right—I saw the improv troupe perform a couple of times last year and they could probably use my help—but it's a foreign and delightful feeling to have someone who isn't me recognize that. Unfortunately, I retired from performing two and a half years ago after a traumatic incident at my bat mitzvah. Nevertheless, I'm flattered.

"Oh yeah," I say. "Maybe."

"First meeting of the year is tomorrow. After school."

Pearl, back from replacing an empty serving dish, asks Evan, "Chicken or vegetable?" He opts for vegetable, which surprises me, then turns back to me as I'm grabbing a rice pudding and walking away. "Seriously, think about it. You'll have even more fun than you did in Nam!"

"That's not possible," I say. "Nam was a blast."

Evan cracks up harder, and I try to hide my smile.

Maybe I *should* join Improv Troupe.

2

"Howdy, pardners!" I say as I approach the table where Leili, Azadeh, and Azadeh's field hockey friend, Roxanne, are sitting.

"Howdy to you too," Azadeh says, popping a grape into her mouth. "What was going on over there with Evan Miller?"

My face gets hot. Neither of the twins is one to dance around the truth, but Azadeh has a slight edge in the candor department.

"Geez, at least let the girl sit down first," Roxanne says. She's an inherently cool person. (See also: shiny stud in nostril, pink streaks in hair.)

"Okay," Azadeh says. She patiently waits as I sit down next to her. "Now, what was going on—"

"Wait," I say, getting up from my seat. "I forgot to get ketchup."

"Come on!" Azadeh throws her hands in the air as Leili and Roxanne laugh.

"Just kidding." I sit back down.

"Now you should actually tell us," Leili says, her perfect eyebrows slightly angled in that jokingly stern way. "We only caught the end, when he was laughing like you'd invented the first joke."

I can't help but smile and I'm sure I'm blushing like a doofus.

Who actually did invent the first joke? And what was it? That seems like something I should know.

"Seriously," Azadeh says. "If it's that effective, I want to borrow what you said to use on other people."

"*Rowr*," Roxanne says, pawing the air like a leopard.

Leili throws Azadeh a curious glance. "Anyone in particular?" she asks.

"No, Lay, no need to be protective. It would just be a general addition to my seduction repertoire."

"Ha," Roxanne says. "Seduction repertoire."

"I'm supposed to be protective," Leili says. "I'm many seconds older than you."

"Yeah yeah, blah blah," Azadeh says, affectionately rolling her eyes.

Azadeh and Leili Kazemi are identical twins, but I've known them since third grade, so it's really easy for me to tell them apart. Azadeh's nose and chin are slightly rounder than Leili's; that's the main giveaway. Also her eyebrows are slightly shaggier than Leili's. Also Leili usually wears a solid-colored hijab, and Azadeh usually wears a patterned one. But really, if you spend more than three minutes with them, it's just obvious. I'm always shocked and offended on their behalf when people can't tell the difference.

"Okay, just to clarify," I say, "I was not *seducing* Evan Miller. But, for those interested, he laughed because I said this thing about how Pearl the lunch lady and I fought in the Vietnam War together." All three of them stare at me blankly.

"Wait, what?" Leili asks.

"It's . . . It was a context-specific joke!" I say. "You would have laughed if you had the full setup leading into the punch line."

"You're so funny," Leili laughs. I know she's amused for the wrong reasons, but I'll take it.

"Hmm, yeah," Azadeh says. "I don't think I'll be putting that in the repertoire. So we were arguing for no reason, Lay."

"We weren't arguing," Leili says.

"You were kind of arguing," Roxanne says.

I take a bite of my chicken stir-fry. It's not as good as I want it to be, but eating with a spork more than makes up for that. I don't understand why we as a society have limited ourselves to the disposable version. Stainless steel sporks, people! Think how much easier it'd be to set the table!

"I heard Mrs. Tanaka is giving a pop quiz today," Leili says, taking a huge bite out of an apple.

"On what?" Azadeh asks. "It's the second day of school!"

"Apparently it's easy," Leili says, "just a keep-you-on-your-toes kind of thing."

"But what is—" Azadeh starts saying before I cut her off.

"Hey, Evan said I should join the improv troupe." Speaking over friends is not what I'm usually about, but I feel like that was a premature subject change. Also, quiz talk makes me anxious.

"Oh wow, really?" Leili says. She's already in the improv troupe and, if the two performances I saw last year are any indication, one of the best improvisers. But that's Leili; she's good at everything she does. And she's in, like, almost every extracurricular group. (You think I'm exaggerating. I am. But also not really.)

"Interesting," Azadeh says. She is definitely *not* in the improv

7

troupe. Though she's a hilarious person, she hates performing or speaking in front of people (and unlike me, she's *always* hated it). I've seen her do a bunch of class presentations over the years, and it's the cutest thing ever: she morphs into a different person, her voice robotic, her face expressionless, her gaze rooted awkwardly to some indistinct spot at the back of the classroom. Pretty much the opposite of how she is the rest of the time.

"Is that so surprising?" I ask.

"No, of course not," Leili says. "Oz and I used to tell you, like, three times a week to join, but then you made us promise to stop asking!"

"Well, yeah, because my performing days are over."

"Right, exactly, so that's why I'm surprised you're bringing it up."

"*I* didn't bring it up," I say, "he did!"

"You know," Azadeh says, "I just heard he and Jess Yang broke up a couple of weeks before school started."

I didn't know she and Evan had been dating. I try not to waste brain cells paying attention to things like that. Jess Yang is the crown jewel of Manatawkin High School's drama department. In that production of *Arsenic and Old Lace,* Jess played the young, pretty fiancée, one of those bland, bullshit female roles men have been writing since the caveman days. She's a good actor, but she wouldn't know comedy if it starfish-suctioned itself to her face.

"Ohhhh," Leili says. "I was wondering why Jess's Instagram feed had gotten so cryptic and weird lately."

"Yeah, that's why," Azadeh says.

"Instagram blows," Roxanne says.

"What are you suggesting?" I ask. "That Evan only asked

8

me to join the improv troupe because he was flirting with me now that he's single?"

"No, no," Azadeh nearly shouts. "But, yeah, maybe that was a small, tiny, little part of the reason."

The idea that Evan Miller would be flirting with me is annoying but also flattering. Guys don't usually flirt with me. Or, at least, the ones I am hoping will flirt with me never do. Not that I put Evan in the category of hope-will-flirts. He's more of a neutral-will-flirt. Which is still an improvement over the please-don't-flirts.

"He can get it," Roxanne says.

"Ew," Azadeh says.

"Well, anyway," I say, "performing isn't really my thing anymore—"

"So you bombed at your bat mitzvah, big deal," Azadeh says.

"Yeah," Leili says, "you need to let that go already."

"Wait, what happened?" Roxanne asks.

The phrase *bombed at your bat mitzvah* should have come with a trigger warning, as hearing it threatens to send me into the fetal position on the cafeteria floor. I take a deep breath.

"Evan's right," Leili says, kindly ignoring Roxanne. "You should join. You're really funny and you'll be great and you're more obsessed with comedy than any human I've ever met."

She makes a lot of good points.

"And I'll be there too," she continues, one hand in front of her mouth to shield us from her apple-chomping, "so you don't have to be nervous."

"I'll think about it," I say.

"You really are funny," Roxanne says, which makes her even cooler than I already thought she was.

"And we're, like, the only people who know that," Azadeh

9

says as she peels off a piece of Polly-O string cheese. "More people should know."

"Well, of course they should," I say.

Azadeh, Leili, and Roxanne laugh.

I knew that line would kill.

3

So, of course I spend the rest of the school day—minus the part where I'm taking Mrs. Tanaka's chemistry pop quiz, which, FYI, is much harder than Leili made it sound—thinking about the possibility of joining the improv troupe. I've broken it down as such:

PROS
    1. I will be a part of a group whose main purpose is to be funny. Seeing as that is my life aspiration *and* my life philosophy *and* maybe the one thing I'm actually good at, I will love being a part of this group.
    2. I will be doing improv, just like two of my all-time heroes, Amy Poehler and Tina Fey.
    3. More time with Leili, who I hardly get to hang out with (see: heretofore-mentioned extracurriculars).
    4. It's run by Mr. Martinez, who is twenty-four and joined the faculty last year as an English teacher. Leili is a little bit in love with him, and though I find her crush unsettling, I also know she's a strong judge of character.

5. They might have snacks at rehearsals. (I remember Leili mentioning once that Mr. Martinez brought gummy worms.)

CONS

1. The idea of performing in front of people is nauseating, and I promised myself I would never ever do it again.

The pros outnumber the cons, but that one con is very *convincing*. (Sorry.)

I do know that once I tell my dad, I'll probably have more clarity on all this. Russ Arthur Friedman is the funniest person I know and my biggest fan. He's the one who got me into comedy in the first place, showing me old Abbott and Costello routines (they're the guys who did "Who's on First?" and if you don't know what that is, you need to google it, like, right now) and *I Love Lucy* instead of *Sesame Street* and *Dora the Explorer*. My dad used to be an actor and a comedian, but he gave all that up when I was born so he could be the stay-at-home parent. By that point, my mom, Dana Melissa Teich Friedman, was the main moneymaker, with a high-powered marketing job. When she and my dad met in college, she'd been an actor like him, but she'd abandoned that to get her MBA. ("We shouldn't *both* have impossible creative dreams," she'd apparently said. She's a very pragmatic person.)

Anyway, one of my earliest memories is sitting on the couch with my dad watching Lucille Ball advertise Vitameatavegamin ("It's so tasty, too!") and being highly alarmed that he couldn't breathe. It turned out he was laughing, but I had no idea what the hell was happening. He saw how alarmed I was, and that made him laugh harder, which made me start crying. "No, Win, I'm happy," he said. "I'm laughing." Which flicked on a lightbulb in my three-year-old brain, and I started laughing too. It's kind of funny, when you think about it, that my first memory of comedy didn't involve laughing at the comedian, but at someone else's laughter. There's some deep philosophical wisdom there, though I have no idea what it is.

I know my dad will be into the idea of me joining the improv troupe—he's always saying the Bat Mitzvah Incident is worse in my head than it actually was in person (untrue) and that I should give performing another try—so I guess it's not clarity I'm looking for so much as the look of approval when I tell him. The huge smile that lights up his face will be the last push I need to get over the crippling doubt lodged in my stomach like the sword in the stone. Dad is the only one who can pull it out. I'm sure of this.

It's only after I get off the bus, make the six-minute walk home, and find the front door locked and garage door closed that I remember it's Wednesday, one of Dad's class days. When I was still little, he started teaching theater and playwriting to children aged four to seven at a local kids' gym called Tumble 'n' Play. He'd gotten a bit stir-crazy taking care of me every day, and this was supposed to "scratch the ol' performing itch." It was only a couple of classes a week at first, me at home with an old lady babysitter named Irene. (I've seen pictures; she looks deranged. I can't believe Mom and Dad were okay leaving me with her.) By the time I started going to preschool, though, Dad's classes had gotten more and more popular (because he's amazing), and over time, he's expanded to doing about ten a week. The kids freaking love him, which is no surprise; he bounces around and does funny voices and regularly blows their minds by revealing to them the depths of their own creative powers. I took his class all four years I could, and I felt so lucky. I knew how jealous the other kids must have been that Mr. Russ wasn't just my teacher, *he was my dad*.

I'm disappointed I now have to wait to talk to him, but I will never argue with having the house to myself. I grab a bag of Fudge Stripes from the pantry, crack open a Cran-Raspberry LaCroix, and sit at the kitchen table, where I take out my phone and turn on an old episode of *2 Dope Queens*. By the time I saw one of their HBO specials and became obsessed with them, the podcast had already ended. But listening my way through the archive of past episodes has become my favorite thing. Jessica Williams and Phoebe Robinson have the best chemistry. Like, you can tell they're actually close friends, which is part of what makes them so hilarious to listen to. I keep telling Leili and Azadeh we should start a podcast. I haven't convinced them yet.

I shove cookies in my mouth and laugh at Phoebe referencing her U2 obsession for the billionth time, and before I know it, I've listened to two episodes, and it's four-thirty. I should probably dig into some of my homework—my English teacher, Mr. Novack, just assigned this book called *Tess of the d'Urbervilles,* which doesn't seem funny *at all*—but first I grab the new *New Yorker* off the counter and flip to the contents page so I can see who wrote this week's "Shouts & Murmurs." My heart does a little leap. It's a Megan Amram! She wrote for *Parks and Recreation,* and then *The Good Place,* and she's amazing on Twitter, and her pieces are some of the only ones that get me LOLing. This week's, about the president shopping on Amazon, is no exception. She makes it seem so easy, but I know it's not; I've been working for over a year now on a piece about how depressing it is to be a pizza box. Dad read a draft and said that though it wasn't quite there yet, it did make him feel very bad for pizza boxes. So that's something, I guess.

I suddenly remember the ideas I daydreamed up during US history for my *Parks and Rec* script, so I open my laptop. In my episode, Leslie Knope has a new friend who she really likes in real life but absolutely despises on social media (this may or may not be based on a girl I know from summer camp) (Rebekah Turteltaub). Obviously I'm not going to be able to do anything with it professionally—*Parks and Rec* has been off the air for a while now—I'm just trying to build my chops. If you're going to be a comedy writer for TV, you have to learn to adapt to different voices. You should read my *I Love Lucy* spec script, where Lucy goes to Costco for the first time.

I'm so immersed in the scene I'm writing (an argument between Leslie and Ben about whether or not it's okay to unlike a pic after accidentally liking it) that I don't hear that my parents are home until they're in the kitchen with me.

"Hey," my mom says, holding a plastic bag, my dad trailing behind her. A peek at the microwave tells me it's 6:05, which makes sense for Dad, but not Mom, who usually isn't home on weeknights till at least seven. "We brought dinner from Valeria's."

"Whoa, nice!" Mexican from Valeria's is even more delicious when it's unexpected. "They let you out of work way early."

"Oh," Mom says, glancing at Dad, then back at me. "Yeah. I wrapped up everything I needed to do earlier than usual."

"Sweet! You guys never get home at the same time."

15

Mom again shoots Dad a look I can't decipher, but he's not paying attention, instead peering down at the junk mail on the counter as if he's never seen a more fascinating stack of documents.

"You okay, Skipper?" I ask. It's one of my nicknames for him. I don't remember how it started.

He doesn't respond.

"Russ," Mom says. "Win's asking you a question."

"Hey!" Dad says, jolting back to attention. "Sorry. I'm great. Super. Splendid. How're you, Banana?" One of his nicknames for me. For a few months of my toddlerhood, it was the only food I would eat.

"Also splendid. I actually am—"

"Win, would you mind grabbing us some silverware?" Mom interrupts. I don't even think she means to, but she has a propensity for buzz-killing.

"Sure," I say, trying not to seem as peeved as I am. "I will grab that silverware good."

"Thanks," Mom says as she takes off her long brown jacket and drapes it over one of the stools near the counter. "And plates."

"And if you wouldn't mind building us a new table while you're at it," Dad says, "that'd be great."

"No prob." I smile, closing the silverware drawer with my hip and carrying forks and knives to the table (this is an instance where having sporks wouldn't make much of a difference). "I'll actually build you a whole new kitchen."

"Oh, wonderful, thanks," Dad says, standing at the counter filling glasses of water from the Brita.

"I'm not sure what you're talking about," Mom says, "but it sounds mean." She doesn't always get our jokes.

16

"It's not, it's actually incredibly generous. Winnie's offered to build us not only a new table but an entirely new kitchen."

"Hardy har," Mom says, "because it's so hard to help set the table." She unpacks the to-go containers, identifying each one and steering it to its rightful spot. I grab the plates. "We got you chicken mole tacos, Win. Hope that's all right."

"Of course it's all right!" I'd be pissed if they hadn't. "Thanks, Mom." As Dad sets down the last water-filled glass, I take my usual seat, transferring my tacos from container to plate with zero sauce spillage (I'm a freaking all-star).

Dad sits down next, and I'm thrown for a moment as I notice how tightly he grips the back of the chair, how much concentration he's applying to the simple act of sitting down. Dad's had some weird health stuff going on over the past year—a hoarse voice, tingly hands, stiff legs—but he and Mom went to a neurologist this summer who said it wasn't anything to be that worried about, which was a huge relief. Something about Dad just now does seem concerning, though.

"Didn't your parents ever teach you it's not nice to stare?" Dad asks, and I look away, trying to play it off like I'd just been zoning out. I run my fingers through my hair to put it into a ponytail, but I don't have a hair tie on me.

"Guess they never got around to that one," I say, letting go of my hair.

"Shame on them."

"All right," Mom says as she sits. "Let us eat."

I stare down at my tacos—they're stunning—and get ready to hit my parents with the Improv Troupe news.

"Could you pass the beans, Russ?" Mom asks, gesturing to the family-style aluminum container practically overflowing with them.

I'm tempted to make some kind of fart joke—and if that's not an indication that I'm feeling loose and in a good mood, I don't know what is—but I decide to stay on course. "So, I actually have some interesting news."

"Ooh la la," Dad says, a second before the wobbly aluminum tin of black beans topples off his palms and lands upside down on the table. "Shit," he says. Bean juice seeps out from under the sides.

"Russ," Mom hisses under her breath, as if he'd doused the table with beans intentionally. She gets up with a huff and grabs an entire roll of paper towels from the counter.

"Guess I spilled the beans," Dad says, somewhat sheepishly.

I laugh. Mom doesn't.

"Sorry," he adds.

"It's fine." Mom scoops up handfuls of beans with a paper towel.

"I'll take one," I say, reaching across the table for the roll.

"No, it's fine, I got it," Mom says, seeming angrier than the situation demands. She overreacts sometimes. I guess part of why she's angry is that Dad has dropped a couple of things recently—carton of OJ, pint of Ben & Jerry's—but so what?

"So this is how it's gonna be?" Mom says to Dad without looking at him.

Dad looks down at the table, then back at her.

"People spill things sometimes, Mom," I say, jumping to his defense because come on, lady. "I think we're gonna survive."

"How many things have to happen before you decide it's worth telling her?" Mom asks.

Dad is smiling and shaking his head, more defensive than amused, and it suddenly feels like this is about more than beans.

"Tell who? Me?" I ask. "Tell me what?"

"Well, obviously I'll be telling her now," Dad says, "thanks to that graceful setup."

"She needs to know what's happening, Russ." *What's happening?* "This isn't a joke."

"I know that, Dana. I'm the one living it," Dad says. "I just wanted to . . ." He looks at me, sighs, and smiles. "So, Win . . . Sorry to be speaking so cryptically in front of you . . . I, uh . . . Well, you remember I went to that new neurologist right before you went to camp . . ."

"Yeah," I say, the only word I can muster as a cloud of dread inches forward above us, blocking out the kitchen light.

"Right. So, I actually . . . It seems like I have some kind of neurodegenerative disease."

"Okay," I say, not at all sure what to make of that.

"And it's possible, though not definite, that I might . . ."

"Just tell her, Russ," Mom says.

"That it might be ALS," he says. "I might have ALS."

4

"What do you mean *might*?" I ask.

It's hard to know how to react because, gotta be honest, other than knowing it's bad enough to inspire hundreds of thousands of people to pour buckets of ice water over their heads, I'm not entirely sure what ALS is.

"It means I *could* have it, but it's not definite," Dad says, totally straight-faced. "That's what the word *might* means." He breaks into a smile.

"Russ," Mom says, cocking her head to the side disapprovingly, hair swinging down below her shoulder.

But the fact that he's able to joke is an immense relief to me, pulling me back from whatever abyss I might have been tempted to stare down into.

"Sorry, sorry," Dad says. "I say *might* because ALS can only be diagnosed by ruling out everything else it could be."

"Have they ruled out everything else it could be?" I ask.

"I mean," Dad says, lifting and dropping his shoulders, "more or less. But." He stares down at his burrito.

"Dr. Yu sounded pretty sure about it, Russ," Mom says before looking back at me. "We just had another appointment today. In the city."

"Oh," I say. "Today?"

"That's the real reason I'm home early."

"Wait, I don't get it. How long have you guys known Dad might have ALS? Did you just find out today? Because right before I left for camp you had that appointment where the doctor said it was nothing to worry about."

Mom and Dad are silent. Mom takes an aggressive sip of water.

"Yeah," Dad says, sounding genuinely guilty, "that's not actually what the neurologist said at that appointment."

My jaw drops, the defining feature of my *What?!* face. I've always believed the only lies that are okay are the ones that end in a surprise party. And even those are kind of sketchy.

"I know, I know." Dad runs a hand through his hair. "I'm sorry we misled you, but we definitely didn't know for sure, and we didn't want it to ruin your fun."

I can't believe this. I always tell him pretty much everything, and he can't even be honest about a serious disease he might have?

"I'm sorry we didn't tell you sooner," he says. "It's my fault, Mom's wanted to tell you for a while."

Mom nods, like *Hell yeah I have.*

My brain can't catch up to the present moment, doesn't know how to process it. Should I be scared? Should I be upset? Should I be angry that they've been keeping this from me?

For simplicity's sake, I go with Option C.

"I mean, you should have told me either way," I say.

Mom lifts her eyebrows at Dad, like *Told you so.*

"I know," Dad says. "I really am sorry. But, in my defense, you haven't been completely in the dark. You've known I've been going to doctors this whole past year, trying to figure out what was going on . . ."

"Yeah, but . . ." He has a point. I have known that. It was

Hanukkah almost a year ago when Dad found himself struggling to light a match to get the menorah going.

"Need help, big guy?" Mom had asked.

"I got this," Dad had laughed. But he couldn't strike the match strongly enough to make a flame.

"Come on, let me try," Mom finally said, easily getting the match lit, much to our collective dismay.

"I think I did something to it playing basketball," Dad said, flexing his hand and staring at it, as if it were an old pal who had betrayed him out of nowhere.

"Yeah, yeah," Mom said. "I know it feels like the end of the world that a woman could do something a man couldn't, but you'll be okay. Now let's do the blessing before the entire candle melts."

I hadn't thought much of it at the time, but then in the following weeks, Dad's hand remained wonky. One morning he was writing a grocery list and kept stopping because "the pen felt weird." I made some stupid joke about *all* my pens feeling weird around me, and that turned into a bit, and it left my mind.

By the time January of this year rolled around, the hand was still weird, so Mom forced Dad to go to a sports doctor to see if he should be wearing a splint or something. He did come home with a splint, but the doctor said he might want to go to a neurologist, too, just to make sure nothing else was going on.

Dad didn't want to, but then he developed this hoarse voice, which seemed like a cold or a sore throat until it refused to go away. So off to the neurologist he and Mom went, then to a few other doctors, and nobody could really pin down what it was. Dad was getting tired of "being a cog in the medical complex," so that was it for a while. Mom and Dad stopped talking about his symptoms, which seemed worse some weeks than others, and I guess I just got so used to it, it didn't register anymore.

"But you went to that first neurologist in February or whenever that was," I say. "They didn't say you had ALS, right?"

"No," Dad says. "That's what made it more confusing. Mom had been googling my symptoms back then and was really freaked out it might be ALS. But that neurologist said it was super-unlikely, that I was too young, and so we ruled it out."

"That doctor was a moron," Mom says.

"He was," Dad agrees. "But it was nice to hear at the time."

"Then in July, when Daddy's legs were feeling stiff, I forced him to get a second opinion. And that's how we ended up at Dr. Yu."

"Oh," I say. I think about me two hours ago, blissfully shoving cookies in my mouth while waiting to tell my father I'm thinking about joining a stupid improv troupe. Two-Hours-Ago Winnie was so naïve. "But if you *do* have it, what does that mean?"

"Not much, really." Dad is suddenly bizarrely chill. "I take an expensive drug, which hopefully Mom's health insurance will continue to cover, and we all go on with our lives."

Mom seems like she has something to add but then closes her mouth and looks away.

"Okay . . . ," I say, mostly reassured by this assessment.

"Yeah. As long as you're cool with me dropping beans on a fairly regular basis, this shouldn't be a problem."

I have a joke forming in my head, but I can't get my mouth on board.

"And we're not telling anyone yet," Mom says. "Daddy doesn't want anyone else to know right now."

23

"Okay," I say.

"Not even Grandma."

"Especially Grandma," Dad says. "For now, anyway. I'm just not ready for that."

"Sure," I say, and it occurs to me that if he hadn't literally spilled the beans (good god, that's so stupid), he still wouldn't be ready to tell *me,* either. Suddenly I'm outside my body, crawling on the ceiling like Spider-Man, staring down as he adds, "You know how many questions she would have."

"Right, yeah," I watch myself say, and I'm suddenly aware of how many questions *I* have. Like, for example:

Is Dad going to die?

No, right? This wouldn't be so casual if he were going to die.

"And, uh," Dad says. "Yeah, that's it. We just wanted to bring you, you know, into the loop. But not to make you worried. Don't worry. Be happy."

I'm whisked back into my body as Mom smiles at me. I can tell she's trying hard to evoke *happy,* but she's a few clicks short.

"All right," I say. "But, so, like . . ." If I throw out enough tiny words, maybe he'll understand my question without me asking it. "If, uh . . . With ALS, what are the . . . What else will . . . ?"

"Oh. What will happen to me?" Dad looks at Mom, then scratches his shoulder, casual as can be. "I mean, it's hard to say for sure. ALS manifests in so many different ways for different people. Likely more of the same. Trouble projecting my voice. Trouble walking. Random impulses to murder family members."

"Ohmigod, seriously?"

24

Dad smiles.

"Not funny," I say, though of course another joke is very welcome.

"Sorry, Banana. I promise ALS won't make me murder you or Mom. But hopefully taking this drug will slow down the progression of things, so I'll stay like this." Mom places her hand over Dad's, and he winks at her. Usually that would be my cue to make fun of them for being gooey, but I decide to give them a pass. "Oh, and do me a favor," Dad says. "Don't google ALS. I don't want you to read random crap on the Internet and start freaking out. Because most of it doesn't apply to me. Okay?"

He seems relaxed about it, and Mom does too, but coming from parents who generally trust me to look at or watch whatever the hell I want, it's slightly disturbing.

As Dad waits for me to respond, for a flicker of a second this thought appears:

Nothing will ever be the same.

But I push it away. Because, really, everything in Dad's behavior seems to be saying that things *will* be the same, that a year from now, the day Dad spilled the beans will be nothing but a funny story we tell from time to time.

"Sure, yeah, no prob," I say. "I will never google anything ever again."

"Thanks, Banana," Dad says, choosing that moment to take his first bite of burrito. "So anyway, how was *your* day?"

5

I really want to google ALS.

But I'm not going to. I will respect Dad's wishes. It's the least I can do.

Though if I *were* to look . . . I mean, I'm not some unsophisticated doof who can't place things in their proper context, Chicken Little clucking her head off that the sky is falling.

Still, he said not to, so as I sit here in bed, I'm mindlessly scrolling through Twitter instead. That's how I know I'm in a weird headspace. I used to be on Twitter all the time, but then it started to overwhelm me. So many smart, funny people saying so many smart, funny things, how could I possibly measure up? I would painstakingly compose a thought, but then the idea that I'd launch it into the black hole of the Internet, to all 126 of my followers, only to have it land with a resounding two likes was enough to convince me not to tweet at all. It's just not for me.

Instead, I go to comedy and pop culture havens like Vulture, sites that don't burden me with the feeling that I should be cleverly participating the whole time. I pop over there now, only to find a long feature on the brilliance of Steven Wright, Dad's all-time favorite comedian. He's this guy with a really low, slow voice who tells amazing deadpan jokes like "You can't have everything. Where would you put it?" You kind of have to hear his delivery to fully get it, but he's totally a genius.

Now, though, he reminds me of Dad, and Dad's possible ALS, a condition whose specifics are readily available to me by typing three letters into a rectangular box:

ALS

I let the letters sit there, my finger hovering over the return key.

It's not like Dad would ever know.

And I'm really curious. His voice has gotten weaker, and his hands, and his legs, but how much worse is it going to get?

I'm interrupted by Enya. She's this Irish New Age singer who was popular, like, two decades ago. Leili loves her—which Azadeh and I make fun of as much as possible—so I have her as Leili's ring and text tone. Saved by the Enya.

Are you making prudent decisions? Leili's text reads.

I'm confused until I remember she's referring to our chemistry teacher, Mrs. Tanaka, who for some mystifying reason uses the phrase *prudent decisions* at least ten times during every class. Oh, to be back a few hours ago, when the biggest thing on my mind was mocking a dingus teacher.

I impulsively respond:

My dad might have ALS.

I know my parents said we aren't telling anyone. But Leili and Azadeh are incredibly trustworthy. And I can't not google it *and* not tell anyone!

I look at the words I texted. It feels like they're about someone else's dad.

The three dots hang out in Leili's word bubble. I can imagine the look on her face: eyebrow squished down, cheek squished

27

up, sort of smiling, sort of not. If Azadeh is nearby, Leili will call out, "Uh . . . Oz, Winnie's being weird," and then they'll huddle around the phone for five minutes discussing how to respond.

Finally, the three dots disappear, only to be replaced by: ???

Leili is the most considerate person I know, and she obviously doesn't want to risk offending me by saying the wrong thing. One of about eight thousand reasons why I love her. I write back: *Not a joke.*

My phone makes beeping noises. Most kids I know do everything in their power to avoid ever having to speak on the phone, let alone FaceTime. Leili isn't like that. She understands when real human connection might be helpful. Like now.

"Hi, Lay," I say, my back up against the headboard.

"Hey," Leili says, sitting on her twin bed in the room she and Azadeh share, her brown eyes brimming with empathy. "Are you okay?"

"I don't know," I say. "I think so. It's weird."

"Aw, Winner." She and Azadeh are the only ones who call me that. It's super-endearing. "Oz is here too."

"Aloha," Azadeh says, popping her head into the frame, her hair wet and floppy. Leili shoots her a quick dagger for her whimsical Hawaiian greeting during this serious moment.

"Hey, Oz," I say.

"So what's going on?" Leili asks.

I didn't think I was feeling emotional, but as my best friends stare at me through the screen, I find a golf ball in my throat, blocking all the words. I swallow twice, creating a little space.

"You know how I'd mentioned that my dad's been having some weird symptoms this past year, like with his legs and hands?"

They nod.

28

"So, yeah, he's been seeing some different doctors, including this neurologist in New York City."

"Wow," Azadeh says. "The Big Apple."

"Azadeh," Leili harshly whispers, accompanied by an elbow nudge.

"Yeah," I say. "So he and my mom just told me at dinner that he . . . you know, like I texted. He might have ALS."

"Oh no," Leili says.

"That's awful," Azadeh says.

They both seem to know exactly what it is, which makes me feel like an idiot.

"You know about ALS?" I ask.

They're silent.

"Yeah," Azadeh says, glancing at Leili. "It's that . . . It's the ice bucket challenge disease, right?"

"And it's neurological," Leili adds.

"Are you just saying that because I told you he saw a neurologist?"

Leili moves her mouth to the side, her go-to thinking face.

"Yes," she says, her eyes returning to the screen.

They don't know either. I'm glad.

"But seriously," Leili continues, "what does ALS entail?"

Leili is the only person on the planet who uses the word *entail* in daily conversation. "I don't actually know," I whisper. "My dad made me promise not to look it up."

"What? Why?" Azadeh asks, nose indignantly scrunched.

"Because he said every case of ALS is different and he doesn't want me to get freaked out reading symptoms that might not even apply to him."

"Well, he didn't say *we* couldn't look it up, did he?" Azadeh asks.

29

My breath catches in my chest. I look toward the bedroom door, paranoid that Dad might have heard. But I hear his and Mom's muffled voices down the hall as they get ready for bed, and I know of course he didn't.

"No," I say. "He didn't."

"Do you want us to?" Leili asks.

My answer is simultaneously *Of course!* and *Absolutely not!* I stare at my door one more time, heart racing like I'm about to shoplift or something, before giving a couple tiny nods.

Leili and Azadeh nod back, and then Azadeh's phone is out, and it's happening. They're both looking down at her screen. "Okay, we got it," Leili says.

I'm reminded of a sleepover at their house in fifth grade, when we stayed up way too late asking the Ouija board stupid questions and patiently waiting for answers, the most memorable being that Leili was one day going to write an award-winning novel called *The Beautiful Dolphin*. Except in this case, I don't know if I want to hear the answer. I pop up from the bed with my phone so I can walk around the room to distract myself.

"Oh geez," Azadeh says as they read.

"It's not . . . necessarily . . . that bad," Leili says, but she has a horrified look on her face.

"It's pretty intense," Azadeh says.

Leili shoots her another dagger. "But you said your dad *might* have it, right?"

"Right," I say. "Yeah. I mean, he didn't want me to look it up because he said a lot of the symptoms wouldn't apply to him. What kind of stuff are you seeing?"

"Um," Leili says. "Nothing that helpful."

"Most of this is pretty horrible," Azadeh says.

I feel like I'm on the verge of a panic attack. "Okay, maybe just show me the screen."

"No, you don't need to . . . ," Leili says. "I get why your dad thought it wasn't worth it to look because—"

"Show me the screen," I say, in my commanding no-nonsense voice. Leili and Azadeh look at each other, using nonverbal twin code to try and decide what to do.

"You sure?" Leili finally asks me.

I nod.

Azadeh bites her lower lip and sighs before holding up her phone. The words, slightly hard to read since it's a screen viewed through a screen, wash over me.

ALS, or amyotrophic lateral sclerosis, is a progressive neurodegenerative disease that affects nerve cells in the brain and the spinal cord.

Okay.

Early symptoms vary but can include tripping, dropping things, abnormal fatigue of the arms and/or legs, slurred speech, muscle cramps and twitches, and uncontrollable periods of laughing or crying.

All right.

When the motor neurons eventually die, the ability of the brain to initiate and control muscle movement is lost.

Hmm.

With voluntary muscle action progressively affected, people may lose the ability to speak, eat, move, and breathe.

My god. THAT'S ALL THE THINGS.

And:

Usually fatal.

"Could you scroll down, please?" I ask. I'm searching the page for how long people survive after diagnosis.

I know most of this probably doesn't apply to my dad, but *if it does,* how long does he have? How long do I have with him? How long how long how long how long why is the one piece of information I need so damn hard to find?

"Maybe put it away now," Leili says.

"No," I say, "I'm fine. I just want to read this."

I can't find the answer. There is no answer.

"We'll put it away," Leili says, guiding Azadeh's hand down out of the frame.

I feel a storm threatening to explode from behind my eyes, so I take off my glasses (were you picturing me as someone who wears glasses? well, I do) and press the knuckle of my left thumb against each of my eyes. I've cried in front of Leili and Azadeh before—we've been besties for seven years, so, obviously—but I don't feel like doing it right now, especially over something that might not even be relevant to my situation. I take a deep breath.

"Well, okay then," I say. "That was educational."

"I'm so sorry, Win," Leili says.

"It's not just me, right? ALS seems like the absolute worst."

"Well, it's not *not* the absolute worst," Azadeh says.

"Yeah." I plop down onto my beige rolling chair and stare at the framed picture on my desk of me with Mom and Dad. I'm holding their hands in front of the house we rented on Cape Cod when I was ten.

"How were your parents?" Azadeh asks, almost like she knows I'm looking at them. "When they told you."

"My dad seemed normal," I say. "Pretty calm, made some jokes. My mom seemed a little more tense. But they both said they didn't want me to worry."

"I'm sure most of what's on here is not applicable to your dad's situation," Leili says.

"Definitely," Azadeh agrees.

I'm not as sure. It said *dropping things*.

And other symptoms may have been in plain view for months, and I've just been completely oblivious.

"It's still a lot to process, though," Leili says. "If you ever want to talk to someone, I'm sure Connie would see you." Connie is Leili and Azadeh's therapist. They love her.

"For sure, for sure," Azadeh says.

Leili and Azadeh started seeing Connie after their mom, who's a gastroenterologist, was involved in this big malpractice suit a couple of years ago. It almost cost her her job and put tons of stress on their family. Their younger brother, Ramin, essentially stopped talking for three months. It was that bad. I'd always felt so lucky that my family wasn't going through something like that. Ha.

"Thanks," I say.

"We can come over if you want," Azadeh says.

"It's almost ten o'clock," I say. "And we have school tomorrow."

"We wild like dat."

"There's no way Mom and Papa would drive us to Winnie's right now," Leili says.

"I would *run* there!" Azadeh lets loose her big, throaty laugh, the one that makes people turn and look when we're at the movies or Luigi's Pizza. It only lasts a few seconds, though, before Leili nudges her and she reins it in. I kind of wish she'd kept laughing.

"Thanks, Oz," I say. "But I'm good."

33

"Well, we should probably sleep soon," Leili says. She looks to Azadeh, checking if she has anything else to say. Azadeh gives a subtle shake of her head, like *Let's give Winnie her space*. I'm fairly fluent in their secret language of nods and glances. "We love you, Win. Call whenever."

"Even if it's three in the morning," Azadeh says.

"Yeah," Leili agrees.

"Just not four in the morning. That's way too late."

Azadeh gets a smile out of me with that one. "Thanks, ladies. Love you." I click off first because I know they won't.

I spin around in my desk chair, part of me hoping my parents will knock on the door and say reassuring things. All is silent, though. They're probably asleep already.

Shit.

I never told Dad about Improv Troupe.

But the more I think about it, the more I can't imagine joining. The idea of performing is stressful enough, let alone when I've just found out my dad might (but probably won't) die. The Steven Wright article is still up on my laptop, and my eyes land on a joke quoted toward the end: *I intend to live forever. So far, so good*.

I look again at the photo of me, Mom, and Dad on vacation. I place a hand over Dad to see what the picture looks like without him.

6

Okay, since you're probably desperate to know, here's the terrible, traumatic thing that happened at my bat mitzvah.

The theme of my party was "Winnie's Funny-Joke-Haha Comedyland" (Dad and I came up with that together), with table names that were all comedy-inspired ("Bridesmaids," "The Simpsons," "Kate McKinnon," etc.), so my sweet father thought it could be fun if I did ten minutes of stand-up during the party. My first reaction? AWFUL IDEA. I was stressed enough preparing my Torah portion, trying to wring every inch of Judaic pathos from my wavery off-key alto, and now I was supposed to make my stand-up debut too?

"Come on," Dad had said, "it makes perfect sense that as you become a Jewish woman, you would embrace your sense of humor, which, for centuries now, has been one of the essential gifts of our people. Besides, you love this stuff, and you're always saying you wish there were a place where you could get your feet wet performing." I had been saying that, but I hadn't actually *meant* it. Yes, I'd been doing impromptu bits with my parents my whole life, and those bits usually killed, but the idea of testing that material on people who weren't them was—how should I put this?—*terrifying*. "Well, here's your chance!" Dad had continued. "There's no friendlier crowd than your family— they're gonna eat up everything you do."

If only that had been true.

I reluctantly agreed, cobbling together a set out of some of my personal Greatest Hits: impressions, characters, my best material on the foibles of middle school existence.

I even started to get excited about it, maybe even a little cocky. So much, in fact, that I didn't follow my instincts and speak up when Dad suggested I do my set immediately after our family entrance. I don't know how many bar/bat mitzvahs you've ever been to, but usually at the beginning of the party, everybody gathers on the dance floor as the DJ announces the bat mitzvah girl and her family, who have been awkwardly waiting outside the room during the first couple of songs. They then enter to something horribly cheesy, like "We Are Family" (don't google it), and everyone cheers, and it's all pretty mortifying. (I had asked my parents if we could skip this part, but they both thought it would be "fun.")

Anyway, the plan was for the DJ to then turn off the music and hand me a mic, and I would stand in the center of the dance floor and tell jokes. *Seems great,* I foolishly thought. Catch everybody while they're riled up and feeling good, after my peers had thrown back a couple Shirley Temples during cocktail hour.

So I stood there on the parquet floor, all my friends and classmates sitting around me, rows of cousins and aunts and Mom's coworkers standing behind them. Leili and Azadeh were just below me, which was helpful, and to my right was my current crush at the time, Rory Tan, a quiet artist boy who I'd recently started having actual conversations with. A few days before the bat mitzvah, we'd even joked about how he was going to dance with me at the reception, and we were going to do the tango, and it felt like maybe we weren't joking. So I was, of course, highly attuned to Rory's presence as I began my first bit.

"Hi, everyone! I'm a woman now!" I shouted. "Hope this doesn't mean I have to start packing my own lunches!" It was an easy joke, and everyone laughed, including Rory. It was to be one of the last genuine laughs I would receive that day.

Throwing on a huge, curly wig with a bow in it, I segued directly into my impression of Gilly, one of Kristen Wiig's most famous *Saturday Night Live* characters. As I said her famous line ("Sorry") and moved my eyes back and forth, I got a huge laugh, but as I repeated that same line over and over again, it dawned on me that the character doesn't work without other actors to play off of. Like, at all. The laughs petered out until I was staring at a brick wall of plaster smiles. I decided to abandon my character bits and go right to my more relatable stuff.

"What's the deal with middle school, anyway?" I asked. (I had recently become obsessed with *Seinfeld*.) "What is it exactly that we're in the middle of?" I hoped this high-concept joke would click with my peers, but other than generous pity laughs from my parents, Leili, and Azadeh, who smiled and nodded with everything they had, the room was silent. Some guy named Steve who Mom works with coughed a few times. I made eye contact with Rory, who quickly looked away.

I knew it wasn't going well, but I thought I could steer the plummeting plane to safety. I went into a riff comparing the way kids treat each other in middle school to the various dinosaur behaviors in *Jurassic World,* and sure enough, I started hearing giggling from some boys just left of my feet. An adrenaline rush of pride coursed through me. I knew the dinosaur stuff would click with them; boys are so predictable.

But the laughter was continuing too long, and when I looked down, I saw Patrick Valenti trying to sneak a peek up my dress, four other dudes—not Rory, thank god—egging him on and cracking up.

I was so shocked I didn't even have the words to call them out on it. I just took a few steps backward and went on autopilot with the rest of my material. It didn't even occur to me that I could end early.

I wish it had, because right after that, I was talking about what life must have been like before tables existed—admittedly some of my weaker material—and over the speakers came the sound of canned studio laughter, like on a sitcom. I assumed the DJ had accidentally hit a button, but he gave me a thumbs-up and a wink, like *I got your back,* and inside I was like *No, please, don't do that again,* but I didn't have the words to stop it. The next two minutes were torture, a sea of horrible sound effects—studio laughter, rim shots, sad trumpet sounds, and, most devastating of all, fart noises—cutting into the spaces between my jokes, and there was nothing I could do to stop it.

The most brutal part is that the sound effects actually got people laughing again.

"That's all the time I have," I said, finally, just how I'd seen it done by so many before me. I waved, there was pity applause, the DJ who'd comedy-gaslit me cued up "Bad Blood," and I beelined out of there to the women's bathroom, where I huddled in a stall and tried to disappear.

Here, of course, was the problem with positioning my set at the beginning. Now I had an entire party to get through. Mom and Dad tried to get me to come out of the bathroom, to convince me it wasn't as bad as I thought, and a half hour later, I succumbed. I suffered my way through "Hands Up" and "YMCA" and candle lighting and unsolicited comedy advice ("You should have been louder," Grandma Mitzie said, "really *shouted* the jokes out, you know?") with the unshakable feeling that I was walking around with egg dripping off my face.

And that's why I swore to never ever perform comedy again.

Oh, and this goes without saying, but Rory Tan and I never danced together.

He and his family actually moved to San Francisco the next month. It was probably unrelated, but it's impossible to know for sure.

7

Dad is buttering toast while listening to NPR, and Mom is out the door to work moments after I step into the kitchen. Just a normal day in the Friedman household.

I'm almost tempted to ask, "So, that whole ALS thing . . . Did that really happen or . . . ?" But Dad starts ranting about something Congress did, and I join in, and it feels regular and routine and reassuring, so I don't.

It's only when I bump into Leili at her locker before school and she gives me a huge hug and tells me she's around to talk about my dad whenever that I have confirmation it definitely happened. I tell her thanks and smile and say nothing else, which Leili knows means I don't want to talk about it. So she makes a quick pivot to the status of my involvement with the Manatawkin Improv Troupe.

"Oh man," I say, tugging on the strings of my green hoodie. "I keep forgetting that's today."

"No pressure," she says, "I just know you were thinking about joining."

"Yeah, totally." I try to ignore the panic rising in my stomach like thermometer mercury. "I think . . . I decided last night that now isn't the best time."

"Of course, sure." Leili gently closes her locker, the opposite of a slam. "It can be kind of cheese-town anyway. Though . . . it might be a nice distraction."

"Maybe, yeah, but . . . Thanks, Lay. You the best."

"Come on," she says, rolling her eyes and blowing me a kiss as we walk in different directions.

Of course, that immediately gets me rethinking my decision.

I think about it pretty much nonstop for the next seven periods, rancid bat mitzvah flashbacks aggressively looping through my brain until I can finally say for sure I'm not going. I know I could be funny, but I'm not in the demon-confronting mood.

"Winnie?" Mrs. Tanaka says, in a tone that suggests it's at least the second time she's said my name.

"Oh," I say, "yes?"

"Would you care to take a stab at the question?"

I, of course, have no idea what the question was, let alone the answer. I know she's asking something having to do with chemistry. Because that is the class we're in.

"I, uh . . ." All eyes are on me, a feeling I generally despise. I stare at the board, hoping for a lifeline, but it's not helpful. There's just one word scrawled up there: *meniscus*. On a different day, that would definitely make me giggle. I take a wild stab in the dark. "I think if you combine—"

"Please pay attention in my class, Winnie," Mrs. Tanaka says, mercifully cutting me off before I can embarrass myself further.

"Yes," I say. "Sorry, I . . . Yes, I will."

I'd usually be mortified by something like this, but today I appreciate the brief brain break.

For the rest of the class, I do my best impersonation of a focused student, nodding vigorously at everything Mrs. Tanaka says, and I keep that can-do spirit going into Mr. Hutnik's US history class, too. When the final tone of the day sounds, I grab my books and head for my locker. I'm not doing Improv Troupe; it's just not in the cards right now. Evan Miller will have to live without me.

"Hey there, soldier," Evan says, as if I've summoned him by thinking his name. He falls into step next to me.

"Oh, hi." I wish I'd said something funny or at least halfway clever. Then again, he's wearing a red Elmo T-shirt underneath his plaid button-down, so this might not be someone I should be trying to impress.

"You're coming, right?" he asks, ruffling his shaggy brown hair in a way that seems practiced.

"I, uh . . ."

"To the first improv meeting. More fun than Nam, remember?"

"Yeah, I know what you're referring to, I just—"

"I already told Mr. Martinez you'd probably be there, so."

Why the hell . . . ?

"Well," I say. "I already told Mr. Martinez you probably *wouldn't* be there, so. Looks like we've got quite a conundrum on our hands."

Evan laughs. "See? So frickin' funny. *Conundrum*. Who says that?"

"Me." Not gonna lie, the rush I get from making him laugh is the best I've felt all day. Maybe Leili was right. Maybe a distraction is just what I need.

"I'll be there," I say.

"All riiiiiiight," Evan says.

42

I'm overcome with nausea and nerves once I walk into the audi-torium, the phrase *WHAT AM I DOING* reverberating in my brain. Aside from the Bat Mitzvah Incident, my last time on a stage was in sixth grade, in the middle school production of *Annie,* pretty much killing it as Annie's dog, Sandy, a portrayal equal parts mischievous and heartwarming. I want to draw confidence from that, but who am I kidding? I was playing a dog. I didn't even have any lines.

"Ahhhh," Leili says, practically galloping my way before en-veloping me in a hug. "I'm so glad you came."

"Yeah."

"It's gonna be fun. Pinky swear." Leili pulls out of the hug and sticks out her pinky. I grab it and pretend to rip it off. She pretends to scream in pain. I pretend to put her pinky in my pocket.

"Thanks, Leili," I say.

"Come sit over here." Leili pulls me down the aisle to the third row, where two girls are standing and chatting. "Hey, you two, this is my friend Winnie. She's really funny."

"Oh, hey," the tall girl facing me says, leaning slightly to see around the head of the girl she was talking to. I remember her from the performances I saw last year, super-confident and super-loud. (I have a naturally quiet voice, so I'm always im-pressed when people don't.)

The black-haired girl she was talking to turns her head and torso toward me. It's Jess Yang. "Hi," she says, barely inter-ested, definitely not remembering me from play rehearsals, be-fore animatedly restarting her conversation with the tall girl.

"That's Rashanda and Jess," Leili says, thrown by their lack of friendliness but trying not to make a deal of it. "But you already know Jess from *Arsenic*—"

"Right, yeah," I say, cutting her off so Jess doesn't hear, which would make me feel more painfully uncomfortable than I already do.

Leili stares toward the back of the auditorium. "Once Mr. Martinez gets here, it's gonna be really fun." I know she feels some personal responsibility for me coming and wants to make sure I'm having a good time. I stare along with her. It's not too late to make a mad dash for the door.

But then Mr. Martinez glides in down the aisle. "All right, everybody, we'll get started in a minute," he says. "Sorry I'm late."

Leili sits and pulls me down into the seat next to her. She's beaming with excitement. "That's him."

I get it. Mr. Martinez is a very handsome man, especially for a teacher. Black hipster glasses. Soulful brown eyes. Light stubble beard. Leili says he's twenty-four, "which means that he's only nine years older than us, so once we're out of college and in the real world, it won't even make a difference," which is where I get grossed out. Come on, he's still a teacher.

He walks up the steps to the stage, dropping his blue messenger bag and organizing some papers before turning around to us. "Welcome back, my friends. Why don't you all join me onstage?"

My organs shrivel into raisins. But Leili is already on her feet, urging me to mine. I head toward the stage.

Evan Miller appears ahead of us, leaping up the stage steps like a frog, his limbs flailing outward, then compressing down to the ground as he shouts "Ribbit!", cracking up at least four people around us. Highly cheesy. I am again tempted to make a run for it.

"Cheesy," the guy ahead of me says to himself, and it's the hugest relief. I realize it's Fletcher Handy, who I had no idea was into performing. We were in algebra together last year, and now we're in the same homeroom and English class. Over the summer, he transformed his curls into a flattop, which I'm about to compliment him on until I remember Phoebe Robinson's book *You Can't Touch My Hair*. Definitely don't want to be the white girl exoticizing his hair. I don't even know him that well.

"Go go," Leili says behind me, lightly shoving my back in her eagerness to prove to Mr. Martinez the depth of her improv devotion.

"I'm going as fast as I can, Lay. Chill out."

"Sorry," she says.

When we get onto the stage, we join the fifteen or so of our peers sitting and facing Mr. Martinez, who's still standing. "So, okay!" His hands gesture wildly as he speaks. "Hello hello! I'm excited to be back with you all. I see lots of faces I recognize, and some I don't, which is great, and I just want to say year two of Manatawkin Improv Troupe is going to be even more spectacular than year one was."

Lots of people cheer, including Leili, who makes a triumphant shrieking sound I've never heard from her before.

"What what," Evan Miller says in a deep voice.

"Now, before we go any further," Mr. Martinez says, "a question for our new folks: Do you all know what improv is?"

"No, I ain't got no idea," Evan says in a Southern accent, getting a huge laugh.

"All right, all right," Mr. Martinez says. "We'll get to the funny stuff soon. I'm asking for real, though." He looks straight at me, so I feel like I have no choice but to speak.

"Um," I say. "Improv is, like, uh, making up things on the spot."

Leili softly grunts with concern, which is annoying, because I know I'm right.

"That's true," Mr. Martinez says, a twinkle in his hipster eye, "but I actually asked a yes-or-no question, so your answer is incorrect. Listening is a huge part of improv."

Dammit! Fell right into that one.

"Ohhhhh," Evan Miller, Tim Stabisch, and a guy I don't know call out in unison, each with one hand cupped around his mouth like a megaphone.

I stare down at the stage, searching for a trapdoor to fall through.

"So let's try again," Mr. Martinez says, his brown laser beams pointed at me. *Oh, please, for the love of all that's holy, move on to someone else.* "Do you know what improv is?"

"Yes," I say.

"Great." He smiles and gives me a thumbs-up, which is simultaneously a relief and extremely patronizing. "What is it?"

"It's when you make things up on the spot. Like, in scenes."

"Awesome. And what's your name?"

"Uh . . . Winnie."

"Uh-Winnie, excellent."

Everyone chuckles, including Leili.

"Just Winnie," I say, my ears hot.

"I know," Mr. Martinez says, grinning. "Just a reminder that our words are important tools. We need to be precise when we use them."

I'm guessing Mr. Martinez didn't have a ton of friends growing up.

"But as to your definition of improv," he continues, "that's exactly right. I always describe it as a hybrid of writing and acting, scenes literally being written *while* they're being performed. When it's done well, it's truly magical, the performers and audience living together in the spontaneity of the moment, all of them witnessing creativity unfolding in its purest form."

Say what now?

"As our veterans remember from last year, we do short-form improv, which is the *Whose Line Is It Anyway?* format, quick structured games to improvise within." Dad once forced me to watch a couple of old episodes of *Whose Line Is It Anyway?* All the performers were talented and funny, but it was a tad corny for my taste. And there were no women. "Like, as a quick example, there's the game ABC. Two people do a scene, and the first line has to start with *A*, the next with *B*, and so on, until *Z*, when the scene ends."

"Amazing," Evan says.

"Beautiful," his friend I don't know says.

"Crocodile," Tim Stabisch says.

"Yes, like that!" Mr. Martinez says. "Sorta. So every week, we'll be learning new games and focusing on different rules of improv, which will help us to get better and better at, as Winnie said, making up things on the spot. And just like last year, we'll do three performances for an audience: one in the fall, one in the spring, and one at the end of the school year." My throat goes from normal to dry within the span of two seconds. "Nothing to stress about, just a chance to show your friends and family what we've been doing. The first one will be in

October during Homecoming week, so we've got our work cut out for us."

October? We're already performing in *October*?

"Um." A cute guy with long bangs I've never seen before, must be a freshman, raises his hand, and Mr. Martinez points to him. "So, like, will we be doing any stand-up as part of this?"

"Ah," Mr. Martinez says, grimacing as if forced to break the news to someone that their bird has died. "A very good question. No. We will not." I breathe an involuntary sigh of relief. "Stand-up comedy is actually very different from improv. It's one person, with prewritten material, getting up onstage to tell jokes. I have a ton of respect for that art form, takes mad guts, but it's not what we're doing here."

And thank god for that.

"Also worth mentioning that improv is different from sketch comedy. When you're watching *Saturday Night Live* or *Key & Peele,* those are sketches, and even though at times they may feel loose and made up on the spot, they're not. That's all written in advance. So we're not here to do stand-up. Or sketch. We are here to do improv. Make sense?"

Long-Bangs Guy nods, then straps his backpack on and walks out of the auditorium.

"Whoa whoa," Mr. Martinez calls after him. "You sure you don't want to at least give it a try?"

"I forgot," Long-Bangs Guy says, not turning around, "I have to, um, mow the lawn." If that's the best excuse he could come up with, he was probably right to leave. Still, can't help but feel overwhelmingly jealous that he's out there and I'm in here.

"Well, okay," Mr. Martinez says, looking genuinely befuddled.

"New record for fastest improv dropout. Anybody else want to leave?"

I think he's joking, but nevertheless, this is my chance.

"In that case, let's get up on our feet!"

Shoot. Missed it.

"You okay?" Leili asks once we've stood, possibly noticing the terror in my eyes.

"Maybe," I say, taking a few deep breaths.

She links her arm with mine and leans into me. "You're doing great."

"If I vom," I whisper, "just stand in front of me and act like nothing happened."

8

"All right," Mr. Martinez says, "let's circle up and start with a quick game of Nameball, so we can learn the names of all our new folks, and they can learn ours. Who wants to start?"

Nameball? Have I magically teleported back to kindergarten?

"I got this," Rashanda says. She bends the fingers of one hand into claws and holds them up for all to see. "Rashanda," she says. Then she winds up and flings her arm like she's throwing something across the stage as she says, "Dan!"

A nerdy-looking dude with glasses, muttonchops, and a *Game of Thrones* T-shirt pretends to catch whatever's been thrown, shouting "Dan!" as he does.

We are playing catch with an imaginary ball. Okay.

Dan holds the ball with one claw-hand before putting another hand next to it and expanding his nonexistent ball into something volleyball-sized. He hurls it with two hands toward us. "Leili!" he shouts.

"Leili!" she says as she pulls the ball of air to her chest. She compresses it down to the size of a pea, held aloft between her two fingers. She flicks it up into the air. "Winnie!"

I stick my palm out to catch the fake pea. "Winnie," I say as I imagine it landing on my hand like a raindrop.

"Uh," Leili says.

"You're supposed to catch it the way it's thrown to you," Evan says from across the circle.

"So, like, between your fingers," Leili says. "The way I threw it."

"Oh," I say.

"That's all right," Mr. Martinez says. "We didn't even explain the rules yet. Now we all know."

It's really fun to be made an example of. I hope it happens at least ten more times because it doesn't make me want to puke at all.

"You need to catch it and throw it to someone else," Leili says, a slight layer of panic in her voice.

"Right, great," I say, curling up my palm and putting my thumb and index finger close to each other. "Winnie," I say, pretending once again to catch the invisible ball because this definitely isn't a waste of time.

"Nice," Mr. Martinez says.

"And, uh . . ." Who should I pass it to? Evan's right across from me, but if I throw it to him, he might think it's because I have a crush on him. Which I don't.

"Just throw it to whoever," Leili says.

Okay, Evan it is. I wind up to hurl it in his direction.

"No," Leili whispers. "You need to change it."

I hate this game. I hate it so much.

"What?" I whisper back.

"Change the ball into something else. Like bowl it."

"Make it into a bowl?"

"No, like bowling. A bowling ball."

I want to come up with my own unique take on how to pass

it, but I've got nothing. It's like I've never had a single idea in my life. Everyone is watching us whisper at each other.

"Okay," I say as I begrudgingly go through the motions of pretending a tiny ball is now a bowling ball before swinging my arm back, then forward. "Evan," I say.

"Evan!" he says, all too eager to crouch down and pick up the ball-shaped air that has rolled his way. He shrinks it down again, shouts "Mahesh!" and then puts it into an imaginary blow gun and blows it across the room. Damn, why didn't I think of that? The guy he and Tim had been sitting with before, apparently named Mahesh, shouts his own name as he slaps his neck in surprise and drops to the ground. Everyone laughs, including me.

Now I can, of course, think of at least twenty more creative things I could have done on my turn: bounced it like a basketball, shot it like a bow and arrow, thrown it like a pie. Bowling was pretty good, I guess, but it wasn't even my idea.

I ruminate on this, not realizing how little I've paid attention to the rest of the game until Mr. Martinez says, "Okay, good, time for a little Zip-Zap-Zop!" Here's my chance to redeem myself. Whatever this game is, I will be the best person who has ever played it.

It turns out it is less about skill or creativity and more about listening, clapping, and shouting. I am not the best person who has ever played it.

I do a little better during the One-Word Story, where we go around the circle telling a story by each adding a word. I introduce the word *arugula,* which becomes a key part of the narrative. Then it's time for a game that actually involves two people in a scene together, and my heart begins to snarl at the bars of my rib cage.

"For all you newbies," Mr. Martinez says, "we sit on the edge of the stage to form the audience, and then the action happens farther upstage. Why do we do it this way? I don't know! We just do." Leili laughs way harder than the joke deserves as we plop down on the stage. But so do Rashanda and Jess and Evan. Most of the group, in fact, seems to be in love with Mr. Martinez.

"Okay, now before we really get into it, I would be remiss if I didn't first explain the most important rule of improv. The rule that will apply to every single game we play, every single moment you have onstage with a fellow troupe member. The rule that, let's face it, is kind of the love of my life." Everyone guffaws. Not me. I'm just trying to remember to breathe. "What is it, everybody?" Mr. Martinez leans forward, cupping his ear with his hand. "All together!"

"YES, AND!" more than half of the room shouts. I think Leili's contribution just ruptured my eardrum.

"That's right, *Yes, and*. The absolute most important rule of improv." I feel a surge of relief, and I realize it's because it reminds me of *Yes Please*, Amy Poehler's book, which I've read four times. Her love for improv always made me curious to try it, until I mentally ruled it out PBM (post–bat mitzvah). But maybe I am supposed to be here. Walking the same path Amy did. "And I'm already tired of hearing myself speak, so does anybody who's not me want to come up here to help explain it?"

Numerous arms shoot up, none higher and more determined than my best friend's.

"Leili. Come on up." Leili simultaneously glows and blushes as she joins Mr. Martinez, nervously fiddling with the bottom of her cardigan. He nods and gestures: *You have the floor.*

"Um," she says, "*Yes, and* means that you say yes to everything your scene partner does, then add something new to the scene to help move it forward."

"Yes!" Mr. Martinez says. "Great answer!"

"Thanks," Leili says. I've never seen her beam this much. (And I've known her for almost a decade.)

She goes to sit back down, but Mr. Martinez stops her. "Hold on a sec, Leili. There's one more thing I want you to help with."

"Oh, okay. Sure." She's playing it cool, but I can tell she's flipping out.

"So, her answer was great," Mr. Martinez says, "because improv is all about agreement." He's really fired up, gesturing even more emphatically than before. "You are not here to shoot down what your scene partner puts out there, you are here to support everything that happens on that stage. No matter what. Your job is to *listen* to each other, to make each other look like geniuses, to build something together that you couldn't have built on your own. And with that in mind . . . let's dive into some *Yes, and* drills!"

"Wooooo!" Nicole O'Connor shouts, her long arms and long index fingers extended toward the ceiling. She's another person I sort of know. She had a small part in *Arsenic and Old Lace*. I do a quick scan of the group in the hopes of finding people who, like me, are radiating anxiety. Fletcher Handy's giving off a distinctly neutral vibe, so that's something.

"This is very simple and exactly what it sounds like," Mr. Martinez says. "I'm going to bring up two of you at a time to do a scene together, and your sole focus will be to *Yes, and* each other. I don't want you to worry about being clever, just agree with your scene partner and add something new with every line."

It's hard to absorb every word he's saying because the fear is taking up so much space in my brain. But I can do this. I'll go up and do a scene with someone and agree with everything they say. That's easy. I'm very agreeable.

Is that even true? Dad sometimes calls me the Mule because I'm so stubborn. Well, whatever, I can do this.

"Before we bring anyone up, Leili and I are going to do a quick demonstration, mainly for our new folks." Leili's eyes open wide. "You down?" She pulls herself together and gives a thumbs-up.

"Super. So, I'm going to initiate a scene, maybe by saying something, maybe by miming a physical activity. Then Leili will affirm the reality of that—YES—*and* add something onto it. Then I'll add to that, and she'll add to that, and we'll have a little scene. So . . . here we go."

"Yeah, girl!" Rashanda shouts. Leili shoots her a small smile.

"Yay Lay," I say, seeing as she's *my* best friend. I think I was too quiet, though. She doesn't respond.

"What?" Nicole O'Connor, sitting next to me, asks.

"Oh, nothing, I was just . . ." I shrug, then look back at the stage, where Mr. Martinez is pretending to dig a hole. He's working hard, wiping his brow with his forearm and stepping on the imaginary shovel's blade to guide it into the ground.

Leili stands next to him, staring at the hole while he digs. "I'm sorry I forgot my shovel," she says.

"Oh, that's okay," Mr. Martinez says. "I mean, we'd be able to bury the body faster if you had, but we should be fine."

Big laugh from all of us, partly out of shock that a teacher would talk about burying a dead body.

"True," Leili says. "But now I can focus more on being supportive. You're doing a great job! That man we murdered will be buried in no time!" She's so earnest and natural in her delivery, everyone loses it.

"Thanks, Mom," Mr. Martinez says.

An even huger laugh, as suddenly the scene is about an incredibly twisted mother and son. "And we'll end that one there," Mr. Martinez says. "Awesome!" He excitedly kicks the air with one of his cooler-than-your-average-teacher two-tone shoes.

"Hopefully that was helpful to see, especially with Leili doing such a fantastic job supporting and forwarding the scene." Leili blushes and shrugs. I have no idea if I could do what she just did. "Let's actually have you stay up here for the next one." Mr. Martinez has no idea how much he's making her day right now. "And let's partner you up with . . ." I stare at my lap as he scans the room. Improvising with my best friend would probably be the gentlest way to launch into this world, but I want to watch at least one more scene to get a better feel. "Rashanda."

Rashanda bounds over to Leili and they share a high five.

"And since Rashanda is as much of a pro as Leili"—the two of them shoot each other a quick look of pride—"we're going to add one other element into the mix. Other than *Yes, and*, the most important thing in any improv scene is your relationship. When I called Leili *Mom* in that last scene, that's what I was establishing. Who are you to each other? Do you love each other? Like each other? Hate each other?"

"What if it's all three?" Evan asks, and everybody cracks up.

"You laugh," Mr. Martinez says, "but that's actually a very wise question. Because most times, in human relationships, it *is* all three. And that's exactly the kind of thing we want to see informing the choices you make in an improv scene."

Oh geez. The agreeing with everything I could do, but infusing a made-up scene with dynamic layers of emotional complexity sounds intimidating.

"This is simpler than it sounds," Mr. Martinez says. "It mainly means you should know *how you feel* about the other person onstage. So for each of these *Yes, and* scenes, we're going to give our scene partners their relationship. What should Leili and Rashanda's relationship be in this scene?"

"Sisters!" Molly Graham-Crockett shouts.

"Sisters," Mr. Martinez says. "Perfect. And obviously, ladies, you've got a lot of wiggle room for what that means. For example, if I were going to be using my real-life relationship with my sister, I would be fiercely protective and loving with all my choices. Because, you know, she's my kid sister, and I'm not gonna let anyone mess with her, not for a second."

Much of the room audibly swoons. I mean, it was sweet, but he was laying it on a little too thick for my taste.

"Anyway. Sisters. You two ready?" Leili and Rashanda nod solemnly. "First scene of the new year. *Sisters.* Go!"

Leili looks very thoughtful and begins some intricate miming, maybe polishing a prized statue?

"Thanks for cleaning those dishes, sis," Rashanda says.

"No problem," Leili says, still polishing. "You know me. I love to clean!"

"Good. 'Cause I have fifty more for you to clean after this."

People laugh, including Mr. Martinez.

"Fifty?" Leili says, incredulous. "That's it?" Huge laugh. That was totally brilliant. Leili is brilliant.

The scene continues to unfold, exploring the strange dynamics of their relationship, with Rashanda giving Leili task after task that she always wishes were more involved. They're *Yes, and*–ing like rock stars, and I'm in awe. I don't think I'm cut out for this at all. I should just start an anonymous blog and call it a day.

Mr. Martinez ends Leili and Rashanda's scene, and everyone claps. "That was awesome," I say to Leili as she sits back down, and I truly mean it. She really is good at everything. It's slightly maddening.

Pair after pair gets called to the stage by Mr. Martinez, improvising with varying levels of success as I get progressively more nauseous, a thin sheen of sweat on my forehead and arms.

I can't do this. I'm going to be terrible at this.

Finally my name is called. "Great," Mr. Martinez says as I'm getting to my feet, "so, Winnie, you'll get up there with . . . Who hasn't gone yet?" Please let it be someone who will be kind and understanding when their partner sucks. "Oh, of course. Mr. Evan Miller, ladies and gentlemen." It's possible the universe heard my plea. Maybe?

Evan leaps up from his seat, two arms in the air like an over-caffeinated Olympic gymnast, as everyone in the room *Woo!*s and whistles. Leili tugs at the leg of my jeans and gives me a nod. It should be a calming sight, but instead it brings me right back to my bat mitzvah.

"Go on," Mr. Martinez says, waving me forward. I've been

standing in the same spot for at least thirty seconds. "Evan won't bite."

"What about that dinosaur scene from last year?" Mahesh says, and most of the group laughs.

"Oh man, good point," Mr. Martinez says. "The controversial dinosaur bite scene." What the hell? "I stand corrected. Evan *probably* won't bite." I don't care how funny and charming he is, if Evan tries to bite me in this scene, I will judo-chop him in the testes.

"I mean, who knows?" Evan says, lifting his arms in a comical shrug as he smiles at me.

"The only thing that's going to bite is my performance," I say quietly. Leili laughs, and to my surprise, so do a couple of other people. Dad always says self-deprecation is one of a comedian's sharpest tools.

"Hey hey, soldier," Evan says as I arrive at his side, his expression quickly shifting from jovial to concerned. "Are you shaking?" he asks under his breath.

Yes. Yes, I am. And I feel light-headed and might pass out at any moment, how about you?

"Not really," I say.

"Don't worry." He gives my arm a playful nudge. "I'll do all the heavy lifting." This is what I'd been hoping for, but hearing him say it pisses me off. Like I'll need him to make me look good. He's wearing an Elmo T-shirt, for god's sake.

"What's a word to inspire their scene?" Mr. Martinez asks.

"Lovers!" Tim Stabisch immediately shouts.

Oh, gimme a break. I feel myself turn red. Evan does a little too.

"Um," Mr. Martinez says, clearly thinking he should ask for

a different word, one that doesn't make the improvisers uncomfortable before the scene's even started. "*Lovers* feels vaguely inappropriate, but adjusting it to *boyfriend and girlfriend* seems fine. Does that work for you two?"

"Sure," Evan says, trying to sound nonchalant.

"Sounds *great*," I say, trying to seem like a brave badass. There's laughter, which I'm into at first before realizing people have interpreted what I said as *Finally! I've been desperate to jump this guy's bones for YEARS!* I turn red again.

"All right, all right, quiet down," Mr. Martinez says. "Let's show a little maturity and see what our two performers decide to do with the scene." Evan and I haven't made eye contact since the word *lovers* was hurled at us. "And remember, guys: no biting."

So much for maturity. He gets a huge laugh, though I notice that Jess Yang, who I'm remembering very recently broke up with Evan, is definitely not finding any of this funny. In fact, she looks like she wants to murder me.

"Okay," Mr. Martinez says. "*Boyfriend and girlfriend.* Go!"

I look to Evan, who's looking at me. I'm waiting for him to initiate the scene—he's the one who was all cocky about doing "the heavy lifting"—but he's gone full deer-in-headlights. I'm quite sure I have too.

Boyfriend and girlfriend. What would happen in a scene with a boyfriend and girlfriend?

Kissing. Hugging. Holding hands. Going on a date. Making out.

I don't want to do any of that! Especially not in front of Evan's ex!

"It's so good to see you!" Evan finally says, throwing his arms out to his sides.

I freeze. I can't hug him right now. I won't.

And I don't necessarily think Evan wants me to, because there's terror in his eyes, a look like *I don't know why I just said that, but I had to say something!*

My instinct is to shout *Get away from me, psycho!* I know it would get a laugh. But I also know the whole point of this exercise is to agree with everything.

All eyes are on me. The ground is wobbly.

"I agree," I finally say, much more quietly than I intended.

"What?" Evan asks.

"I agree," I say again, a little bit louder. The room is silent. Oh shoot, I forgot to add something. I only did *Yes* instead of *Yes, and.* "It's really good to—" I unfortunately start speaking at the same exact time as Evan, so I stop midsentence.

"Oh no, you first," Evan says.

"It's okay, you go," I say.

"No, seriously, you . . ." He flings his hand in my direction.

I'm no improv expert, but I know this is the bad kind.

I can see Evan's faith in me slowly diminishing, like air hissing out of a balloon. He's realizing he made an awful mistake asking me to come here.

"Okay," I say. "I was going to say it's really good to see you, too. Because you're my boyfriend. And because I miss your cooking." Aha! There we go: *Yes,* it's good to see you, *AND* I missed your cooking. Boom!

"Aw yeah," Evan says, visibly relieved that I've given him something to work with. "My cooking is really good, isn't it? And guess what? While I was away, I learned how to make lasagna! Yeah, boyyyy!" Evan does a little showboaty dance about his lasagna, which gets people laughing.

Once again, I'm at a total loss for how to respond. *Agree.*

Agree. Agree. "Oh yeah, you did learn how to make lasagna. That's great."

"Uh . . . duh," Evan says. "I just said that."

People roar, which is essentially them laughing at me, which essentially feels awful, and I really don't know why I came here. Maybe there's a sledgehammer backstage I can use to bash my brains out.

"And all right," Mr. Martinez says. "Let's end that one there. Good work, guys."

I slink back to my seat, wishing Mr. Martinez had called our scene out for the mound of feces it actually was. Calling it *good work* feels completely patronizing.

"That was your first try," Leili whispers as I sit down. "You're just getting the hang of it."

I can't get words out, so I just shake my head and stare forward with my arms balanced on my knees, trying not to cry.

9

I'm only half paying attention as Mr. Martinez explains the next game. It's called Freeze. Two people do a scene until someone else shouts "Freeze!" and replaces one of them, mimicking whatever position their body is in at that moment. Then that person starts a brand-new scene using that body position to help dictate what it's about. I don't totally understand, and it doesn't matter anyway because I'm not getting up there again. Or ever coming back here. If I learned one thing from my bat mitzvah, it's that you *can* stop in the middle. The suffering can end. I'd leave right now if I could, but Leili's mom is giving me a ride home.

Freeze begins, the scenes washing over me like background noise. I can't stop replaying what happened. I said *I agree*. I literally said *I agree*. The mortification is so palpable and all-consuming, surgery might be the only way to get it out.

"Are you gonna go up there?" Leili whispers at me, her head still facing the improvisers.

"No way," I say. "Fool me once . . ."

"You need to, Winner," she says. "Everyone has bad scenes."

"I can't, Lay. I just can't."

She shrugs.

I watch as Fletcher approaches the stage after shouting "Freeze!" He taps out Tim Stabisch, who's in a goofy dancing pose from whatever was just happening in the scene I wasn't paying attention to. Fletcher takes Tim's position and immediately justifies it by making it seem as if he's being blown backward by wind. It's very convincing and very hilarious. His scene partner, Mahesh, joins in, spinning around and screaming.

"Freeze!" Mahesh is replaced by Leili. She assumes his position and becomes a passive-aggressive yoga instructor. Hilarious. I truly don't know how she does it.

"Freeze!" Fletcher is replaced by Nicole O'Connor. (And again, Leili kills.)

"Freeze!" Leili is replaced by Molly Graham-Crockett.

I can't wait for this game to be over. I sneak a peek at my phone: 3:47. Shouldn't be long now.

"Freeze!" Leili shouts, and I'm thinking, *Okay, we get it, you're very amazing at this. How about you spread the wealth a little?*

But then I feel her hands on my back, gently urging me to my feet.

"Go," she says. "You have to do this."

I stare at the stage. Molly Graham-Crockett is frozen with a worried look on her face, hovering over Nicole O'Connor, who's in a crawling pose, like she's searching for a lost contact lens or something.

"Leili, no," I whisper, my head starting to get that swimmy underwater feeling.

"You're the funniest person here," she whispers back. "Just go."

I wish I actually felt that way right now, but nevertheless, Leili knows the way to my brain, and her over-the-top flattery has the desired sobering effect.

I look again at Molly and Nicole, hoping inspiration will strike. The only thing that occurs to me is that Nicole, on all fours, could be a dog or a cat. But that's stupid.

"Leili? You going back up there?" Mr. Martinez asks, trying to figure out why the game itself seems to have frozen.

I suddenly remember: I have experience playing a dog. I was Sandy in *Annie*, dammit!

"Um . . . ," Leili says, trying to gauge how much emotional damage she'd inflict by volunteering me to go, thereby leaving me no choice. I save her from having to make that decision.

"No, I am," I say, already halfway to Nicole, forcing my body to keep moving before my head can reconsider.

"Oh, good," Mr. Martinez says.

I tap Nicole and take up her position.

I bark.

Molly immediately gets it and starts patting my head. "Aw, what a good little doggie."

For a moment, I'm blank before realizing I know exactly what to do. One day during *Annie* rehearsals when I was feeling particularly down about playing a dog with no lines, Dad encouraged me to come up with my own backstory for Sandy. And what I ended up with was that Sandy is incredibly resentful of Annie, of having to tag along all the time, and, also, always paranoid that Annie is out to get her. Dad and I have refined this bit together over the years; we actually still do it from time to time. "You think *you've* got a hard-knock life, girl?" I'll say to him. "Try being a frigging dog!"

I stare Molly down, taking two steps away from her. "Don't put me in a box, okay? I'm more than just your 'little doggie.'"

Oh god, I've just broken the cardinal rule of improv by not agreeing. But everyone watching erupts in laughter, startling me. My doggie legs momentarily tremble.

Molly is taken aback, even her freckles looking bewildered, and seems at a loss for what to say next, which for some reason eases my nerves. "I'm sorry, doggie," she finally says. "Don't you like it here at the park?" She gestures to our surroundings.

"Of course I like it at the park," I say. "The park is the best. I love the frigging park." More laughs. "I just feel a little nauseous." I eye Molly with disdain. "Did you put something in my food?" Sandy's constant suspicion that Annie has poisoned her food is one of the main bits Dad and I do. There are yet more huge laughs, each layered with a note of surprise, like people were not at all expecting me to be this funny.

I want to savor this feeling forever. I want to bathe in it. I want a wizard to cast a spell that turns this feeling into a person so I can marry it.

"No!" Molly says, almost laughing herself. "Of course not!"

"You better not have," I say, dead serious. "I know where you live." I can pick out Leili's voice in the laughter that follows, even though she's heard me do this bit before.

"You need to trust me, doggie." I'm not sure why Molly isn't coming up with an actual dog name for me, but whatever. "I've been your owner for twenty years!" Whoa, twenty years? How old a character is she even playing?

"Yeah, twenty years of *pain*!" I shout.

People are practically rolling with laughter. Even Mr. Martinez.

As the scene continues, the laughs stay pretty consistent: I've got tons of Sandy material to draw on from years of doing this bit with Dad. I keep waiting for someone to freeze us, but nobody does.

I notice, though, that Jess Yang isn't even smiling, let alone laughing. It's disconcerting. And Rashanda, sitting next to her, is chuckling a bit but clearly trying not to for Jess's sake. Whatever.

"Okay, let's stop there," Mr. Martinez says a minute later, bringing me out of my dog trance. "That'll be the last Freeze scene of the day. Great work, guys. Really nice." I suddenly realize how much pain my knees are in from being on all fours so long. But it doesn't matter because people are cheering and *Woo!*ing as I get to my feet, and Molly holds out her hand for a high five.

"That was awesome," she says.

"Yeah, you too," I say, slapping her hand, suddenly feeling shy. "Sorry I was so mean to you."

"Are you kidding? That was HI-larious."

I keep my head down, smiling as I walk to my seat and plop down next to Leili. "You were so good!" she says.

"Thanks," I say. "And thanks for pushing me to go up there."

"I knew you'd come through."

I appreciate her confidence in me, but it also occurs to me: What if I hadn't?

"Guys, believe it or not," Mr. Martinez says, looking up from his phone, "that's all the time we have for today." Many of my troupe mates emit disappointed moans. "I know, I know, but we'll be together again next Thursday, and I am so excited. In the meantime, I want you to try and get your hands on a copy of . . ." He digs around for a while in his messenger bag before producing a purple book, colorful letters in its title. "This! It's called *Truth in Comedy,* and it's brilliant. It pretty much lays out all the key concepts of improv. If we had anything resembling a budget, I'd have copies for all of you, but since we don't, people can take turns reading this one if you can't get your own. Who wants it first?"

Many hands shoot into the air, including mine, but it's Nicole O'Connor's that he sees first. Her arms are otherworldly long.

"Great. Nicole, you'll get it today, then someone else will get it next week."

"Woooooooo!" Nicole says for the second time this afternoon as she gets the book and holds it up like she's one of those hopped-up contestants on *The Price Is Right.*

"Well, great," Mr. Martinez says, seeming like he wishes he'd given the book to someone else. "Anyway, till Thursday!"

There's a buzz of chatter as everyone stands and makes their way back down to the auditorium seats to get their stuff. "That was so funny," a short-haired girl, I think her name is Shannon, says as we walk down the steps.

"Oh, thanks." I want to say the same to her, but literally all of her scenes involved repeatedly asking her scene partner where they should go for breakfast. She seems like a sweet person, though.

"Yeah," Mahesh says from behind me. "That was completely ridiculous, in the best way."

"Thanks," I say again. I'm not used to compliments from people I don't know. I can't believe the past six minutes happened. Dad is gonna be so psyched.

Which reminds me, for the first time since entering the auditorium, that my dad has been diagnosed with a terrible disease. It's like leaving Disney World to find a decimated war zone outside.

"Aren't you glad you came?" Leili asks as we grab our back-packs.

"Yeah, totally," I say.

"Isn't Mr. Martinez wonderful?"

"He is."

A hand lands on my shoulder. "Yo!" Evan says, jolting me out of my own brain. "That was unreal!" My system isn't quite sure what to do with all this praise. I look down at my feet as I thank him.

"I knew you had the goods," he says. It's stupid, but I'm so relieved to hear that, to know I didn't let him down. "That dog character was amazing. You were so great."

"You really were," Leili says.

"Thanks," I say for the eighteenth time in the past two minutes. I'm finding it hard to respond with anything more than that. I want to make a clever joke or say something self-deprecating, but in my overwhelmed state, none of that's possible. Part of me is worried that if I say too much, I'll jinx it.

"Hey, give me your number," Evan says. "I took a picture of you improvising that I want to send you."

He wants my number.

Evan wants my number.

Should I give him my number?

Leili's eyebrows are raised so high they're nearly hidden by her headscarf. It's exactly how I'm feeling too.

"Oh," I say. "Um, sure." I give him my phone number, then he holds up his screen.

"Look what I put you in as," he says, unable to contain a Cheshire cat grin.

My contact info is labeled *Dog Girl*.

I understand this is meant to be some kind of tribute to

the fantastic performance I just gave, but after the two-second burst of flattery endorphins has worn off, I'm thinking maybe being listed in his phone with my actual name might be nicer than *Dog Girl*.

Evan is still grinning like a puppy dog himself, which, in spite of my annoyance, is pretty endearing, so I smile and say, "Ha, yeah, nice."

"EVAN!" Tim Stabisch roars from the back of the auditorium like a monster. "YOU COMING?"

"BE RIGHT THERE!" Evan barks in his own version of Monsterese before turning back to us. "All right, I gots to jet." He holds up two hands, one each for me and Leili to high-five, which we do. "Later, guys." He does this deliberately goofy run up the aisle, elbows all over the place, which is one part funny, four parts huge dork. Still kind of charming, though.

"Wow, he totally likes you," Leili says.

"I mean," I say, "maybe not. He only wanted my number so he could send me a photo."

"Uh, yeah, but why was he taking photos of you in the first place?"

"That's . . . a good point."

"And has he even sent you any photo yet? I think he just said that so he could get your number."

"I don't know, lemme check." By now, everyone has filed out of the auditorium except for Mr. Martinez, who's sitting in the aisle seat of the first row writing in a notebook. My phone buzzes just as I'm taking it out of my bag, a photo from a number I don't know along with a message: *you funny, gurl.*

"He actually sent it," I say to Leili, but she's absorbed in her own phone, a concerned look on her face. "What's up?"

"Oh," she says, extracting her eyes from the screen to look at me. "It's nothing."

"You can tell me."

"It's . . ." She glances over at Mr. Martinez to see if he's listening. He's not. "It's Azadeh. Being annoying."

"What'd she say?"

"She's getting a ride home from Roxanne instead of with us. They're, like, besties now."

"Awww, don't be jealous, Lay," I say, partially because I'm feeling it myself.

"It's not that."

"She's finally getting her revenge, huh?" When the three of us met in third grade, Leili and I became friends first, and there was a tense week or so when Azadeh hated me. I still have this hilarious note she wrote me: *She's my sister, not yors.*

Leili laughs, knowing exactly what I'm talking about. "She totally is! Maybe I should—" Her phone lights up in her hand. "Oh shoot, my mom's waiting outside. Let's go."

As she leads the way up the aisle, I sneak a glance at the photo Evan was so eager to send. It's me on all fours, angrily shouting at Molly Graham-Crockett. Not the most flattering photo—my hair is vaguely rat's-nesty and light's reflecting off my glasses so you can't see my eyes—but I'll take it. Dog Girl lives.

10

"Lucy! I'm home!" I call out as I walk in through the side door. I feel like I'm back in kindergarten, busting with excitement to show Dad what I made at school today. (It was mainly unimpressive family portraits.)

"Hey hey," he says. "In here." He's in the family room watching a Hannibal Buress stand-up special from a few years ago, laughing so hard at every joke that it immediately lifts my spirits. My dad's laughter is one of my favorite things in the world—and also, this is not a man worried about a fatal diagnosis.

"Ah, so good," Dad says, wiping a tear away after Hannibal spends a minute riffing on how horrible it would be to have triplets. "How are you, Banana?" he asks, pausing the TV. He's the picture of relaxation, his arms draped on the back of the couch.

"Good," I say, sitting down near him. "I'm good."

"Great," he says. "That's great."

"How are *you*?" It comes out sounding more loaded than I intended, but my dad doesn't seem to notice or care.

"Pretty good," he says. "You know I love me some Hannibal. Once you texted that you'd be staying after school, I figured I'd keep up our tradition on my own."

On Tuesdays and Thursdays, Dad is back from teaching by the time I'm home from school, so, assuming I don't have to stay after for a *Turtle Times* meeting (I write caustic movie reviews), we sit and watch something before we start making dinner. We've been working through a rewatch of Season 1 of *The Marvelous Mrs. Maisel*. Dad says Mrs. Maisel reminds him of me (which I like, even though I think it's mainly because we're both short, brunette, and Jewish).

"I appreciate that. Tradition is important."

"Indeed," Dad says. "What'd you have to stay after for? Newspaper?"

"Well, actually . . ." I hear a drumroll in my head. "I joined the school improv troupe today."

Dad cocks his head to the side, like maybe he's misheard me. "Excuse me?"

"Yeah, I . . . I decided to try it."

"Wait a second, wait a second," he says, a half grin forming on his face. "Just to clarify: You're aware that Improv Troupe involves performing, right? In front of other people?"

"I am," I say, unable to hold back a grin of my own.

"My daughter, Winnie, who swore she would never ever perform again ever in her life, has joined a *troupe*? The kind that ends with the letter *e*?"

"I mean, I've only been to one rehearsal so far, and it was today, so don't get too excited—"

"I'm gonna get *very* excited!" Dad takes an arm off the couch to hold it out for a high five. It reminds me of Evan Miller. "This is awesome, Win! You belong in that group. I've always said so, haven't I?"

"You have." I high-five him.

"Following in the family legacy. What pushed you over the edge? Did Leili finally convince you?"

I think about Evan encouraging me to join. For some reason, I don't want to get into that with Dad.

"Pretty much," I say.

"Wow, I owe her a drink."

"That's a weird thing to say."

"*You're* a weird thing to say."

"Thanks." Calling out my dad, even when he isn't actually that worthy of being called out, is one of my favorite things to do.

"Seriously, though, this is so exciting, Win. I can't believe you didn't tell me and Mom sooner."

"I didn't decide to join until yesterday, and I was gonna tell you last night, but then . . ." It hangs there in the air for a second before Dad changes the subject.

"So the first rehearsal was today? How did it go?"

"Ugh," I say. "It started out atrocious, but then it got amazing."

"Wow, better than I would have expected. My first improv rehearsals were almost exclusively atrocious."

"Really?"

"Yes, really! I was awful. Even once I got better at it, I still had terrible wanna-roll-into-a-ball-and-hide performances. It's like a muscle you have to build. What games did you guys do? Any Arms? That was always my favorite."

"What is Arms?"

"You know. It's that game where you bring up two volunteers from the audience to be the arms for two performers. So, like, I would put my arms behind my back . . ." He gets himself up from the couch to demonstrate. "And you—just stand up real quick—you come behind me." He gestures with his head.

"We're doing this right now?"

"Come on, it's nothing weird, let me just show you." As always, I go with my dad's flow. I take a few steps and get behind him. "Okay, now slide your arms into these holes." He flaps his elbows, highlighting the gaps between arms and body.

"Can't you just explain it in words?"

"Winifred. Please. I promise this will be fun and not creepy."

"All right, all right." I put my arms through his, my nose buried in his gray polo shirt, just below the collar. Smells like the forest. Like fresh air. Like home.

"Okay, now you move your arms around however you want, and I have to justify what you're doing."

My eyes have started to produce tears. Maybe because soon his arms might actually not be under his control. Or maybe because I'm worried this closeness won't always be available to me. "That's kind of cheesy, Dad," I say, somehow making my voice sound normal.

"So what? Cheesy is good sometimes!"

I half-heartedly move my arms back and forth.

"Okay, that's a start," Dad says. "So while you're doing that, I say something to justify it. Like 'I call this lazy-man piano playing!'"

What we're doing is even cheesier than I thought it was fifteen seconds ago, but I decide to throw him a bone anyway, interlocking my fingers and shaking my hands in the air like an old-timey athlete celebrating victory.

"*Now* we're talkin'!" Dad says. "I am a champion! I am a winner! Hooray for me!"

I pull my hands apart and start pointing in random directions. I obviously can't see anything, as my face is still buried in Dad's back. I wish there were a way to wipe my wet face on his shirt without him feeling it.

"You lost!" Dad says. "And you lost too! You suck! You suck! You all suck!" I point a finger into my dad's chest. "I don't suck!" I point it forward again. "But you do!"

I laugh in spite of myself.

"Wait a sec, is somebody back there laughing at this *very cheesy* improv game?"

I raise my right hand and give Dad's face a gentle smack. His stubble is prickly. "Hey," he says. "Don't make me be violent to myself." I lightly smack the other cheek. "Hey!"

"Why are you hitting yourself?" I ask.

"Oh, don't even go there, Win." It's well known within our family that as a kid, Dad hated nothing more than when his older brother, Noah, would say that while grabbing Dad's hands and propelling them into him.

I smack both cheeks at the same time. "You don't like yourself or something?"

Dad turns around and lifts me up as he growls like a grizzly, then hurls me onto the couch. I'm laughing, happy and genuinely surprised; it's been at least three years since he's done that to me.

"If you poke the bear, you're gonna get hurt," he says, growling but maybe also wincing and more out of breath than I would have expected.

"You okay?" I say, my own smile fading.

"Yeah," Dad says, trying to laugh it off. "That just . . ." He flexes his right arm at the elbow a few times. "I'm good."

"Okay. I can slap you again if that's helpful."

He continues to look at his arm for what feels like a full minute before responding. "What? Oh. Ha. No, thanks."

He takes his phone out of his pocket and glances at the screen. "I should probably get dinner started," he says. "Wanna help?"

"Not really."

"That's fine, I'll just get the robot to do it."

"Okay, great."

Dad walks over to the fridge to gather ingredients, and I join him, trying to ignore the way he reaches out to the counter to make sure he doesn't fall.

"Winnie joined the school's improv troupe today," Dad says, a few minutes after we sit down to eat dinner.

"Wow," Mom says, her face lighting up. "That's great. The ban on performing has lifted?"

"For now," I say. "I think. Maybe."

"Amazing. I didn't even know your school *had* an improv troupe."

"Yeah," I say. "I've told you about it before. Leili's in it."

"Oh, that's right, that's right," Mom says, slurping a single spaghetti noodle into her mouth. "How'd she convince you to get back in the game?"

"She paid me."

"What?" Mom looks concerned.

"That was a joke."

"Oh. Okay." Mom makes that face like *I don't understand what passes for humor these days in this house, but all right.* "So why did you actually decide to join?"

I stare down at specks of Parmesan cheese that missed my

plate and landed on the table. Can't we just celebrate this personal milestone and talk details later? "I don't know, I just did."

"Come on, Win," Dad says. "You can give Mom a better explanation than that. You said Leili wore you down, right?"

"Right," I say. It sounds better than the actual reason, which suddenly seems pathetic. *I joined because a boy I barely know told me to.* Ugh.

"Go Leili," Mom says.

"We owe her a drink," Dad says, repeating his not-that-funny joke from earlier.

I love our family, but sometimes I wish I had someone to roll my eyes with other than Dad. A little jokester brother named Johnny. Or a scrappy little sister named Madge. When I was eight or nine years old, I bugged my parents constantly about not wanting to be an only child until finally Mom looked at Dad and then at me and said, "You know, we didn't want that for you either." They had tried to have a second child, she explained, but she'd had two miscarriages. Neither she nor Dad wanted to go through that again, so they stopped trying. So. A little TMI for age nine, but I stopped asking.

"And how was your day?" Mom asks Dad.

"Oh, me? Good. Fine. Classes this morning went well."

"Did you call to make that appointment?"

"Oh shoot, no, I didn't."

"Russ," Mom says.

"I will. I'll leave a voice mail later. I totally forgot."

"This isn't a joke. I can do it if you—"

"No, I got it, I got it," Dad says. "I just . . . I got it." This is a long-standing dynamic between my parents. Mom is more on top of things. Dad is less so.

"Okay," Mom says, lifting a forkful of salad into her mouth. "Just actually do it."

"I said I got it, Dana." Dad doesn't get snappy regularly, so it's always notable when he does. This time I think he even surprised himself. He's suddenly very focused on the last meatball left on his plate.

I want to ask what appointment they're talking about, but now the subject seems off-limits. We eat in silence for five minutes before I get up the courage to ask to be excused.

As I'm walking to my room, I see that I have nine new texts: one from Leili, and *eight* from Evan. It catches me so off guard I trip up the steps.

"You all right?" Dad says, from the kitchen.

"Totes McGotes," I say, using the banister to pull myself back up.

Once firmly planted on my bed, door to my room closed, I look at my phone.

Leili's text is simple and to the point: *Azadeh = SUPER annoying.*

Hah why? I text back before looking, with a combination of excitement and dread, at the eight separate thoughts Evan felt he needed to transmit to me.

Did you like the pic? he texted at 6:17 p.m.

You were seriously so funny today

I can't look at my dog wo thinking about it

And wondering if he hates me

Haha

He texted again at 7:04 p.m.:

I'm starting to think you gave me a made-up number

And I'm texting these things to a stranger

Sorry, Stranger

That was twelve minutes ago.

I drop the phone on my bed because I'm nervous I'm going to accidentally respond before I'm ready. He's definitely flirting with me. You don't send eight texts to someone if you're not flirting.

Right?

But does that mean he's pretending he thinks I'm funny so that I'll go out with him?

Or does he have a crush on me *because* I'm funny?

I hope it's that.

It better be that.

Dad is often a helpful resource on questions such as these. I've always felt more comfortable talking with him than Mom. Mainly because Mom gets so invested in every real-time detail and then I feel all this pressure to keep reporting back, whereas Dad can give good advice—mainly about the moronic male perspective—and then forget the conversation happened by the next day.

Not that I've even had so much experience. The closest thing I've had to a relationship was with this elfin boy named Asher Fisk who I met at Camp Valley Island Mountain the summer before high school started. He was my first kiss, and he made charcoal sketches of me, and he had gorgeous dimples, and he referred to many things as "wicked," and he always wore a hemp shell necklace, and when camp ended, we decided to make the long-distance thing work (he's from Maine), which it did up until February, when he stopped responding to my texts

80

and calls for a full week and then sent me this long, annoying email about how he'd started dating some girl at his school "which, really, when you think about it, makes a lot more sense, right?"

Dad explained that many boys are stupid dipsticks in high school and that it was completely acceptable for me to entertain fantasies of pushing Asher Fisk into a cement mixer. It was very helpful. I want to go downstairs and ask him about Evan's texts, but I don't want to accidentally stumble back into Tenseville. And also he's got way more important things to worry about.

A bigger question is: How do *I* feel about Evan? (I mean, assuming he actually does like me and think I'm funny and I'm not reading way too far into all of this.) I guess he's cute. Goofy-cute. Thinking back on it, I didn't have a crush on Asher until he started talking to me all the time in the dining hall and leaving cryptic drawings of birds and pinecones on the steps of my cabin (which seemed charming then but now just seems weird), so maybe this is kind of like that. Maybe my destiny is to never end up with boyfriends who I have crushes on first.

Not that I actually have a crush on anyone right now. I spent much of the past summer pointlessly pining after Dev Ahmad (along with every other girl at camp). He was handsome and good at magic tricks, but what really got me was that his magic act was hilarious, and not even in a dorky way. But he was making out with Michelle Jorgenson all summer, which I was actually okay with, since she's super-shy, so it felt like a nice message to send to the younger campers. Like, you can be a quiet person and *still* get the hottest guy in camp.

I don't know, I probably just came up with that rationale so

I wouldn't have to feel bad that Dev never had any interest in me. And never laughed at my jokes. For example, I once told him during a pottery elective that if he ever needed a rabbit for his act, I could supply him with one from the family of bunnies I was raising in our bunk bathroom. "Don't you think that's a little . . . inhumane?" Dev asked. He looked so serious that I couldn't get up the nerve to tell him I was joking. "Yeah, I guess you're right," I said, looking back down at my pottery wheel. It was then that I became convinced Dev didn't actually write his own act, but that's another story entirely.

The thing is, Evan *does* get my jokes. And that's actually kind of awesome. I stare down at his last text: *Sorry, Stranger.*

Not a problem, I text. *Do you want some candy, young man?*

The joke is a bit of a reach. The three dots pop up immediately.

Haha No I don't take candy from strangers.

He got it.

He's cooler than I thought.

It's two Snickers and a Pixie Stix tho, I write. *Kids love Pixie Stix.*

OK I changed my mind I'll take it, he writes.

I laugh. *So easily convinced.*

You actually picked 2 candies that I really love haha, he writes.

Well, there was poison in all of it, so you're dead now. Should have listened to your parents' advice.

He texts the openmouthed Xs-for-eyes emoji.

Haha, I write. This feels good. This is fun.

We joke back and forth like that for a little while, speaking of absolutely nothing of substance, until I realize it's been almost forty-five minutes of texting. I also realize I've gotten so wrapped up in our conversation that I never responded to a Leili text that came in twenty minutes ago.

She skipped dinner! Leili wrote, followed by another text, presumably after I'd failed to respond: *Hulllooooooooo?*

Sorry! I say. *I'm texting with Evan. Can't believe Oz did that.*

Leili fires back a shocked-face emoji.

I know, I say.

He reeeeeeeeally likes you.

Right? The whole thing is weirding me out.

It's not weird it's cute, Leili says, followed by a bear emoji.

Are you ignoring me? Evan texts, followed by four winky faces. Oops, I'm bad at texting multiple people at once. (I know, what kind of twenty-first-century human am I?)

I am, I say. *It was a test. You failed.*

AW DANGIT, Evan says.

Gotta go, Leili says. *Azadeh's home.*

Give her hell, I say. She sends back a heart and a fist.

Then, to Evan: *I should get going, more kids to poison.*

Going for Stranger of the Year Award, he writes. It makes me laugh out loud, which is not the easiest thing in the world to do.

Already won twice actually. Going for the threepeat. That's a sports word I heard Mike Muscone say to Matthew Lee before class once, and I filed it away in my brain for a moment just like this.

Evan sends a cry-laughing emoji.

Blammo! Preparation + timing = comedic genius.

I'm gonna find you at school tomorrow, he says.

There are many creepy ways to read that, yet I receive it the way he'd intended: a tiny, cozy campfire that lights up my stomach. Is Evan Miller going to be my boyfriend? This is nuts.

Not if I spend all day hiding in one of the utility closets, I say.

You just gave away your hiding spot.

AW DANGIT, I say. Nothing I text will top that, so I triumphantly toss the phone away to prevent further communication. I overshoot, though, and it smacks directly into the headboard, then bounces off the mattress and onto the floor.

I pick it up and see that three new cracks have formed across the screen.

The funny thing is, I don't even mind.

"Aw dangit!" I say aloud.

11

Is it possible that I spent an entire weekend texting with Evan Miller and now am scared to see him in person?

Yes. It's very possible. Because what if real life doesn't live up to our invisibly transmitted hilarity?

Okay, that wasn't the *only* thing I did all weekend, but pretty close. I also devoured that book *Truth in Comedy* in one sitting after finding out Dad still had his copy from college. Every time I stumbled on a note he'd written in the margins (like "<u>SIM-PLIFY</u>"), I got chills. It's so cool to be following in his footsteps (or, you know, fingerprints). The book was really good, though now I can't remember a single thing I learned. I might have read it too fast.

Wait! Here's something: *Don't make jokes in improv!* The book explained that improv is more about listening and paying attention and making connections and finding the humor that way, which I love. Because it's true. If you pay attention, as I have been doing my whole life, funny things are happening *all the time*. The things people say, the way they interact, the stupid customs humans have.

Like, for example, saying "Good morning." It's a little aggressive. I don't know what kind of morning you're having—it might be a *terrible* morning—so who am I to force a label on it? That's why I just say "Morning." Or I pose it as a question: "Good morning?" Occasionally I'll do "Have a good morning," though that's still pretty pushy.

See? Maybe that's not hilarious, but it's a universal moment that we never really stop to examine. Our days are *filled* with those! And thinking about them makes life so much more satisfying. And by *satisfying,* I mean bearable.

Because, let's be real, our lives are filled with many *un*funny things too. Like, even genuinely upsetting things. But when you filter them through the lens of comedy, you can turn pain into laughter. Dad first taught me that in third grade. Leili, Azadeh, and I had just become friends, and resident dick Mike Muscone decided to coin annoyingly obvious nicknames for us: Ukulele, Mazda, and Pooh (as in "Winnie the"). Unfortunately, the names caught on like wildfire with the rest of the class.

"Aw, Banana," Dad had said when I came home crying one day. "I'm sorry. It's funny how that inevitably happens, isn't it?"

This was not the comfort I was looking for. "It's not funny, it's mean. I'm really sad about it."

"No, of course. That's what I meant. Not funny haha, funny sad. That kids always do this to each other." I just stared at him. "Look," he said, "I've always found the best thing to do when something is making you upset is to see if there's any way to turn that into something funny."

The next day at school, I came prepared with a nickname for Mike Muscone: Muskrat. Leili and Azadeh thought it was hilarious. We started using it. Soon the whole class was on board. It somehow neutralized the entire nickname situation, and within a week or two, everyone was being referred to by their preferred names again. Not only that, but it made Leili and Azadeh and me much closer.

So. That was a very long-winded way of saying: I think improv is going to be a good fit for me.

And lo and behold, moments after I step off the bus, I see the best friends I was just thinking about stepping off theirs. Our buses usually show up within the same four-minute window, but it's never as magically precise as this. It feels like a sign from the universe or something. Leili and Azadeh are deep in solemn but animated conversation, and they don't notice me approaching, so I leap toward them and shout, "BOO!"

I immediately regret it. They both startle, looking authentically frightened for at least two seconds, and even once they realize it's me, they don't smile.

"Why did you do that?" Leili asks very genuinely, almost confused.

"Sorry," I say. "I don't know." What was I thinking? Scare humor isn't even my thing!

"That was straight-up terrifying," Azadeh says. "And you know I don't scare easy."

"I'm really sorry," I say. "I thought it would be fun."

"It wasn't," Leili says.

"Yeah, I get that." I pretend my glasses need adjusting because I don't know what else to do. "Anyway, morning."

"Morning," Azadeh says as she starts walking toward the school entrance and Leili and I fall into step next to her.

Leili doesn't say anything. Either I really annoyed her with that scare or there's still some resentment after Azadeh skipped out on family dinner last week. Probably both.

"Good weekend?" I ask. I was so wrapped up in trying to come up with funny bits for Evan that I wasn't in touch with them much.

"Definitely," Azadeh says.

"Well, of course it was for you," Leili says. "You were barely home."

"Lay, I said I'm sorry!"

"No, don't worry about it. I love hanging out with Mom and Papa and Ramin while you're out having fun. Everybody wins." Wow. I mean, Leili and Azadeh squabble all the time, but this seems particularly intense.

"I'll make it up to you," Azadeh says, "I promise."

"Fine, fine. It doesn't matter. I gotta get to homeroom."

"We're in the same homeroom!" Azadeh looks to me, like *What is with her?* I pretend I don't notice. Past experience has taught me it's best not to take sides.

"Well," Leili says, "how am I supposed to know if you're gonna decide to skip it at the last minute or not?"

Azadeh tips her head back and lets out a Hulk-like grunt of frustration as I hear a "Happy Monday!" from my right and my heart ping-pongs. Evan Miller appears at my shoulder wearing a purple-and-blue argyle sweater that looks surprisingly cute on him.

"Hi hi hi," I stop to say, immediately realizing that Leili and Azadeh have continued walking. I call after them, but they're too enmeshed in their own conversation to realize I'm not with them anymore.

"Just the human I was looking for," Evan says, wrapping an arm around my shoulders and pivoting me back the way I came. "Come with me."

It's jarring, in a nice way, as no guy other than my dad has ever put an arm around me like that. Even Asher Fisk.

"Wait," I say, "my homeroom is in the B Wing."

"We're not going to your homeroom."

"Um," I say. It's fun to be wanted, so I smile, but I'm confused. "Where *are* we going?"

"Top secret," he says in a gruff federal agent voice as we weave around a pack of loudly laughing football players. It's like I've suddenly found myself on a roller coaster, and it's exciting, but also terrifying, because *How many loops does this thing have? How big a drop?* Texting all weekend is one thing, but actual one-on-one contact before the school day's even begun? Are we gonna make out? Did I remember to brush my teeth?

"Hold on," I say, stopping in the middle of the hall. "I actually don't want to miss class. And I haven't even gone to my locker yet. So."

"Whoa," he says, smiling. "I've never seen you this serious. Don't worry, I promise. Just come with me."

"Watch this, I can be even more serious," I say, furrowing my brow as much as humanly possible, which gets a laugh out of him. I definitely forgot to brush my teeth. I bet my breath smells like scone. I think I'm shaking. "Now tell me where we're going. Or else."

Evan gives an exaggerated shrug. "It's a surprise! So just— It's a school-sanctioned activity, okay?" He better not be trying to tutor me or something. "You won't get in trouble. Pleeease?" He makes what I imagine he thinks is a very adorable face, smiling without showing teeth, eyebrows raised high. And he's right. It is very adorable.

"Okaaaaay," I say, and now he genuinely smiles, his whole face lighting up like a jack-o'-lantern.

"We're gonna have to pick up the pace," he says, looking at his phone. "We're gonna be late." He starts walking much faster than before, so I have to sort of run to keep up. I follow him through the lobby and straight toward . . . the school office?

Guess we won't be making out.

This is weird.

He swings open the glass-windowed door and holds it for me as I tentatively walk in, the white-haired lady behind the desk shuffling papers and staring at me with a *Can I help you?* look.

I have no idea what to say, seeing as I have no idea what I'm doing here.

"Cutting it close, Evan," the white-haired lady says as she spots him behind me.

"Nice to see you too, Ms. DiMicelli," Evan says, in an exceedingly sweet voice, clearly the one he uses to kiss grown-ups' asses, before winding his way around the desk—something I've never in my life seen a student do—to walk deeper into the office. *What is happening?* "Hi, Ms. Moore," Evan says to the other secretary, who's curly-haired and slightly younger than Ms. DiMicelli.

"Morning, Evan," she says without looking up from her computer.

"Come on," Evan says, gesturing wildly at me. "Back here." I look to Ms. DiMicelli and Ms. Moore, thinking they might object, but they've stopped paying attention.

"Are you planning a heist?" I whisper to Evan once I've

awkwardly scampered over. He just smiles, which is a tad infuriating. I'm already thinking up ways to return the favor, maybe a "surprise visit" to a room of rabid raccoons.

The homeroom bell rings, so now I'm officially late to class. Evan glances over to Ms. DiMicelli, who gives a little nod. "Here we go," he says to me before pushing a button on the wall next to us, leaning in, and starting to speak.

"Good morning!" he says. "Please stand for the Pledge of Allegiance."

Ohmigod. The morning announcements. *He's* the one who does them! Duh. I knew his voice was familiar. He stares at me as he recites the Pledge, a big exaggerated smile playing on his face, a look more suitable for performing the opening number of a musical.

So . . . is this why he brought me here? To watch him while he announces? Is that what I seem like? A watcher? I guess it's fun, in a way. Like a behind-the-scenes peek at how it all happens.

As Evan transitions into the actual announcements— reading from a printout on the wall reminders about Yearbook and French Club and Back-to-School Night that he spices up with his own asides ("And, Frenchies, don't forget to bring your berets!") (weak)—I start wondering if this is part of his courtship ritual with every girl he likes. Did Jess Yang stand in this exact spot last year? So that Evan could dazzle her with his delivery?

I'm pulled out of my own head when I realize Evan is talking about the improv troupe. "Yes, that's right, kiddos, we meet Thursdays after school in the auditorium, and this is your last chance to join and be a part of the shenanigans!" Shenanigans.

Ugh. "But you don't have to take my word for it . . ." I realize with horror that Evan is giving me an *Are you ready?* look.

Oh no.

"I brought my dog Spot to let you know why the Manatawkin Improv Troupe could be just the extracurricular you've been waiting for." Evan nods and points to the microphone part of the wall. "Take it away, Spot!"

I'm supposed to speak? Right now? To the whole school?

My heart is pounding. I try to get a deep breath. Evan's body gets all wavy, then solidifies. I want to say something, and I want it to be funny. But I have no idea what that is.

"Uh . . . Spot?" Evan asks.

In the midst of this paralysis, though, my nerves take a backseat to something else: my anger, that I've been put in this position in the first place. If he'd only let me know *last night* while we were texting, I could have dug into my Sandy repertoire and absolutely destroyed. But instead I'm supposed to manufacture brilliance out of thin air?

Also, side note: Spot is the most clichéd dog name of all time. But whatever.

"Sometimes Spot gets a little shy," Evan says into the wall. He can tell that I'm nervous but not that I'm angry. Because I'm hiding it well. *Why am I hiding it?* "Spot, why don't yo—"

"I'm not shy," I say into the microphone, nudging him to the side as the words explode out of me. Evan stares warily, suddenly uneasy about what I might say next. "I was just relieving myself on a desk. Geez!"

Evan grins at me, reassured. "Oh wow, sorry, Spot, I didn't realize you were . . . doing that."

"Yeah, well, you never realize anything that I'm doing," I say, not returning the grin. "Because you're a terrible owner. The worst."

"Oh." Evan is slightly thrown, but he's trying to roll with it. "That's not true."

"It is! This guy only gives me off-brand dog food!" I say, leaning closer to the microphone. "Never the good stuff."

"But . . . ," Evan says. "Can you even taste the difference?"

"Of course!" I shout. "All dogs can!" Evan chortles into his hand as creative inspiration courses through me. "This guy's idea of a quality chew toy is the cardboard from a toilet paper roll."

"What's the problem with that?" he asks.

"What's the problem? I want something that squeaks, man! Squeaks are the whole point!"

Evan is now legitimately cracking up, which feels pretty great. I'm actually feeling like I might laugh too.

"I'd honestly rather live with a *cat* than with you," I say. "And that's saying a lot. Because cats suck!"

"I'm sorry!" Evan says in between laughs. "I'm truly sorry, Spot!" I have to say, I'm impressed by how well he's playing along. "But we've gotten way off track. I brought you here to talk about the Manatawkin Improv Troupe."

"Oh, right," I say. "That. I don't care if you join. Whatever."

"Okay then. There you have it, friends. Join us after school on Thursday. That's all the news this morning. Have a super day!"

Evan presses the button to turn off the PA system and looks at me with awe and wonder. "That. Was. Incredible."

I can't believe that just happened. I want to jump up and down. I want to scream. I want to wrap my arms around Evan and squeeze. "Thanks," I say.

"I knew I made the right decision bringing you here," Evan says.

He *did* make the right decision. He knew I was funny, and he picked me, and he laughs at my jokes, and he is wonderful, and I don't know why it took me this long to see that.

"I mean, I knew you'd be funny," he continues, "but I didn't know you'd be *that* funny. I'm so proud. Ms. DiMicelli, Ms. Moore, wasn't that hilarious?"

"Quite," Ms. DiMicelli says, adjusting the position of the visitor sign-in clipboard. "Reminds me of my own dog, actually. Kermit. He's completely ungracious."

Wow.

"It was very . . . interesting," Ms. Moore says without glancing up.

Well, two out of three ain't bad.

"And sorry I had to keep it a surprise," Evan says, giving me a sheepish smile, "but I was worried otherwise you might have chickened out. And I knew you could handle it."

When he puts it that way, I actually understand. Because I might not have had the guts to do that. No, I *definitely* wouldn't have. But he was right: I could handle it. I *did* handle it. "Oh yeah, no," I say, "don't worry about it."

"Ms. DiMicelli," Evan says, "could you give Winnie a late pass for homeroom?"

I get to do bits *and* skip homeroom with no consequences?

I could get used to this.

"Of course." Ms. DiMicelli writes one out and hands it to me over the desk. "I'm not going to be able to look at Kermit with a straight face tonight." She winks, which I normally hate coming from grown-ups, but this one seems different. Pure.

I'm not sure how to respond, so I just say, "Oh. Yeah. Tell him Spot says hi."

But this is one comedic leap too many for Ms. DiMicelli, who stares at me for a few seconds, puzzled, before she says, "Well, okay," and returns to her computer.

12

I walk into Mr. Novack's English class as nonchalantly as possible, thirty or so seconds after the homeroom-is-over tone has sounded, stopping at his desk to hand him my late pass.

"Oh. So you *are* here," Mr. Novack says. He's only been my teacher since last week, but so far, he's lived up to his reputation of being a pompous dick.

"I am," I say. "Sorry about that."

He sighs, as if my tardiness is the pulled Jenga piece that knocks down the whole tower, and starts scribbling in his attendance book.

After a few seconds, I realize my presence is no longer needed, so I take my seat and place *Tess of the d'Urbervilles* on my desk. I'm still coming down from the high of five minutes ago.

"Hey," I hear from behind me to the left. "That was you, right?"

I turn to see Fletcher Handy, the guy who was so convincingly blowing in the wind at improv.

"Oh, hey," I say, feigning ignorance on the off chance he's talking about something else. "What was me?"

"The dog. On the announcements."

"Oh yeah. Evan just, like, pulled me into doing that. I—"

"It was really funny," Fletcher says, though if it weren't for the nod and closemouthed smile that followed it, he could just as easily have said, "The capital of South Dakota is Pierre."

"Thanks," I say.

Wanda Pechofsky taps me from my right. "Did you just say that was you?" We've been going to school together since sixth grade, but this might be the first time she's ever spoken directly to me. "On the announcements? The angry dog?"

"Um," I say, feeling my face flush as I turn toward her. "Yeah."

"That was freaking hilarious," she says. Wanda leans to the purple-haired girl on her other side, Danielle something, and points at me. "The dog was her. It was . . . uh . . ."

"Winnie," I say.

"Winnie, yeah," Wanda says. "Winnie was the dog on the announcements."

"Oh," Danielle says, blinking, confused. "Really?"

"Yo!" Matthew Lee says from the back row. "*I want something that squeaks, man!* We were all laughing our asses off."

A surge of energy moves through and around me like a force field. Like I've crossed over into some alternate reality.

"Yeah, we actually paid attention for once," eternal asshole Mike Muscone says. "Nice job, Pooh."

What. The. Hell. Is. Going. On.

"All right," Mr. Novack says, closing his attendance book, having finally completed the thousand-word essay about my late arrival, "let's open to page eight in our copies of *Tess of the d'Urbervilles*."

As I flip to the right page, I'm nearly floating. The past minute was so much like a fantasy I've had on repeat in my brain for years, it gives me joy chills. And also kind of makes me want to throw up.

Yes.

I'm so happy I could vomit.

The joy continues through the rest of the morning. I'm never gonna do Ecstasy, because it puts holes in your brain, but I imagine this might be what it's like. Every time I'm convinced I dreamt the whole thing up, someone goes out of their way to tell me how great I was and that they never knew I was so funny (even Mr. Barker, one of the gym teachers, who had previously given zero indication he knew of my existence). It's a touch unsettling; if I were going to program my own personal matrix, this is what would happen in it. Which leads me to wonder: Have I entered my own personal matrix?

I keep hoping I'll run into Leili and/or Azadeh before lunch, because they would be helpful proof that this is reality, but it doesn't happen. They each text me excitedly, though—Leili with an *OMG* and Azadeh with a *what the what???*—saying it was awesome and wondering why I hadn't mentioned I'd be doing it.

By the time I walk into the cafeteria, I'm desperate to talk with them, so I'm thrilled to remember Dad packed a lunch for me and I won't have to waste time going to buy one. But as I sit down across from Leili, Azadeh and Roxanne are cracking up about something and don't even acknowledge my arrival.

"Hey, Winner," Leili says, this fake sort of smile glued to her face.

"Hi, Lay," I say. "What're they laughing about?"

"Hard to say. Some inside joke, I think."

I completely forgot about the way the day started, with Leili and Azadeh bickering as we walked into school.

"No, no," Azadeh says, gasping for air, a hand on Roxanne's arm. "It's not— I can explain, it's just about something this girl Siobhan on our team always does." Are Azadeh and Roxanne . . . flirting with each other? I thought Roxanne was straight. At least, she was dating this guy Rodrigo for a bunch of months. Still, maybe they're flirting. Azadeh came out last year. She told me while we binge-watched *Jane the Virgin* at my house ("I think I love Gina Rodriguez," she said. "She's so great," I said. "No, but . . . really," she said), but I've definitely never seen her flirt with anyone before. Suddenly their inside joke goes from annoying to adorable.

"Yeah," Roxanne says, snorting, "we're making a joke about how Siobhan and I fought in Vietnam together."

Right. Back to annoying. Leili and I look at each other. "So how was your morning?" I ask over the guffaws.

"Fine," Leili says. "It was— Oh!" Her irritation dissipates, as if she just remembered she won the lottery. "You were so funny on the announcements!"

"Yes!" Azadeh says, pulling herself together and reaching across the table to grab my hand. "Ohmigod, Winner, you're my hero!"

"*So* funny," Roxanne agrees.

My irritation dissipates too.

"We weren't even paying attention to the announcements," Azadeh says, "and then Leili heard your voice and nudged me, which at first I thought she was just doing because we were fighting—"

"We weren't *fighting*," Leili says, "we were having a disagreement."

"We were pretty much fighting." Azadeh holds out her arms and nods her head like *Come on, we can all agree on that, right?* "But then I realized it was your voice on the announcements, and we got nervous for you, but then you were saying the funniest things, and we weren't even the only ones laughing!"

Her shock that other people found me funny would be offensive if I didn't feel exactly the same way.

"Lots of people were cracking up in Mrs. Kalanithi's class, too," Roxanne says. "Like *Hahahahahaha*." She tries to act out how they were laughing, and it's flattering but uncomfortable.

"The curse is broken!" Leili says, raising a baby carrot in the air like a magic wand. "You performed for so many people! And it went great!"

"Well, I mean, I couldn't even see the audience," I say.

"Don't try to belittle it! It was really cool, Win. You should have told us you were gonna be doing that."

"Seriously," Azadeh says. "We might have missed it if it weren't for Leili's bat-radar hearing."

"I didn't know I was gonna be doing it," I say. "Until, like, literally, moments before."

"What do you mean?" Leili is tripped up by the logic of that.

"I mean Evan pulled me away in the hall but wouldn't tell me why and it was, you know . . . to do that. To do that part of the announcements."

"Aww," Azadeh says. "That's pretty sweet."

"He didn't even tell you he was about to have you perform?" Leili asks. "You had to come up with that on the spot?"

"But," Azadeh says, confused, "that is what improv is, isn't it?"

"Right," I say. I'm embarrassed that didn't even occur to me.

"Well, normally you know when you're going on," Leili says. "But I'm so proud you were able to get through it."

"If someone did that to me," Roxanne says, "I would have no idea what to say. I'd be all, 'Uh, can I just say the Pledge again?'"

Azadeh laughs, and we fall into a brief, awkward silence. Leili looks like she's about to bring up something new when—

"Spot! There you are. I've been looking for you everywhere." It's Evan. He and Tim Stabisch grab two empty seats next to Roxanne. "Cool if we join you?"

"Uh, sure," Leili says, though they've already lowered themselves to the table, so it doesn't seem like her answer really mattered one way or the other.

"Whaddup," Tim says. He's wearing a T-shirt that's covered with tattoos, as if to make the wearer seem like a shirtless tattooed person.

"Y'alls hear Winnie on the announcements this morning?" Evan asks, pulling a wrap out of his lunch bag. "She killed it!"

"Yeah, she was great," Azadeh says. "We were just talking about that."

"Sweet," Evan says. "Nice job last week, by the way."

"Oh," Azadeh says, confused as to why she's being complimented. "Were you . . . Were you at field hockey practice?"

"You do field hockey, too? Wow, that's impressive."

Evan thinks Azadeh is Leili. Even though this happens all the time, I feel particularly mortified. Leili gets what's happening, but Azadeh is for some reason taking longer to catch on.

"Oh. Well, yeah," Azadeh says, "it's the main thing I do, but—"

"I think you're thinking she's me," Leili says, leaning her head forward so that Evan, who's a couple of seats down, can see her. "Hey, Evan."

"Oh!" Azadeh laughs, her impressively good nature a skill

she's developed over time to combat the world's twin idiocy. "That's why I had no idea what you were talking about."

"Whoa!" Evan looks back and forth between the two of them. "Twinsies! I didn't know you had a sister. You should join Improv Troupe too," he tells Azadeh. "We could do so many cool twin bits. Or, like, scenes about clones and stuff."

"Nah, not really my thing," Azadeh says.

"Well," Evan says, taking a huge bite of his wrap, "just think about it."

Does he encourage literally everyone he meets to join Improv Troupe?

"Twins are hot," Tim Stabisch says, messily spooning soup into his mouth.

I look across the table to Leili, trying to mind-meld so I can transmit an image of Tim's head and torso being snapped off by a *T. rex,* but she's looking down at her pita chips and hummus.

"Almost as hot as fabric tattoos," Roxanne says.

Tim is unsure whether or not to say thank you.

"Yo, Winnie," Evan says, skillfully changing the subject, "everyone keeps asking me who was the voice of Spot this morning."

"Oh really?" I say, trying to seem humble and surprised.

"Yeah. I tell them it was Ms. DiMicelli." Evan cracks up at his own joke. "I'm totally kidding! Of course I tell them it was you. We gotta do something to celebrate."

"Smoke a huge bowl," Tim says, taking the straw from his milk and using it to blow bubbles in his soup.

"Shut up, dude." Evan elbows him and soup splashes onto Tim's shirt.

"Hey!" he says. "This is a new shirt, jerkwad."

"It's fine. The soup looks like another stupid tattoo."

"Up yours," Tim says.

Leili, Azadeh, Roxanne, and I are silently looking at each other. Our table has been commandeered by a couple of morons, and it's my fault.

"Sorry about him," Evan says to all of us but mainly to me. "Brought up by wolves, this guy."

"*Ow-ooooooo,*" Tim howls.

I try to think up a witty response, but nothing comes.

I am very good at improv.

13

"Okay, okay," Mr. Martinez says, hushing everybody. "I have an announcement to make."

All of us sitting onstage go silent, drawn in by the promise and possibility of the word *announcement*. "I knew that'd quiet you guys down." Mr. Martinez smirks, twinkle in his eyes that I know Leili, who's sitting next to me, is loving (because she's specifically referenced it many times).

We've already gone through our warm-up games, all of which felt slightly less mortifying than they did last week. I'm not sure if that's because I'm used to them or because I feel more confident or what, but let's just say during Nameball, I changed a tennis ball into a human-sized orb of light, so. Yeah. Progress.

It's been three days since I woofed my way into my classmates' hearts, and I've been eager for another comedy fix. I thought maybe Evan would ask me to do the announcements again, but he hasn't. He has, however, continued texting me and sitting at our lunch table (which I apologized to Leili, Azadeh, and Roxanne for; they've all been way more understanding than I would have been) and generally giving every indication that he really, really likes me. Which I think I'm into.

"So," Mr. Martinez says. "I was really happy with the work everybody did last week, and it confirmed to me that we're ready to challenge ourselves a bit more, stretch our wings a little further. I went to a fantastic conference this summer and learned some new tricks, which I want to impart to all of you." He puts a finger in the air and takes a dramatic pause. "We're going to do some long-form improv."

There's a murmuring among the group, both excited and confused. I am one hundred percent psyched. Long-form improv is what they do at the Upright Citizens Brigade Theatre, which Amy Poehler cofounded.

"For those not in the know," Mr. Martinez says in my direction, which I sort of resent, "long-form improv is far less structured than short-form. You usually get one suggestion from the audience, and that's the seed of inspiration for all the scenes that happen during that performance. We're going to focus on a specific improv form known as a Harold, which consists of—"

"Wait, what'd you say it's called?" Rashanda asks.

"It's called a Harold," Mr. Martinez says.

"Like the name?" Mahesh asks.

"Yeah. Funny improv people came up with it, so they decided to name the art form with an actual name."

"That's weird," Jess says.

"Ha, well, it doesn't matter, it's just what it's called." Mr. Martinez seems both amused and defensive. "Anyway, when you do a Harold—and if you've started reading *Truth in Comedy,* you'll learn more about this—you have a series of scenes, which at first may seem like they're all about different things, but as the Harold progresses, it's the players' job to make connections between those scenes, until by the end, it all feels like it's related. Does that make sense?"

Not really!

I must not be the only one thinking that because he says, "Well, it will soon. And look, if we can get the hang of this, our first performance in October . . . will be all long-form."

A buzz percolates through the group as Leili looks at me like *I guess we're supposed to think this is cool?* Some people nod enthusiastically, and Evan and Dan Blern are high-fiving like a couple of nerds.

"I know, I know," Mr. Martinez says. "It's very exciting, but our show is soon, so if we want to do this, it's going to require a lot of focus and a lot of concentration. But don't stress out about it. The performance will be more like a low-stakes experiment. A chance to show your friends and family what we've been up to. But we will have to work hard to get there."

These mixed messages are gonna give me a panic attack.

"All right, enough talking! I figure the best way to start learning is to just dive in. Today we'll do scenes inspired by a single word. No relationships provided like last week—that's for you and your scene partner to figure out in the moment. Don't forget to *Yes, and*! Let's start with . . . Molly and Leili."

Leili, usually so unflappable, shoots me her wide-eyed *Yeesh* face.

"You got this," I say. She and Molly bravely hop into the playing space, Leili nervously bouncing on the balls of her purple low-top Chuck Taylors.

"Can we get a word?" Mr. Martinez asks.

"Tunafish!" Dan Blern shouts.

"Okay then. This scene will be inspired somehow by the word *tunafish*. Take it away, ladies."

Leili immediately springs into action, holding her hands together and flinging them forward. It takes me a second to realize

106

she's fishing. Molly doesn't get it, though. "Hey," she says. "What are you . . . Are you okay?"

"Yeah," Leili says. "Hoping to catch a big one today."

"Oh," Molly says, clearly still confused. "Me too." She holds her hands together like Leili is, not having any idea why she's doing it.

Leili tenses up her body. "I think I'm getting a bite!" she shouts, pulling back on her pretend fishing rod.

"Oh!" Molly says, the lightbulb finally turning on. "Like a fish?"

"Yes, I think I'm catching a fish!" Leili spells it out for her.

"What kind of fish is it?" Molly asks.

"Okay, let's pause," Mr. Martinez says. "This is actually a good educational moment. One of the major rules of improv is: *Don't ask questions.* Because when you do that, as Molly did a few times, you're forcing your partner to come up with everything in the scene. It's much more helpful to invent and add information to the scene. *Yes, AND,* right? Do you see what I mean, Molly?"

"Totally," Molly says, nodding a lot and seeming devastated.

"Don't be discouraged. There really are no mistakes in improv—they're all opportunities to take the scene in new directions. But asking questions is actually kind of a mistake. Don't do that. Okay, great, continue."

Molly stops asking questions, but the scene doesn't get much better. Even Leili can't save this one. After them, duo after duo does a scene that is sort of a sloppy mess. Without predetermined relationships, locations, whatever, everyone kind of flounders. People are trying to *Yes, and,* but lots of scenes devolve into long, boring conversations, like Shannon and Fletcher debating for a solid seven minutes about whether or not they should go get a sandwich.

Evan livens up his scene with Nicole by making some hammy jokes in goofy voices, which get some good laughs, but then a considerably-less-enthusiastic-than-he-was-an-hour-ago Mr. Martinez cuts them off. "Okay, that's— Yes, let's stop that one there. Thanks, guys." He seems a little beaten down. I don't think this is going how he imagined it would. "That actually reminds me of another important rule: *Don't try to be funny.*"

If I hadn't already read that improv book, I'd be a little confused right now. But I have, so I nod along with what he's saying.

"I know that seems counterintuitive, but even though improv is often funny, you shouldn't *try* to be funny. The laughs should come naturally by committing to the scene, by supporting your scene partner, not by interrupting the scene to tell a joke or do a silly voice." He's very obviously subtweeting Evan, who is staring straight ahead, possibly trying not to cry . . . ? Yikes. "I guess what I'm saying is, just try and play the scene as real as possible, and that honesty will very likely be funny to the audience."

I get what Mr. Martinez is saying, especially about not telling jokes, but Shannon and Fletcher were committed to their sandwich debate, and it was definitely not funny.

"And on that note, let's bring up two performers who haven't gone yet to demonstrate what an honest and real scene looks like. How about Jess and . . . Winnie."

Okay. I don't completely get long-form, but I sort of do, and hopefully that, plus whatever funny instincts I've been tapping into this past week, will take me through this. A few people cheer for me, which, not gonna lie, feels pretty fantastic.

Granted, Jess Yang isn't the ideal scene partner, seeing as she's continued to give me nothing but the cold shoulder, probably because she knows I'm text-flirting with her ex-boyfriend. She rolls her eyes as she walks toward me. Gimme a break.

"Hi," I say once Jess is standing next to me.

No response. And an expression on her face best described as disgust.

"Can we get a word for these two?" Mr. Martinez asks.

I'm trying not to be intimidated, even though Jess is at least four inches taller than me and strikingly pretty, with thick black hair and black boots with heels.

"Sad," Rashanda says, staring at me. I know she's taking a dig, but I can't think about that. I need to focus.

"Great. Sad," Mr. Martinez says. "Remember: be honest, be real. Agree with each other. Cool?"

"Definitely," Jess says.

"Sure," I say.

"Okay, go for it."

I've been thinking all rehearsal that I'm going to be this character I do for Dad called Sue the Super-Talkative Hygienist, based on, well, a super-talkative hygienist named Sue who works with my dentist, Dr. Rogers. ("Not to be confused with *Mister* Rogers!" is a nonfunny joke he makes more often than is comfortable.) Sue will always hit you with some serious TMI while you've got a sharp tool in your mouth and can't possibly respond.

But by the time I lift my imaginary dental pick and turn to Jess, she's quietly crying. I gotta say, she really is a good actress, because even though I know we're about to do a scene, for a split second I wonder what happened. The crying actually works well for my bit, as I can pretend I accidentally hurt her while in the process of cleaning her teeth.

"I'm so sorry, honey," I say, channeling my best nasal Sue voice.

"No, *I'm* sorry," Jess says, turning to me with *actual freaking tears* running down her cheeks. "I'm so sorry about your dad."

"What?" I say, completely thrown.

"I heard he died."

You know how in the movies when a bomb explodes, and everything suddenly goes mute except for a high-pitched whistle sound, as if you're actually experiencing what the exploding of a bomb does to your hearing?

Right now feels like that.

"It's so terrible," Jess continues. She does some more authentic crying.

I'm frozen.

Why did she say that? Does she know about my dad?

I catch Leili's face, and she looks kind of stunned. If Jess knows, then who else does? I should say something, but not only have I dropped my Sue persona, I don't have any words at all.

"Here," Jess says, pretending to set something down in front of me. "I baked you a cake to make you feel better."

"Thanks," I say.

"Oh, you poor thing," she says. "You're speechless, I know. Your dad was a great man." Why the hell is Jess Yang talking about my dead dad in an improv scene? Is this some kind of terrible coincidence?

"He was." Jess stares, waiting for me to add more, but my mind is a black hole.

"Okay, let's take a pause moment," Mr. Martinez says, "so we can look at what's happening. Jess, great job with a strong initiating line, bringing up Winnie's dead father. Love that. But I still want to know more about who you are to each other."

"I'm coming up with things," Jess says, "but she's not adding anything."

"Right, sure," Mr. Martinez says. "But improv isn't about placing blame, it's about working together. That said, Winnie, I *would* like to understand more about your father. How did he die? Did you know it was coming or was it sudden and shocking? What was your relationship with him like? What will happen to you now that he's gone?"

I nod as I look down at my pink Vans, my vision blurred.

I can't speak.

"But even more important," Mr. Martinez says, "is the relationship between the two of you. Because that's the relationship we're watching onstage. What I'm extrapolating thus far is that there's some animosity between your characters, so as we pick up the scene, let's play with that." He gestures for us to continue.

"You should have some cake," Jess says. "It might make you feel better."

I shake my head, eyes still on the floor.

"Come on, eat some," Jess says, digging an imaginary fork into an imaginary cake and holding it in front of my face. "Take a bite."

"I don't . . . I can't right now," I say, somehow finding my voice.

"Way to lean into the animosity," Mr. Martinez says, "but try to move the scene forward, too."

"Okay," I say to Jess. "I'll have some." I pretend-chew the pretend cake.

"Isn't it delicious?" she asks.

I want this scene to be over. "It's great cake."

"No, it's not. My baby brother made it. It's terrible."

"Oh," I say, too bewildered to harness the anger that my shock and sadness have morphed into.

"I can't believe you thought it was good," Jess continues. Some people laugh.

"All right," Mr. Martinez says. "Let's stop right there. That, uh, was an interesting one." I must be doing a good job at hiding how overwhelmed I am because Mr. Martinez doesn't seem to have noticed. He just thinks I'm bad at improv.

"But okay!" Mr. Martinez says. "That's it for today, but this, uh, this was a good start. We can work with this. You were all really brave, and, uh . . . yeah. See you next Thursday!"

You were all really brave, and, uh . . . yeah. Inspiring words from our leader.

"Oh! And for those who have been asking if there are any good videos online to see what a Harold is like, I answer: sort of. It's really hard to capture on film the magic of being in that room during an incredible improv show. It's ephemeral that way; you either were there to see it, or you weren't. But, that said, if you insist on watching something, you should google the UCB show *ASSSSCAT*. That's, uh, four Ss in *ass*."

People laugh, but I've barely taken in any of what he's said. As everyone steps down from the stage, gathering their bags and coats, I float toward Leili, who takes my hands and looks

112

into my eyes. "Are you okay? That was so mean. She's not usually like that."

"Did you tell her?" I ask.

"Tell her what?" Leili asks.

"About my dad."

"What? Of course not."

"How did she know, then?"

"I don't think she did," Leili says. "It seemed like an awful coincidence."

"Hey," Evan says, appearing next to us. "Unbelievable, right?"

I nod, moved that he's so definitively on my side in this.

"Like, what a dick, right?"

"I know," I say, even though it's odd that he's calling Jess Yang a dick.

"Calling me out like that in front of everybody." Evan shakes his head and purses his lips. "Just for making a few jokes. So out of line."

And then it dawns on me: he's not talking about my scene with Jess. He's talking about Mr. Martinez. I'm kinda mad he's so oblivious, and kinda glad he didn't notice how bad my scene was.

"Yeah," I say.

"I hate that, you know?" Evan says. "I've been in improv since day one last year, I'm one of the best performers—at least I happen to think so—and he has to make an example of me?"

"Not cool at all, bro," Tim Stabisch chimes in, just as worked up as Evan, if not more so.

"Yeah," Leili says. I can tell she's saying it sarcastically, but most people wouldn't know that.

"He probably used you as an example because he knows you can take it," I say. "Because he knows you're one of the best."

Evan seems to like this rationale. "Maybe," he says.

As the four of us walk out of the auditorium together, I see Dad's gray Honda Civic parked at the curb outside, waiting for Leili and me.

I'm so sorry about your dad.

A golf ball forms in my throat. I swallow it away and ask Leili how Yearbook's going, hoping I'll be able to pull it together by the time we step into the car.

14

I derive immense comfort from the cereal aisle.

I'm standing in it now, letting the rainbow of cardboard and cartoons wash over me. It's a simple place. A good place. Aisle 7 of Stop & Shop.

For years now, Dad and I have gone food shopping every Saturday morning. It might be my favorite tradition. (I live a wild and reckless life.) And within that tradition, this subtradition has sprung up of me taking a few minutes to absorb the view of all the cereals, as if mulling over my choices, even though I rarely deviate from the usual course: Life. Why? Uh, because it's the best. Delicious and perfectly textured, sweet but not too sweet. Just like me!

Actually, I first tried it after Grandpa Harvey died when I was seven. His was the first death I'd experienced, and it really rocked me. I was scared my parents were next. Then me. So, when I saw it up there on the shelf, the word *LIFE* calling out to me in bright rainbow letters, of course I had to have it. This was the answer to all my problems! I would literally feed my parents and myself *more life*!

I've come to understand that isn't actually how it works.

Though there's still a small part of me that is thinking Dad should be eating at least a couple bowls of this a week.

"She's thinking hard, ladies and gentlemen," Dad says as he and his half-full shopping cart slowly turn the corner into my aisle. He's wearing his faded T-shirt with this orange 1980s video game character called Q-Bert on it. "Could *this* be the day she chooses something other than Life? Let's watch and find out."

"You don't know me," I say with faux attitude. "It might be a Honey Nut Cheerios day."

"Yeah, right," Dad laughs. "I think the last day you enjoyed those you were still in a high chair."

He is, as per most of the time, correct. "That may be, but I'm just saying, you never know. People change."

"Sure they do," Dad says.

I grab a box of Life and daintily place it in the cart in between two cartons of eggs and a jar of pickles. "Okay, my business is done here."

"So much for *People change,*" Dad says.

"Well, that's Life," I say.

Dad boos me. "We all know you're just in it for the puns."

"What's wrong with that?"

Dad surveys the contents of his cart and checks it against the list on his phone. "I think we've got nearly everything . . ." Tomorrow is Mom's birthday, so we're having some people over for brunch to celebrate—including Grandma Mitzie (Dad's mom)—none of whom know about his ALS. I know he's anxious about it, but he's trying to pretend he's not. "I need you on cracker and pasta detail, I'll go hit up the freezer, and then we'll be good."

"Perfect," I say. "I'll meet you up front."

"BREAK," we both say.

The cracker and pasta sections hold no emotional charge for me, so I move quickly, filling my arms with our usuals (Triscuits for Mom, rice crackers for Dad, Ritz for me, penne, spaghetti, and elbows for all of us) before heading to the front. Normally, whichever one of us is done first gets in line, but the lines are all pretty short this morning. So I awkwardly stand near a rack of gum, pretending I'm thinking really deep thoughts.

"Hey," a voice says, and when I come out of my fake-deep-thought reverie, I see Fletcher Handy in a red vest pushing a dolly stacked high with packages of toilet paper.

"Oh, hey," I say. He stops walking and nimbly steers the dolly so it's not blocking the front aisle.

"Hey," he says again.

We stand there for a moment. I feel stupid that I'm holding so many boxes.

"I didn't know you worked here," I say.

"Yeah. It's . . . You know, it's a job."

"Yeah. Cool."

He gestures to the dolly. "I'm on toilet paper duty."

"I see that," I say, trying not to laugh at that phrase. Because scatological puns, though not my preferred humor, can still be hilarious in the right context.

"What?" he asks, noticing the strange half smile I was unable to rein in.

"Oh no, it's . . ." My face gets hot. Please, dear god, don't force me to stand here and explain this. "*Duty* kind of sounded like . . . sorry . . . I'm a five-year-old."

"Oh, *toilet paper duty*? Like, you heard it as *doody*, like poop, instead of *duty*, like work?"

"Right," I say, mortified to have it spelled out like that.

"Oh yeah," Fletcher says, barely smiling. "I never thought of it like that."

Well, good, because now it doesn't seem funny at all.

"But anyway," I say, changing the subject in the hopes that my face might revert to a lighter shade of crimson, "are you liking Improv Trou—"

"Got a real carb situation going on here, huh?" Fletcher interrupts, pointing to all my boxes. Guess the crimson's gonna stick around a little while longer.

I look down as if I had no idea there was anything in my arms. "Oh, uh . . ."

"I didn't mean that in a dick way," he says, shaking his head. "I just meant it as an observation."

"Oh, of course, yeah." I'm actually not offended. I just feel embarrassed that my stupid box-holding has been called out. "I, uh, it's for my family. I'm on carb duty."

"Carb duty. Ha, nice." He smiles the first real smile I've ever seen him smile.

"I should actually go find my dad. He's taking his sweet time."

"Oh, sure, yeah, do what you gotta do." He's already maneuvering his dolly back into action. "See ya around."

"See ya." I've known Fletcher since the beginning of freshman year, but that's the longest conversation we've ever had. By a long shot. My carb load and I move toward the other end of the supermarket.

When I turn down the freezer aisle, it's empty except for one shopping cart, so I look down the next aisle instead. There're a couple of people—an older dark-haired woman, a young father with a baby in a carrier—but no Dad. Huh.

I go back to the first aisle, thinking I'll check out the contents of the one cart there, see if it's ours, but before I've even made it halfway down the aisle, I freeze. (Pun truly not intended.)

Just past the shopping cart, Dad is lying on his side on the floor.

It is not a fun thing to see.

"Daddy," I say, using a name I haven't uttered in at least five years as I rush over to him.

"Hey, Win," he says, grimacing in pain, three boxes of frozen chicken sausage scattered around his body. I'm so happy he can speak.

"Ohmigod, are you okay?" My voice is trembling. "What happened?"

It feels like a stupid question the second I say it.

"I fell," he says, with just a touch of snark. "My right foot stiffened up, and I— So stupid."

"It's not stupid. People fall all the time—I fall all the time." My heart is racing, and I'm not sure what to do, and I can't comfort him because my arms are still overflowing with goddamn crackers and pasta. I drop it all and crouch down next to him, where I see for the first time that he's bleeding from a spot just above his eyebrow. "Oh god."

"It's not a big deal. My head grazed the side of the freezer on the way down."

"I should probably go get some help." I look up and down the aisle, those terrible fluorescent lights shining on us. How can there not be a single other person desiring frozen goods? "Did this just happen?"

"No. A minute or two ago." The thought of Dad lying here

119

helpless for even that long shatters me. "You don't need to get anybody," he says. "Nothing's broken. I just need a hand getting up."

Technically no one outside of our family knows about his diagnosis, and I'm sure he's worried we'll know someone who's shopping, and it'll turn into a thing.

"Okay," I say. I wrap my arms around his torso, awkwardly trying to lift him to a sitting position. Dad grunts in pain, and I pull my hands back as if I've been burned. "I don't think— I mean, you're not supposed to move someone after they've been injured like this. In case you had a concussion or something."

"It doesn't feel like a concussion."

"Well," I say, even though I don't think that's something you can assess by feel. But the last thing I want to do right now is argue with him. I stare down the aisle, trying to will someone into existence to come help us.

A man walks by, and I shout out.

"Excuse me! We need some help over here!"

"Win, don't," Dad says.

The man stops, and it is only once he turns into our aisle and starts slowly ambling our way with his shopping cart that I realize he is approximately ninety years old.

"Yes, what is it?" the man says loudly. He's wearing pleated khakis and a blue polo shirt. It might actually be unsafe for him to help Dad get up. We need somebody else.

"What's he doing on the floor?" the man asks. I feel Dad looking at me, and I know he doesn't want me to make this a big deal. I look ahead of and behind us, hoping for someone else, anyone else, who can help.

The man points. "You dropped some crackers."

I can't stand here anymore. I dash down the aisle and scan the front of the store, almost immediately finding who I'm looking for. "Fletcher," I call out, seeing his lanky frame steering an empty dolly in the opposite direction. He stops and turns, blinks twice. "Can you come with me?"

Fletcher doesn't ask any questions, as it's probably clear I'm not asking for produce guidance, and moments later, he's taking in the strange tableau in the freezer aisle.

"We, uh, my dad fell," I say. "Dad, this is Fletcher. He just joined the improv troupe too."

Dad grunts as he pushes himself up to a sitting position. There's a thin trail of blood connecting his forehead and cheek. "Good to meet you, Fletcher," he says, looking sheepish as he extends a hand from the floor. "I'm Russ."

"Nice to meet you," Fletcher says as they shake hands. Dad is about to let go, but, much to his surprise, Fletcher transitions seamlessly into pulling him up into a standing position.

"Oh, thanks," Dad says, leaning on the freezer to stabilize himself.

"No prob," Fletcher says.

"Well done," says the man in pleated khakis, who for some reason is still standing here.

Fletcher nods.

"Yeah, thanks," I say. I feel so relieved I found him so quickly.

Fletcher is already bending over to pick up the six boxes of crackers and pasta, which he places in the cart with an almost balletic athleticism. "Can't leave without your carbs," he says, giving me a quick smile (the second I've ever witnessed from him), then bending down again, this time to pick up the sausage boxes. "Did you want all of these?" he asks.

"Uh, just one, actually," Dad says. "The others, you know, sprang out and knocked me over."

"Yeah, gotta watch out for that spicy sausage," Fletcher says, placing a box in our cart and the other two back on the freezer shelf in what seems like one fluid movement. It's bizarre; he almost seems like a different person from the guy I spoke to five minutes ago next to the toilet paper. "Here," he says, taking a tissue from a small packet he's pulled out of his back pocket and handing it to Dad. Fletcher carries around tissues? "Just to clean up some of the blood on your . . ." He points to his own forehead.

"Oh," Dad says, newly alarmed, "is there . . . ?"

"Just a little," Fletcher says.

I take the tissue and dab at Dad's face. He tries to be stoic but winces a little.

"So, you all good?" Fletcher says.

"Fine, thank you," the man we don't know says.

Dad and I stare at the man, then at each other, and Dad is making his holding-back-a-laugh face, which is comforting on a deep level I can't begin to articulate.

"Glad to hear it," Fletcher says to Ol' Khakis before turning to Dad and me. "What about you two? Good?"

"I think— Yeah, I think we're good. Thanks so much, Fletcher," Dad says, extending his hand.

"No prob," Fletcher says again as he shakes Dad's hand for the second time in two minutes.

"Really, thank you," I say, and I truly mean it. I think what I'm most grateful for is how few questions he's asking. And how nonjudgmental he seems.

Fletcher gives me a thumbs-up. "See ya in school."

"Yeah, definitely," I say. "See ya."

"I think I'll continue my shopping as well," the ninety-something-year-old man says, pivoting his shopping cart back the way he came.

"Okay," I say. "Thanks for your . . ." I'm not sure how to finish that sentence . . . *annoying unhelpful comments*? I don't think he heard me anyway.

Dad and I silently watch the man until he's left our aisle, on to greener shopping pastures.

"I'll miss that guy," Dad says.

"Ha, me too." I laugh, and clearly I was holding in a lot of tension, because it comes out really weird, like a cockatoo mating call or something.

"And your friend Fletcher. God bless him."

"I know," I say. "I don't even know him that well."

"Can't believe he had a packet of tissues on him."

"That's what I was thinking!"

"So, shall we?" Dad nods his head toward the front of the store and the checkout lines, as if he's ready to jump back into our usual rhythms and pretend nothing traumatic just happened.

"Uh, are you sure you're all right? Should we call Mom?"

"I think I'm fine," Dad says. "We'll tell her what happened, but calling would just freak her out. And on her birthday weekend, no less."

I can already hear Mom's incredulous voice asking Dad why the hell he didn't let her know right away. But again, he's the one who just fell, so I'll leave it up to him.

"Okay," I say. "Do you want me to push the cart? Since . . . ?"

"Nah, I got it," Dad says, a little more forcefully than I would have expected.

"Okay, great. I was just offering in case— Yeah, great."

Dad and I don't say anything else as we walk toward the checkout lines. I deliberately slow down my pace so we can be side by side.

15

"You sure I can't help?"

"Back away, woman!" Dad shouts at Mom as he stands at the stove guarding the eggs in his pan. He's being funny, but he's also nervous, so it comes out super-loud and intense.

"Okay, okay," Mom says, hands in the air. "Geez, somebody ate their Wheaties this morning."

"Sorry," he says, "but the birthday girl does no work on her birthday. That's the rule."

"Well, if you bite the birthday girl's head off," Mom says, "there won't be a birthday girl. So."

Dad chomps at the air like a dinosaur.

I'm watching all this while covering the kitchen table with a My Little Pony tablecloth that Dad and I found at Party City. Even though Mom and Dad are being a little snippy with each other, it's mainly good-natured, which is about eight billion times better than the fight they had most of the day yesterday once we got home from Stop & Shop.

Dad was able to keep his fall a secret for exactly zero seconds, as a purplish goose egg had sprouted on his forehead by the time we walked in the door. As I'd expected, Mom could not wrap her head around the idea that Dad would get injured and not call her immediately. Especially since it turned out this wasn't his first fall. Back in July, right before I left for camp, he'd gotten a huge bruise on his elbow that he'd told me was from "being whacked with a prop" by one of his students. Not the case, Mom informed me. How much else don't I know?

"Win was there," Dad said, justifying his most recent post-fall behavior. "We had the situation under control."

"I can't even— Let's talk about this later," Mom said before proceeding to do the most passive-aggressive grocery unpacking of all time. You can't actually slam a fridge, because it always closes with that gentle suction of air, but she came close.

"I didn't want to worry you on your birthday weekend," Dad said as she set the pickles in the fridge so hard I was sure the jar would shatter.

"I said we'll talk about it later. And that's bullshit, and you know it."

I've gotten over the novelty of my parents cursing, but when they're cursing *at each other,* something I've only witnessed a couple of times, it still shakes me to my core. It seemed like Mom was reacting a little too strongly, considering Dad was the one with ALS who'd fallen in the freezer aisle, but I stayed out of it.

I caught bits of their arguments the rest of the day, so I knew Mom wanted Dad to start using a cane, and he said he wasn't ready for that. Not sure if I am either, to be honest. My father, sauntering through town with a cane. Kind of badass in a way, I guess.

But now Mom and Dad seem to have worked through whatever it is they had to work through, which is good because people will be arriving for the brunch soon, and the stress of

126

watching Dad try to hide his ALS from them is anxiety enough for one day.

"Oh, you guys," Mom says now, smiling as she notices the My Little Pony tablecloth.

"Only the best for you," I say.

"Glad my sister's not coming today."

When Mom was five, she baked Aunt Michelle's favorite My Little Ponies in the microwave during an ill-conceived game of Tanning Salon. They came out as melted, deformed pony monsters, and Aunt Michelle didn't talk to Mom for a week. It's obviously one of my favorite stories.

"She's gonna FaceTime us later," I say, "and this tablecloth is the first thing I'm going to show her."

"Noooooooooo," Mom says, as if in slow motion.

The doorbell rings, and Dad's shoulders tense up as he spoons his egg-spinach scramble out of the pan and into a bowl. "It's not eleven yet, is it?" he asks.

"Nope," Mom says, already heading out of the kitchen to the front door. According to the oven, it's 10:24. And if I had to bet, I'd say it's Grandma Mitzie. She's always early.

"Hi, Mitzie!" we hear Mom say after she opens the door.

Yup.

"Do you smell something?" Grandma Mitzie asks. "Something smells bad out here."

And yup. No "Happy birthday" or "Nice to see you," just an immediate commentary on how our home has assaulted her olfactory glands.

"Oh boy," Dad says, cracking an egg for his next batch, then accidentally missing the bowl and sending yolk oozing onto the kitchen floor.

"I got it," I say, rushing over with paper towels before he can attempt to do it himself, possibly creating another catastrophe before a single guest arrives.

Out of all the people coming over, I know Dad's definitely most anxious about his mother. He even put a Band-Aid over the bruise on his forehead.

I get it. Grandma Mitzie is the very definition of a tough cookie. She's got a huge heart and she loves me so much and she's absolutely hilarious, often by accident, but she's also, um, how should I put it?

Mean. She's mean.

I guess the slightly nicer way to say that is she's judgmental, but I'd rather be honest. She's just mean. And most of the time, I don't even think she realizes. She spends half the year a few towns away from us in Springfield and the other half down in Florida. Mom once pointed out that Dad is visibly less stressed from November through May, and I was like *That's ridiculous,* but then I realized she was right. I don't know how I'd never noticed it before.

When I was eavesdropping yesterday, one of the main points being argued was when Dad should let Grandma Mitzie know about his diagnosis. Mom was lobbying for telling her in person sometime during or after the brunch, but Dad was pushing hard to wait until November, when Grandma was back in Florida.

"Are you kidding me?" Mom said. "You're going to wait three months to let your mother know you're seriously ill?"

"I think it's in everyone's best interests," Dad said.

"You mean *your* best interests."

"Well, yeah."

Mom let out a huff of air. She's very good at that.

"Come on, Dane," Dad said. "You know what will happen if I tell her. My mom will be over here every day, asking a billion questions I don't have the answers to, generally stressing me out, which is the last thing my body needs right now. And what's not good for me is not good for you and Win, either."

"Fine," Mom said (and this is where I had to scurry away down the hall because I heard her approaching the very bedroom door my ear was pressed against), "do whatever you want. As per usual."

Mom is often making these comments about Dad doing whatever he wants, and it pisses me off. He's the one who gave up his entire acting career to move to the suburbs and stay at home with me, so right there is a super example of him doing what he *didn't* want.

Mom and Grandma enter the kitchen, still talking about the smell.

"It's like a . . . like a fish smell," Grandma says, wearing her usual scowl. "Or maybe it's your fertilizer. What kind of fertilizer do you use?"

"I couldn't tell you, Mitzie," Mom says. She always goes into her interactions with Grandma with an upbeat attitude and a smile, and she's always beaten down within fifteen minutes. Faster than usual today.

"Oh," Grandma says, handing Mom the two boxes she's remembered she's holding, one a white bakery box and the other small and wrapped. "Here you go, dear. It's a chocolate babka and then a little something for you. Happy birthday."

"Thanks, Mitzie." Mom's smile is only half sincere, but Grandma doesn't see that because she's just spotted me.

"And oh! Here's my little Winnala. How are you, my love?"
She hugs me and mushes her lips into my cheek, and her perfume makes my eyes sting. But that's always what happens, so
it's become kind of comforting. When I'm a grandma one day,
I'm gonna wear so much goddamn perfume.

"Hi, Grandma. How are you?"

"Much better now," she says, as she always does upon seeing
me, finally unclenching from the hug. "You're not wearing your
hair down today?" She lightly swats at my ponytail. "For this
special occasion?"

"It appears not." Looks are incredibly important to Grandma
Mitzie. If it's not a comment about my hair, it's a comment
about an outfit she doesn't like. When I call her out for being
negative, she'll say, "What? Better me telling you than someone
out in the world, right?" To which I think: *Um, how about* no
one *tells me?*

"Hey, Mom," Dad says without turning from the stove,
where he's moving eggs around in the pan, an obvious bit of
busywork so he can put off engaging with her a little longer.

"Hello over there," Grandma says. "Am I getting a hug, or
do I have to come over to you?"

"Just doing some cooking so that there will be food for our
guests to eat," Dad says.

"Well, I know that." Grandma walks over to Dad, who leans
his cheek in as she gives him a side hug. I think he's nervous
about making any sudden moves in case it reveals that he's not
so great at making sudden moves. And that he has a Band-Aid
on his forehead. Grandma doesn't see it. Instead, she peers at
the stove, then the rest of the kitchen, like a sanitation inspector
making a surprise drop-in. "What can I do to help? Anything?"

"We're good, Mom," Dad says. "Sit down, relax."

"Yeah, do you want anything to drink?" Mom asks.

"Oh, come on, it's your birthday," Grandma says, already opening the fridge, "I can get myself something." I've always been in awe of my grandmother's ability to say something as if she's doing you a favor when it's actually the exact opposite. "Is this fridge cold enough?"

My mom opens her eyes wide at Dad and me, like *Kill me now.*

Twenty minutes and twenty underhanded Grandma comments later, I'm finishing arranging all the bagels and spreads when the doorbell rings. Mom practically sprints to get it, and I'm delighted when I hear Leili's and Azadeh's voices. Of course they're here right on time; Leili wouldn't have it any other way.

"Hiiiiiii," I say, bounding into the front hallway to greet them.

"Hey," Leili says.

Azadeh just flips her chin up at me, like she's pretending to be tough.

"I'm so happy you girls are here," Mom says.

"Happy birthday, Mrs. Friedman." Leili hands Mom a tray of Koloocheh, these amazing Iranian cookies, covered with Saran wrap. "Our mom made these for you. They're really good."

"Yeah, really really good," Azadeh says.

"That's so sweet," Mom says. "Please tell Pari thanks."

"My grandma's here," I say quietly, mainly to give them a friendly warning, as I steer Leili and Azadeh away from the kitchen to the family room, where we plop down on the couch.

No sooner have we plopped than Azadeh has her phone out, smiling hugely, thumbs blazing.

"She's so ridiculous," she says, holding the phone out so Leili can read.

"Ha, she definitely is," Leili says. "But put that away. We just got here."

"Roxanne?" I ask.

"Yeah," Azadeh says, shaking her head. "She's just— Yeah." She looks to Leili, like *Should I tell her?* Leili looks back: *I don't know, geez, do whatever you want!* Azadeh puts her phone in her lap, leans toward me, and whispers something in an incredibly quiet voice.

"I couldn't hear a single word of what you just said," I say.

"Me neither," Leili says. "And I'm sitting right next to you."

Azadeh crawls to the far end of the couch, where she can see into the kitchen to make sure no one's listening, then back to where she was. "So, um, Roxanne and I are kind of . . ."

"Ohmigod!" I say, definitely too loudly. "I *knew* you were flirting!"

Azadeh grins and covers her face. "We were."

"This is amazing, Oz!"

"Well, it's still new. It might not even be a big deal. I'm only telling you and Lay right now."

"I'm honored," I say, looking to Leili, who nods and smiles. "This is so freaking great, I can't even handle it. Tell me everything!"

And of course Grandma Mitzie chooses that moment to join us.

"Hello hello," she says, rattling the ice cubes in her juice glass as she carefully lowers herself onto the couch between

132

Leili and me. "Wait, let me see if I can get this . . ." She narrows her eyes and darts them back and forth between Leili and Azadeh. "You're Leili," she says, pointing at Azadeh. "And you're . . . Wait, no."

She does this literally every time she sees them. And seeing as they've been my best friends since third grade, that's a lot of times.

"Grandma," I say.

"Wait, wait, hold on," she says, one hand on her chin. "I think I can do this." Leili and Azadeh remain politely still, as if they're having their portraits painted. I get the same mortified feeling in the pit of my stomach that I always do when Grandma does this. "It's those darn scarves that make it so challenging."

There it is. I was hoping it wouldn't be a headscarf-mentioning day. Alas, not to be. "You really can't say that, Grandma."

"Oh, it's fine," Azadeh says.

"It's not!" I say.

"What, mentioning their scarves?" Grandma asks. "They're wearing scarves, what's the big deal? Do you know how many little boys in yarmulkes I've confused in my lifetime?"

"What does that even mean?" I ask.

"It means that when multiple people wear the same piece of clothing, it can get confusing. But if you want me to not say it, I won't—whatever you want."

That's Grandma's sorcery at work: somehow I'm the bad guy for suggesting she shouldn't imply that my twin best friends look extra-similar because they're in hijabs.

"Okay, wait, you're Leili," she says, pointing at Leili, "and you're Azadeh."

"Ding ding ding!" Azadeh says.

133

"I also have this freckle right here," Leili says, pointing to her chin. "Which is a good cheat." They tell her that every time, and it's far more generous than Grandma deserves.

"Oh yes, that's right," Grandma Mitzie says. "But I like to try and get it without cheating." She winks at them, another one of her uncomfortable trademarks. "So how are you two doing?"

"We're good," Leili says.

The doorbell has rung a couple of times since the conversation with Grandma started, though I've been too focused on damage control to pay attention to who's shown up. Now Ed and Cory, two of my parents' best friends, walk into the room.

"Hey hey," Cory says, making ironic jazz hands, Ed sauntering in behind him holding a bottle of water.

I actually gasp in excitement upon seeing them, and I'm pretty sure Leili and Azadeh do, too. Cory and Ed are the best. They went to college with my parents, where they were in shows and theater classes together, and Cory was in Laugh Riot with Dad (he's hilarious). Unlike my parents, Cory and Ed stuck with acting, and now they both have successful careers. Cory's guest-starred on a bunch of TV shows and been in so many commercials, and Ed (who I should mention is a stunningly beautiful human) has been in the ensemble of a bunch of Broadway shows. It's incredibly cool, and it also means they're usually busy or out of town, which is why it's so awesome whenever we see them.

Leili, Azadeh, and I bound off the couch like frisky puppies. "What's going on, Winnie?" Cory says as he hugs me. I inhale the masculine musk of his cologne as his beard hairs rub against my forehead.

"Not much," I say. "Actually, I just joined the school improv troupe."

Cory pulls back so he can look at my face. "Whaaaat? That's awesome!" Cory and Ed have always been two of my biggest cheerleaders. I've often thought that my bat mitzvah set might have played out differently if only they hadn't had to miss it because Ed was in *Kinky Boots* and Cory was shooting an indie film. "Leili, up high," he says, throwing up a hand that she doesn't see because she's too busy enjoying her hug with Ed.

"Oh, what?" Leili says.

"You got Winnie to join Improv Troupe with you," Cory says. "Up high."

"Oh! Yeah." She lets go of Ed and slaps Cory's hand. "It wasn't totally my doing, but I'll take the credit."

"Gurrrrl," Ed says, giving me a hug with his muscular dancer arms. "That's huge. You're finally fulfilling your destiny."

"Well, I don't know about that," I say, even though I immediately feel like he's one hundred percent accurate.

"Hello, gentlemen," Grandma Mitzie says, large smile on her face as she walks over. She loves Cory and Ed maybe even more than we do.

"Mitzie!" Cory says. He hugs her so hard he lifts her off the floor a little bit. I can never tell if he's truly delighted to see her or just pretending. He's a good actor.

"So glad you boys had a break in your busy schedules to come play with us." *Play with us?* Ew. Grandma always says weird things like that when they're around.

"Oh, you know we would play with you all the time if we

could, Mitzie," Ed says in a flirty way, which is highly distressing even though I know he's gay.

"No flirting with my mom in front of me, please," Dad says (and thank god for that) as he walks into the room, giving his all to make it seem like a casual saunter before planting himself near the wall.

"Hi, Mr. Friedman," Leili says.

"Hey, Leili."

"Hi, Mr. Friedman," Azadeh says.

"What's new, Azadeh?"

"Not much." I know my best friends are trying to act as natural as possible, but I catch them sneaking little glances at him, trying to spot evidence of his disease.

"Ohmigod," Grandma says. "Russ, what happened to your head?" Guess it was only a matter of time.

All eyes turn toward Dad, but he's ready for it. "I cut it shaving."

"You . . . what? You were shaving your forehead?"

"You'd be surprised," Dad says. "It gets pretty hairy."

Azadeh laughs loudly, then covers her mouth once she realizes she's the only one.

"Don't joke." Grandma strides toward Dad. "You've got a Band-Aid on, what happened?"

"It's nothing, Mom," Dad says. "I bumped into a door when I wasn't paying attention." Mom and her longtime best friend, Paige, walk into the room, with Paige's seven-year-old daughter, Ava, right behind them.

"Okay," Grandma says, seeming entirely unconvinced.

"Mitzie, you remember my friend Paige," Mom says, not so subtly trying to change the subject.

"Hi, Mitzie," Paige says.

"Nice to see you," Grandma says, flipping back into the same mode she was in with Cory and Ed, as if the last couple of minutes never happened.

Paige nods, and there's an awkward silence of at least five seconds.

"Anyway," Dad says, "food is ready, so head into the kitchen, everybody."

It's another five seconds before anybody moves.

16

The eating part of Mom's birthday brunch is pretty uneventful. I mean, there's definitely some tension between Mom, Dad, and Grandma (who at one point says through a mouthful of bagel, "Good thing you're not seated near any doors, Russ. Wouldn't want one to bump you again!"), but it's subtle enough not to ruin everyone's good time.

With most of the food consumed and the table littered with used napkins and muffin crumbs, Paige holds up her mimosa and toasts Mom for being "a superwoman in every respect," whatever that means, and her personal hero, and Dad follows that up with his own toast, recalling for maybe the eight hundredth time how he first met Mom in a student-directed production of *Romeo and Juliet*. She was Juliet, Cory was Romeo, and he was Mercutio. "I'm just so grateful Cory isn't into women," Dad says, and we all laugh even though he's made that joke before. "This story might have turned out very differently if he were."

"No way," Cory says. "The chemistry between you two was undeniable. I mean, Dana and I might have slept together a couple of times, but it wouldn't have been a long-term thing."

"You wish," Mom says.

Leili and Azadeh are playing it cool, but I assume they're

just as shocked as I am to hear adults casually talking about sleeping together.

"No, but seriously," Dad says. "Happiest birthday to my smart, beautiful wife. Dana is the best thing that ever happened to me, and I feel so lucky that she's—" For a moment, I think he's choking on a stray piece of bagel, but then I realize he's holding back tears. Oh god.

"Look at you, Russ, getting all emotional," Ed says.

Of course now there are tears in my eyes too, and a quick peek at Mom confirms that she's not holding it together either.

"No, no," Dad says, smiling, "I just thought of something sad I read in the news. Totally unrelated to Dana."

"Oh sure, yes, of course," Ed says.

Dad finishes up his toast and never actually releases any tears. I help him put candles on the chocolate peanut butter ice cream cake we got Mom (it says "Happy Birthday to the Queen"). We all sing to her, barely on-key. I slice and serve the cake. Grandma brings the chocolate babka to the table. I offer to refill people's coffee. Only Ed and Leili take me up on it. (Leili drinks coffee, Azadeh and I don't. We're not as sophisticated as her.)

After cake, Leili, Azadeh, and I hightail it up to my room, not realizing seven-year-old Ava has followed us. I give her my phone to play with, and her attention is instantly absorbed, her index finger flying across the screen at lightning-fast speed while she sits cross-legged on my bed in between Leili and Azadeh.

"Sorry for the weird parts down there," I say as I rotate back and forth in my spinny desk chair.

"Nothing was *that* weird," Leili says.

"I love it," Azadeh says.

"Your grandma is a little intense."

"You mean racist?" I say.

"Eh. Our grandmother's pretty much the same person, just racist and judgmental about different stuff."

"Are all grandmas that way?" Azadeh asks. "That's eerie."

"You think your dad's gonna tell her about his—" Leili starts to ask.

I rapidly shake my head, not wanting Ava to hear.

"About his what?" Ava asks, not looking up from the phone.

"New job," I say. "He got a new job."

"Oh," Ava says, disengaging as soon as she hears it's something she doesn't care about.

"I don't know," I say. "I hope so. I feel like she should know."

"Well, I don't want to be there for *that*," Azadeh says.

"Dad was telling us the other day," Leili says, "how not so long ago in America, they used to not tell cancer patients that they had cancer."

"Wait, what?" I say.

"Yeah," Azadeh says. "They would tell the parents or the spouse, but not the person who it was happening to. They thought it would only make things worse if the person knew they had cancer."

"Does your dad have cancer?" Ava asks, this time looking up from the phone.

Dammit. We keep forgetting Ava has ears.

"No," I say quickly. "He doesn't. His new job involves working with kids who have cancer."

"Oh," Ava says. "A boy in my school had cancer. Jake Reese. But he's better now."

"That's good," Leili says.

"What are you even doing on there?" I ask Ava.

"Playing *Feather Frenzy,*" she says. "It's really fun."

"I didn't know I had that."

"You didn't. I downloaded it."

I give Leili and Azadeh a look like *What the hell?* Which reminds me of what I actually wanted to talk about up here. "Wait, so, Oz . . . you and Roxanne!"

"Yeah," Azadeh says, smiling down at my bedspread.

"That's— This is— Like, Roxanne is so cool! How long has this been going on?"

"We started getting closer at summer practices," Azadeh says, "but it only became something . . . more . . . like, in the last two weeks. It's really new."

"I just found out three days ago," Leili says.

"You were so relieved," Azadeh laughs.

"I wasn't! Well, maybe a little. If Roxanne's your *girlfriend,* I don't have to be jealous the same way I would if she's your *best friend.*"

"You don't have to be jealous in either case," Azadeh says, reaching past Ava to playfully shove Leili. "She's not, like, stealing me away from you, dodo."

"I thought Roxanne was straight," I say.

"So did I," Azadeh says. "I'm the first girl she's ever been attracted to."

I put both hands on my head and make my *Whaaaaat?* face.

"I know, right?" Leili says.

"This is the best thing ever," I say. "Can I . . . be nosy for a second?"

"Maybe," Azadeh says.

"You two have, like . . . kissed and stuff?"

Azadeh gets red, smiling with her hand over her eyes. "We have."

"Aaaaaahhhhhhhh! Oz!"

"I really like her."

"My parents kiss sometimes," Ava says, in between dramatic swipes.

"Hey, are you gonna tell your parents?" I ask. (Azadeh came out to them last year. "I think Mom's gonna need some time to get used to the idea," she had said, "but of course Papa's fine with it. He's always trying to show how 'woke' he is. His words.")

"At some point," Azadeh says. "I just don't want to tell them I'm in a relationship until I'm sure it actually is one. Same with the field hockey team."

"Oh wow," I say, the realization dawning on me, "this is like on *Friends* when Monica and Chandler started secretly dating!"

"That's what I said!" Leili practically jumps off the bed.

"Uh, yeah," Azadeh says, "except not, because I'm not keeping it a secret from you two."

"Don't ruin it," I say. "This is exactly like *Friends*."

"It really is," Leili says.

"Um, you're getting a text," Ava says, holding my phone out. "From Evan."

"Oh," I say, trying to keep my tone neutral even though I'm actually thinking, *Gimme my phone back, what did he say?!*

How was the peacock? he's texted, followed by a bird emoji and a fork-and-knife emoji. We were texting all day yesterday, a delightful distraction from Dad's supermarket fall. When I mentioned we were having a birthday brunch for my mom, he

142

asked if we'd be serving any meats. *Only peacock,* I said. Hence his text.

"What super-funny thing did Evan say today?" Leili asks.

I can't help but hear the sarcasm, but I pretend not to. "Oh, it's stupid."

"Seems like *you're* sort of seeing somebody too," Azadeh says, but unlike Leili, her tone is playful and affectionate.

"Oh no," I say. "It's not really like that."

"Come on, Winner," Leili says. "Even Ava knows it's really like that."

Ava looks up and nods, then returns to her game.

"Okay, maybe it's like that, I don't know. But I don't want to be annoying about it. Like, I really am sorry that he and Tim invaded our lunch table this week."

"Evan's fine," Leili says. "It's Tim who's the dingus. But it's not a big deal. You and Evan are actually really cute together."

I feel myself blushing.

"Are you going to write back?" Ava asks, holding the phone in my face. "Or can I go back to playing?"

"Oh." I want to respond, but I don't want to seem like I'm putting Evan ahead of Leili and Azadeh. It's silly because Azadeh seems to have no problem texting Roxanne while she's with us. But I don't want to follow her down that road. At least not yet. As Leslie Knope once said, "Ovaries before brovaries. Uteruses before duderuses." I tell Ava she can keep playing, then look to see if Leili's registered my bold act of sisterhood. Unclear.

"Okay," Ava says. "Why does your screen have cracks on it? It makes it hard to see some of the feathers."

"I threw my phone the other day. Do you want to keep using it or not?"

"I do, I do," Ava says, going back to her app.

"So, are you and Evan going to, like, go on a da—" Leili is in the middle of asking when we hear a huge thud from downstairs, followed by Grandma Mitzie screaming.

"What was that?" Leili asks.

But I'm already out my bedroom door and cascading down the stairs. I peek into the family room, which is empty, then dash into the kitchen, where Dad is lying on the floor surrounded by everyone else, Grandma and Mom hovering directly over him, both looking sheet-white.

"Ohmigod," Grandma is saying. "Ohmigod."

"I'm fine, Mom," Dad says. I don't see any blood on his face this time. "I just . . . Can you give me a little space?"

"Here," Cory says, ushering Grandma aside, then crouching down and using his masculine beardy energy to lift Dad to his feet.

"Thanks, Cory," Dad says, wobbling slightly. Ed and Mom are standing behind him, in case he topples over again.

"Of course, man. You okay?"

"Yeah. Just thought the brunch was getting boring. Tried to spice it up a bit." Everyone laughs (not Grandma), in that unsure way where you can tell they're all sort of nervous.

"Mission accomplished," Cory says.

"Seriously, though," Dad says. "I think I just slipped on something."

It's a good effort on his part, but nobody's buying it.

"Is this what happened the other day, too?" Grandma asks. "Is that why you have the Band-Aid on your forehead?"

"Mom," Dad says, "it's not— Let's not—"

"Let's give him a minute, Mitzie," Mom says, taking charge.

"Fine, fine," Grandma says, eyebrows raised as she takes a step back.

Having just experienced one of Dad's falls less than twenty-four hours ago, I feel like the veteran of the group, who should be offering expertise from time spent on the battlefield. Really, though, Fletcher Handy did most of the helping yesterday, so maybe I don't have much advice beyond *Let's give Fletcher a call!*

"Here, this might help," Paige says, worming her way into the inner circle to hand Dad a paper cup of orange juice. She teaches second grade, where I imagine juice is the answer to many traumatic situations. "In case your blood sugar is low."

Leili and Azadeh appear in the doorway with Ava, who—likely sensing the tension in the room—runs to Paige and hugs her legs, causing her to accidentally slosh some of the orange juice onto the floor just as Dad is about to take the cup.

"I got it, I got it!" Grandma shouts, bounding toward the paper towel roll, grateful for an activity into which to funnel her panicked energy. Within seconds, she's on all fours in between Dad and Paige, sopping up the minor OJ spill.

"Thanks, Paige," Dad says, taking the now-slightly-less-full cup from her. I know he's mortified. Falling in front of me, Fletcher, and some old man is one thing, but this is different. His wife. His best friends. His mother. They may not know the details yet, but his secret is out.

Everyone hovers around for a little while longer, making sure Dad is all right, before Paige says she and Ava should head home for when Ben (her husband, Ava's dad) gets back from his business trip, and the whole brunch deflates. Ed and Cory say they've gotta hit the road before traffic back to Manhattan gets too bad. Leili and Azadeh always have lots of family over for Sunday night dinner, so they need to help cook and set up. Part of me thinks they're glad to leave, and I don't blame them; Grandma is the only one who doesn't seem to be going anytime soon, so it's still pretty tense here. I feel bad that Mom's celebration is ending on such a downer note.

"So now can we talk?" Grandma asks, seconds after Leili and Azadeh have exited the premises.

Dad takes a deep breath. "Sure."

He, Mom, and Grandma sit down at the kitchen table, and I take that as my cue to get the hell out of there. I attempt to do some of my chemistry homework, then pace aimlessly around my room, half trying to hear the slow-motion car crash going on downstairs. At one point, I'm pretty sure Grandma is sobbing, and that's when I start frantically scrolling through my phone for music. I put on "Hold On" by Wilson Phillips, an old song I first heard and fell in love with in one of my all-time favorite movies, *Bridesmaids*. It's super-cheesy, so I always start out listening to it ironically, but then it actually ends up making me feel good.

There's random meowing in the middle of the first chorus, and I look down to see a text from Evan: *So?*

I forgot to respond to his earlier text.

Tastes like chicken, I write before chucking my phone onto the bed (much more carefully than last time).

As I wait for him to write back, I move around at the foot of my bed, doing my version of dancing. It involves lots of head-shaking. Fists in the air. It's not something I'd attempt in public.

"Don't you know, don't you know things will change?" Wilson or Phillips asks. "Things'll go your way, if you hold on for one more day."

I don't think any amount of holding on is going to make Dad better, but it's nice to pretend for the duration of the song.

17

"Hey. Winnie. Hey," Fletcher says from behind me as Mr. Novack works through his self-important attendance-taking.

"Hello. Fletcher. Hello," I say, turning around.

Since he came to Dad's rescue at Stop & Shop, he and I are like actual friends now. Funny how that happens. I still know close to zero about him, but every day this week we've had a quick, pleasant conversation during homeroom, usually about nothing.

"You going today?"

"Yeah," I say casually, as if I haven't been thinking about improv since the moment school started Monday morning, about the chance to redeem myself after that heinousness with Jess. I don't think I've ever anticipated Thursdays this much in my life. "You?"

"Yeah, I'll be there. Sucking it up like I do every week."

"You don't suck." I mean that. Maybe he hasn't fully nailed any scenes, but he's always so committed and in it.

Fletcher shrugs. "It's cool. My thing is physical comedy."

At first I think he's messing with me, but his face remains dead sincere. And then I remember him being whipped around by imaginary gusts of wind, and it makes sense.

The PA speaker crackles to life. "Please stand for the Pledge to the Flag," Evan says. I turn away from Fletcher toward the ol' Stars and Stripes. Mr. Novack has his hand on his heart and a look of defiant pride in his eyes. He's really into the Pledge.

It's weird listening to Evan over the loudspeaker knowing he's kind of maybe my boyfriend. I mean, nothing is official, but last night, we went a step beyond texts and Instagram messages.

He called me.

We were texting about improv rehearsal and what we thought it'd be like, and then suddenly my phone was yodeling (my default ring). I almost didn't pick up, it was so overwhelming.

The first ten seconds were odd, clipped sentences and long pauses. "Do you feel like you're listening to the morning announcements?" Evan asked.

"That's a stupid thing to say," I said.

He laughed, and then I laughed, and then it felt more normal. Evan said that with Mr. Martinez calling him out last week and all, he was really nervous about improv. It was the first time I'd heard him express vulnerability about anything. It was nice, like he felt he could open up to me.

"I'm nervous too," I said. "My main memory from last week is getting fake cake shoved in my face, and I feel like anything I did well that first week was just good luck."

"No way," he said. "You're really talented."

That was nice too.

"I've just never done long-form before," he continued, "and I might be really bad at it." We talked about it awhile, and the strange part is, knowing he was so uneasy actually made me feel calmer.

Now PA Evan is making some dumb joke about athletes

needing to get order forms in for their varsity jackets or else they'll have to make their own jackets at home out of construction paper. I don't fully get it, but it makes me smile just because of how confidently he says it. So different from the worried dude I talked to last night. And none of these people listening to the announcements have heard that side of him. Makes me feel cool, like I'm in on a secret.

And it's definitely a better secret to be in on than the Dad-is-seriously-ill one. After the Weekend of Falls, Mom threatened to leave Dad if he didn't start acknowledging the reality of his situation. I don't think it was a serious threat, but it was still pretty intense and served as a kind of wake-up call for him. As a start, she said, he needed to get a cane because she couldn't handle him falling every other day. I actually agreed with her, though I stayed quiet because I didn't want to get entangled in their fight (more than I already am).

So when I got home from school Tuesday, Dad was waiting in the doorway with an iridescent cane, the metallic blue at the top blending into metallic purple in the middle and metallic pink at the bottom. It reminded me a lot of my bike in elementary school and clearly it reminded Dad, too, because he'd attached to the handle of his cane the same white streamers that had once protruded from my bike's handlebars. Not only that, but he was decked out in his white suit and white top hat (he'd had to get a white suit as a groomsman for Cory and Ed's wedding; the hat was his own idea) and a monocle like the Monopoly guy.

"Wow, Dad," I said, cracking up.

"Whattaya think of the new look?" he asked, attempting to spin the cane but then thinking better of it after getting a little wobbly on his feet.

"I think I love it," I said. "What's with the monocle?"

"I've always worn this," he said, totally deadpan.

"Oh, right, but you usually wear it on your other eye."

He seemed so genuinely pleased with his cane that I assumed he'd gotten over whatever reservations he'd had. But when I came home from school yesterday and put away my jacket, I saw his cane in the closet. Less than an hour later, when Dad walked in from teaching his theater class, I asked about it. I didn't want to be annoying, but I knew how important it was to Mom.

"Oh," Dad said. "Yeah, I forgot to bring the cane. But I don't really need it there, anyway. These days I spend most of class sitting down." When I'd been to his classes in the past, he pretty much *never* sat down, so clearly he'd had to adjust. Or maybe he was bending the truth a bit. Either way, I didn't want to be too pushy about it.

"Please don't tell Mom," Dad said. "I *have* been using the cane when it's really necessary."

I hated being in that position, having to lie to Mom on Dad's behalf. But I also got that this wasn't the easiest situation for Dad to be in.

"Fine," I said. "But I *am* telling her you stopped wearing the monocle."

"No! Don't do it! She says that monocle is the only reason she married me."

"Well, I relate. It's the only reason I chose you as my dad."

"That makes no sense."

"Thanks," I said.

I don't know how freaked out I should be. I've thought on the daily about googling ALS for myself, but then I remember what I read on Azadeh's phone that night, and I can't do it.

Dad seems to want to pretend nothing has changed. It's a bit we do well together, our banter helping to relieve the pain. So, if he wants to keep putting that out there, I will *Yes, and* till the cows come home.

Support your partner no matter what, right?

Just like every week, Mr. Martinez isn't there yet when I arrive at the auditorium, so I immediately scan the rows for Leili, who has a steaming cup of coffee in her hand.

"Where'd you get that?" I ask.

"Stole it from the teachers' lounge," Leili says, all non-chalant, taking a sip.

"What? Really?" Leili's driven but she's also a rule follower.

"Well, not exactly stole. Mrs. Fumarola got it for me." That's more like it.

"Of *course* she did." Mrs. Fumarola is the yearbook advisor, and Leili is her all-time favorite student. That's not hyperbole. She goes around telling people.

"Hey, if you worked your butt off on Yearbook ten hours a week, I'm sure you could be her favorite too."

"Any other perks besides free coffee?"

Leili makes her mouth-to-the-side thinking face. "She gave me a Kind bar once."

"Yeah, I'll pass." Evan is perched on the back of a seat in the front row, speaking in a weird voice and cracking up Dan Blern and Mahesh, seated below him on either side. He doesn't look like someone who's feeling anxious, but then maybe this is what that looks like for him: ham dials turned up to eleven.

"You can go sit over there with him if you want," Leili says.

"What? Gross, no. I want to sit with you."

"Okay, just giving you the option."

"You're a ridiculously impressive human being, you know that?"

"I do." Leili smiles.

"Hey, are you okay, by the way?"

"What do you mean?"

"I dunno. Just, like, with Oz dating someone. I didn't know if that was weird for you or not."

"It's not weird."

"Oh. Okay. Good."

"I'm happy for her."

"Of course, yeah. I am too."

"Hello hello," Mr. Martinez says, palpably shifting the energy in the room as he strides down the aisle. "Sorry I'm late. Let's all get right up onstage." Mr. Martinez vaults onto the playing space, giving us a good look at those surprisingly-hip-for-a-teacher two-tone blue shoes.

"Here we go," Fletcher says from behind me as Leili and I take the stairs.

"Oh hey," I say.

"Time for some improv duty," he says.

"Huh?"

"It's from the, uh, when we were at the supermarket. Like toilet paper du—"

"Oh yes!" I say. I wish I'd gotten his reference right away. He probably feels ridiculous now. "Improv duty. Totally."

We arrive onstage, everyone standing in a circle. There's a spot right next to Evan, but I don't want to ditch Leili for a guy. So she, Fletcher, and I end up standing together on the opposite side from him.

Evan pouts out his lip while motioning me over with his

head, which makes me smile. It's too late now, so I laugh like he's making a joke and redirect my attention to Mr. Martinez, who has begun speaking.

"So I want to start by reiterating how brave everyone was last week," he says. "I really threw you all into the long-form fire, so to speak, and you all did good."

"Did *well*," Evan says in a jokey disciplinarian voice, which gets a nice laugh, even though I think it's kind of rude to correct a teacher.

"Ha, yes," Mr. Martinez says, "pardon my grammar. You all did *well*. Gotta love a good adverb stickler." He points at Evan, somewhat sarcastically, and Evan bows his head. "But this week, we're going to get back to some of the basics, do some exercises and drills, probably no time for long-form scene work."

Leili looks disappointed, and several students good-naturedly boo.

"I know, I know." Mr. Martinez smiles and gestures with his hands, like *Keep it coming*. "Get all the boos out. But this will make us better improvisers. You think Steph Curry played his first game and then said, 'Okay, I'm all set, I got this basketball thing all figured out now'?"

I side-glance at Leili—my *Explain this to me, please* look—who quietly says, "He's on the Warriors."

"The what?"

"It's a basketball team."

"Oh."

"Heh," Fletcher softly chuckles, clearly having overheard.

"Of course not!" Mr. Martinez says. "Dude's already won multiple championships, and he's still out there every day, coming up with new ways to challenge himself, doing drills, shooting baskets from half-court with a blindfold over his eyes. And that's what I want for all of you: to always be improving."

Though I had no idea who Steph Curry was a minute ago, I'm finding myself weirdly inspired. I *want* to improve. I *can*. I will be the Steph Curry of improv. Somebody get me a blindfold.

"All right, enough of me jabbering. Let's get our Nameball on. And in the spirit of Steph, I'll start it off . . . with a basketball." Of course that inspires cringe chills because, come on, it's super-cheesy, but mixed in with those chills is a fiery determination that must be kind of like what athletes feel when they are doing sports. (I'd be more specific in my simile construction, but my involvement with athletics has been limited, and the involvement I have had, I've tried to block out.)

Nameball is followed by Zip-Zap-Zop (the clapping-shouting game) and One-Word Story, and by the end, I'm feeling ready to, like, do twenty slam dunks.

"Okay!" Mr. Martinez says. "Our main exercise today is going to be about creating and exploring our environment within the scene. Obviously in improv we don't have actual sets or actual props, so we're always miming. And, no joke, scenes can be made or broken by the level of the improvisers' commitment to the physical reality of the scene."

"Miming?" I say to Leili, who nods.

"Shit yeah," Fletcher says, more to himself than me.

"And this means exploring the environment on your own but also paying close attention to what your partner has discovered. It's still *Yes, and,* but on a nonverbal wavelength. For example, if your scene partner establishes that there's a table right over here"—Mr. Martinez swirls his arm around like a spastic wizard casting a spell—"and you don't notice so you just straight-up walk through the table, that's going to take the entire audience out of the scene. You feel me?"

Everyone nods. Only Molly Graham-Crockett responds aloud: "Totally."

"Instead, you say *YES*, there's a table over there, *AND* there's *plates* on that table too!" I've never seen someone so excited about plates, real or imaginary. "So that's what this exercise will be all about. Don't worry so much about the scene, worry more about discovering the environment."

"Totally," Molly Graham-Crockett says again.

"Now which of our intrepid improvisers want to go first?"

"Hey," Fletcher says as he shoots his hand up in the air. It's the most confident I've seen him since the supermarket aisle.

"Great," Mr. Martinez says, as visibly surprised by Fletcher's confidence as I am. "Anyone else?"

My arm shoots into the air before I've consciously decided to volunteer. "Winnie." Mr. Martinez is again pleasantly caught off guard, and hearing him say my name jolts me into reality too. Not sure why I threw my hand into the air. I think seeing Fletcher so confident made me feel like I wanted to be a part of whatever was about to happen. As I move into the circle, I catch a look on Evan's face that might be jealousy, which, though it wasn't my intention, is not unpleasant.

"So here's the deal," Mr. Martinez says. "Fletcher's going to start the scene by doing some activity to establish an environment. Totally nonverbal. Then Winnie's going to come in and add something. And then Fletcher can build on that and so on and so on . . .."

"So no talking at all?" I ask. I am not, nor have I ever been, much of a mime. What have I signed up for?

"I mean," Mr. Martinez says, "you can exchange some words here and there. But the words shouldn't be what the scene is about, if that makes sense. What the scene is about should be happening in the physicality."

"Um, okay," I say, glancing over at Fletcher, who's staring straight ahead, nodding his head to the beat of some song only he can hear.

"All right?" Mr. Martinez asks, looking at both of us with care and concern, like he genuinely wants to make sure we're fully equipped for this exercise in make-believe. It's endearing.

"Sure," I say at the same time as Fletcher says, "Oh yeah."

"Great. Let's get you two a word."

"Heat!" Jess Yang shouts. I can't help but think she's trying to steer Fletcher and me into some kind of romantic scene in order to screw with Evan. I'm not normally so paranoid, but she was a total a-hole to me last week. So.

"Heat," Mr. Martinez says, stepping aside. "Go for it."

The wheels in Fletcher's head spin for a few moments before he nods definitively and starts to grimace. At first I think it's because he can't think of anything, but then I realize he's already started. He exhales as he undoes the two top buttons on his shirt, even though he's wearing a T-shirt with no buttons. As he moves his imaginary collar back and forth and loosens his invisible tie, it's completely obvious to me and the whole room that this type of improv is Fletcher's sweet spot.

His miming is truly next-level. It's like I can see every detail of the scene he's setting, with him as this dude coming home from work on a hot day, taking a load off. Fletcher takes a few steps and struggles to open a nonexistent window, followed by the screen, and then looks authentically relieved as he sticks his top half outside the window frame. I'm so absorbed that Mr. Martinez has to whisper my name to remind me that I'm supposed to join in.

I don't know how to contribute to this mastery, so I just extend my arm, cupping my hand as if I'm holding a glass of lemonade. I move it from side to side to indicate there's ice inside. I don't think it achieves the effect I'm going for.

"Hey," I say to Fletcher, whose back is to me as he continues to cool off outside a window that's not actually there.

"Huh?" he says, so convincingly that I'm thinking maybe he forgot I was in the scene with him.

"Oh, here," I say, trying not to speak too much as I hand him the glass.

"Cool, thanks." Fletcher turns around and takes the glass from me, then tilts it as if to pour the lemonade all over the ground. Of course, he had no idea it was lemonade. Or that it was a glass. I see that his free hand is now in a fist, suspended in the air a little way down from the other hand, and I realize he's decided I've handed him some kind of pole. He hefts it into the air with a grunt and uses it to open a high-up window above us. He is clearly a mime genius. "Get a breeze going," Fletcher says as he leans the huge pole against the wall.

"Right," I say, no clue what to do next.

Luckily, it doesn't matter because Fletcher slaps his neck and scowls, and I instantly get it. A fly. It just came in through the newly opened window. I'm telling you, next-level.

I'm excited because I've had an idea, thinking I'll take out a flyswatter, but again, Fletcher is a step ahead of me, retrieving the huge pole thing from the wall and starting to flail it around. Hilarious. And much better than an obvious flyswatter.

"Oh shoot, sorry," Fletcher says as his hands jerk, like the invisible pole has made contact with something above us.

"That was a new chandelier," I say in a frustrated voice, which gets a huge laugh.

"I know," he says, placing the pole down at his feet, then looking around the room with intensity, as if he actually is tracking a buzzing fly. "That's why I said sorry."

"Try this," I say, holding up the invisible flyswatter I'd intended to bring out earlier.

"A welding torch?" Fletcher says. "You crazy? You're gonna burn the house down."

It's so surprising and delightful, I can't help but laugh.

"Stay committed to what's happening," Mr. Martinez tells me. "It's going great."

I put the swatter-turned-welding-torch down. "You're right," I tell Fletcher. "I don't know what I was thinking."

"Don't move," he says, his attention laser-focused on me.

"Huh?" I turn my head in his direction.

"I said don't move!"

"Oh." I freeze, contorting my face in this goofy way that gets some laughs.

"It's on your head," Fletcher whispers. "I think I can get it."

His commitment to this moment is so deep that I find myself raising my own game, exploring the comedic potential of my physicality in ways that would make Lucille Ball proud. I screw up my face and hunch my neck, staring upward as if Fletcher's imagination has manifested an actual fly on the top of my skull.

The whole room is rapt as he steps closer to me, silently, gracefully, a hunter stalking his tiny prey. He raises one hand in the air, as if ready to smack the fly. Which should be concerning, as that means he'll soon be smacking me in the head, but I'm so in the scene, I don't even care. Fletcher wraps his hand around my wrist, as if to ground himself before he swings.

A chill rolls down my spine as Fletcher's hand, simultaneously strong and soft, touches my skin.

"Okay, here we go," he says, raising his other hand higher in the air.

"And let's end it there," Mr. Martinez says. "Before Winnie's parents file a lawsuit against me." Everyone laughs. I don't because I'm still shaking off the scene, wishing it could have gone on a little longer. Fletcher takes his hand off my arm. My wrist feels like it's glowing. "Nice work, you two. That's the level of commitment we're talking about with this stuff. Excellent. Set the bar real high."

I look at Fletcher, who looks how I feel, blinking and reorienting himself to his surroundings, the fire of thirty seconds ago nowhere to be found. He gives me a bashful smile as we walk back to our spots in the circle. I smile back.

"That was really good," Leili says to Fletcher and me.

"Thanks," Fletcher says.

"Were you actually going to smack Winnie in the head?"

"I was wondering that too," I say.

"Nah," Fletcher says. "The fly was gonna get away before I could do that. I was thinking I might smack myself a bit, though, if it had gone on longer."

"Wow," Leili says.

"All right," Mr. Martinez says, "who wants to follow that up?"

Evan practically leaps into the center of the circle, a man possessed. He and Mahesh do a scene where they play video games in a basement. Evan's trying really hard to push the buttons on his pretend controller in a way that seems realistic, but he mainly seems spastic. Which is sort of endearing. Mahesh is sloppier and unspecific, looking much more like a dude with twitchy fingers than someone playing a video game.

Once their scene is done, Evan heads back to his spot in the circle and gives me a look and a big smile, like *How'd you like THAT?* I move my hand back and forth like *It was so-so,* and Evan's face falls. I quickly smile and mouth *I'm kidding* as I give him two thumbs up.

The rest of the scenes are all fine—my favorite is with Leili and Dan Blern, who are paleontologists carefully uncovering dinosaur fossils; Leili accidentally uses the wrong brush and a rare bone crumbles hilariously in her hand—but none of them can match the brilliance of Fletcher Handy.

As Leili and I pack up (Dad is picking us up today) once rehearsal ends, I'm excited to tell Fletcher how great he was and how fun it was to improvise with him, but he's already dashing out the auditorium door.

"Dan Blern always smells like Cheetos," Leili says quietly as I watch Fletcher disappear. "Have you ever noticed that?"

"Maybe sometimes," I say.

"He's a nice guy," she continues. "I just really smelled it during our scene."

"Hey, girl," Evan says, startling both Leili and me by inserting his head in between ours. "You were really funny today. You too, Leili."

"Thanks," Leili and I say at the same time. Evan seems a little jumpier than usual.

"Did you like my scene with Mahesh?" he asks. "It was kinda stupid, right?"

"Oh," I say. "No, it was great. So funny."

"Yeah. It was good," Leili says.

"Hey, do you wanna maybe hang out sometime?" He spits it out so quickly that it almost seems like he's directing the question at both me and Leili. But then Leili takes a few steps away, and Evan doesn't tell her not to.

"Oh," I say, heat rushing to my face. With all the texting we've done lately, I assumed this is the direction we were moving in, but it's still a surprise. "Yeah. Sure."

"Yeah?" Evan says, visibly relieved. Until this moment, I didn't realize just how nervous he was. It's sweet.

"Yeah, totally. Let's, you know, hang out sometime."

"She said yes!" Evan shouts up to the high auditorium ceiling.

18

"So you'll text when you're ready for a ride home, right?" Evan's mom asks into the rearview mirror.

"I already told you," Evan says, "Winnie's parents are picking us up."

"Oh, right, right, sorry," she says, her brown bob cut gently undulating as she shakes her head. "I keep forgetting. Hard to keep all you kids' plans straight."

It's Friday night, and Evan and I are sitting in the first row of his mom's tan minivan on the way to the movie theater. It's a little weird since no one's in the passenger seat, like she's our chauffeur, but Evan doesn't seem to care.

I'm very nervous. When he suggested we hang out, I didn't think he meant something as official as this. I've never gone on a movie date in my life. I always thought of it as something only our parents' generation did.

But that's part of what makes it charming, too. We're, like, going on a proper date. I'm wearing an outfit approved via text by Leili and Azadeh. (*Classy but hot,* Azadeh wrote. *Clot,* Leili added.) I'm even wearing some light pink lipstick, given to me by my aunt last Hanukkah, and Mom's eyeliner.

"All right, have fun, you two," Evan's mom says as we pull up to the multiplex.

"Thanks, Mom," Evan says, having already slid open the door and gotten one foot outside it.

"Thanks so much, Mrs. Miller," I say.

"Sure! Have fun," she says for the second time. She's so routine about the whole thing, it makes me wonder how many girls Evan has done this with before. At the very least, he had to have come here with Jess. Probably others. Or maybe she's just been through it with Evan's three siblings.

We walk into the lobby, stepping around popcorn crushed into the carpet, and stop at a ticket machine. Evan pushes a series of buttons and swipes a credit card. He takes the first ticket that comes out, and when the second drops into the slot, I grab it.

"Oh," he says. "No, that's— That's just a receipt."

I look at it and immediately feel foolish, realizing he's only purchased a ticket for himself.

"I didn't know if . . . ," Evan says. "Shoot, sorry. I didn't want to assume."

"Oh, of course," I say. Honestly, I'm fine with it. Glad, even. The idea that a guy is supposed to pay for his date is antiquated and, frankly, pretty sexist.

I punch through the same screens Evan just did until I find the comedy we're seeing, a new one starring Will Ferrell and Tiffany Haddish that I'm really excited about. They're two of my all-time favorite people, mainly because of, respectively, *Elf* and *Girls Trip,* both of which Dad and I are obsessed with.

"Ohmigod, I won!" I say as my ticket comes out of the machine. "I won!"

"Wait, seriously?" Evan asks excitedly. "Did they give you a free gift card or something?"

"Oh, uh, no," I say, deflating. "It's . . . It's actually just my ticket. That's a joke my dad and I do sometimes."

"Ah, I get it now," Evan says. "That's funny. I thought maybe you really did win something."

"No."

"That would be kind of funny if you had, though. Like if you randomly got a new car."

"Right, yeah," I say. "Definitely."

"Hey, you want something to eat? My treat. If that's okay."

"Sure. Thanks." I'm happy to move past my misunderstood attempt at humor as quickly and gracefully as possible. Evan usually gets my jokes, so I'm not gonna dwell on one misfire.

"So, are you a popcorn girl?" Evan asks. "Or do you lean candy?"

We're almost to the snack counter when I see that Jess Yang is behind it. She looks different, her thick black hair up in a bun, but it's definitely her. I almost choke on my own spit.

"Um," I say. "Wait."

"What?" Evan asks. He had to have noticed her, right?

"I didn't know Jess works here."

"Oh." Evan looks at Jess, then back at me. "Yeah. She does. Not a big deal."

"But maybe we want to get our snacks from the counter on the other side? Don't know if you've noticed, but Jess doesn't really like me very much."

"Well, that's just because she's cuh-razy. Seriously. She was really nice when we were going out or whatever, but then she turned total psycho. Like in your improv scene, remember?"

Of course I remember. "Isn't that even more of a reason to buy food from someone else?"

165

"I guess. But I'm all about facing your fears, you know?" He puffs his chest out like a superhero and speaks with the gruff rasp of Batman. "Do you want to face your fears with me, Winnie?"

I'm about to say "Not really," but he takes my hand and says, "Come on."

So, yeah, we're holding hands. Which would be nice, except . . . does the first time it happens really have to be as we approach his ex-girlfriend? I let go.

Two girls ahead of us walk away with a bag of Sour Patch Watermelons and a huge soda, and now it's our turn.

"What are you doing?" Jess asks Evan without so much as glancing at me.

"Uh . . . *buying food*?"

Jess shakes her head, snorting out air. "Fine. What do you want?"

"Oh yeah, we never decided," Evan says, looking at me. "What do you want?"

I want this interaction to be over, like, yesterday. Is what I want.

"I'm good with whatever," I mutter, staring down at a lone gummy bear on the floor. I am painfully uncomfortable.

"Do you like Buncha Crunch?" Evan asks me, somehow ignoring the expression on Jess's face (like she wants to wring his neck).

"Sure, yeah."

"That didn't seem very convincing," Evan says to Jess, as if she's supposed to join in on a lively discussion about my movie candy preferences. Good god. He turns back to me. "Goobers, then? Are you a Goobers girl? Heh heh."

166

"There's a line behind you," Jess says. I'm trying to steal glances at her when I can, trying to decide for myself how much of a psycho she really is. She actually seems more annoyed than crazy.

"Buncha Crunch is fine," I say. "Let's just do that."

"Cool cool," Evan says, taking out a plastic *Pirates of the Caribbean* wallet. Of course he has a *Pirates of the Caribbean* wallet. "One Buncha Crunch." Jess grabs a box and smacks it down onto the counter. "Anything to drink?" Evan asks me. "I been really into Cherry Coke lately, but—"

"Sure, great."

"How much do you think you'll drink? So I know what size to get."

I'm compelled to look into Evan's eyes because I'm starting to think this is a bit. It has to be. Why else would he be dragging this out so much?

I don't think it's a bit.

"All the sizes are huge," I say. "Just get a small."

"Nice. Good point." He turns back to Jess. "All right, one small Cherry Coke, if you please."

As Jess fills a hugely small cup and Evan holds his debit card out in the air, I try to extract myself from the cringiness and get back into the headspace I was in moments ago, on a date with a guy I like who likes me back.

"*Gracias*, Jess," Evan says as he grabs the candy and soda. "*Hasta* later."

"Bye," I say to Jess without making eye contact and then, more quietly, "Sorry."

We step away from the counter, and everything starts to feel better. I look at Evan, at his short-sleeved plaid button-down and tight-ish jeans and his hair that looks shaggy without seeming dirty. He looks really good. "See what I mean?" he says as a short man in a tie rips our tickets. "She's totally nuts."

I want to say "I wouldn't be happy either if I had to serve snacks to my ex-boyfriend and some new girl," but instead I just say, "Hmm."

"But it's not even that," Evan continues. "You're way funnier than her."

Gotta give him credit, he definitely knows the right things to say.

"I've seen her do some funny things," I say, though, because I don't want to tear her down entirely.

"Yeah," Evan says as we walk into the theater, which is already at least two-thirds full. "But she's more of an actor than a comedian. And you're, like, the real deal. Let's sit up here."

We walk up the aisle steps and go into the third row from the back, squishing past a bunch of people before we sit down.

"Ahhhh." Evan leans back in his seat—this whole multiplex has those fancy recliner chairs—and pushes the button until he's in full recline. "That's what I'm talkin' about!"

I push my button a little so I won't seem like a party pooper, but I don't really want to lie down. It always makes me sleepy, and I actually want to watch the movie.

Evan lifts his chair up until it's exactly parallel to mine.

"Whaddup," he says.

"Nuttin'," I say.

"Want a sip?" he asks, pointing the straw in my direction immediately after he's taken a huge gulp of cherry soda. It occurs to me that sharing a beverage is actually a very intimate act. Putting our mouths on the same piece of plastic. Not that far off from kissing.

Oh man. We're probably going to kiss tonight.

How soon will it happen? Before the movie even starts?

"No sippy?" Evan asks.

"Oh sure," I say, grabbing the cup. All I can think about as I drink is Evan's mouth and how soon it might be touching mine.

"It's better at the movies, right?" Evan asks.

"Hm?"

"Cherry Coke. Tastes way better at the movies than anywhere else."

It actually tastes bland and watered down. Sometimes people just say things, and I don't even think they know why they're saying them.

"Yeah," I pretend to agree. "Though I personally think it tastes the best while hunting. Shoot a big deer, then drink a Cherry Coke. Delicious."

He laughs at this one. Thank god.

"You hunting," he says. "That's hilarious."

"What? I can't hunt?" I ask, pretending to suddenly get very serious. "I could hunt."

"No, sure, yeah," Evan says, squirming. "Just that you don't seem like someone who would want to, like, pick up a gun and shoot animals."

"That's sexist."

"Ahh, I really didn't mean it like that, I'm sorry—"

"Evan," I say, putting a hand on his arm. "I'm kidding."

"What? Oh." He smiles, radiating relief, like *Of course you were.*

"I mean," I say, "it is kinda sexist, but I also agree that me hunting is hilarious."

Evan narrows his eyes at me in this wistful way and puts his mildly clammy hand on mine. "You're not like other girls." I recognize the cheese factor—I think he's literally quoting from some movie—but it's sweet. Though, when you really think about it, why is that a compliment? I am like other girls. I'm like Leili. I'm like Azadeh. And I'm *trying* to be like my heroes, almost all of whom were once girls.

That doesn't seem like fun first-date banter, though, so instead I say: "Aw shucks." Evan starts leaning toward me, awkwardly straining over the recliner arm, and I realize the kiss is coming, it's about to happen. I hope my breath smells all right. I brushed my teeth and everything.

Just as his mouth comes close to mine, the first preview starts with a shatteringly loud and bass-y explosion and we both startle apart, then laugh at ourselves for startling so much, and even though I think we both still want to kiss each other, the moment is temporarily gone, so we both look at the screen as if our mouths weren't millimeters apart mere moments ago.

"That was so loud," I say, but it's a trailer for an action movie, so it's still loud, and Evan doesn't hear me.

When the trailer ends, Evan leans into me and says, "That looks sick."

I couldn't agree less. I've always hated action movies, especially the humorless kind like the one we just saw four minutes of, all guns and noise and determined faces. I've never understood how you could enjoy watching something that has not a single funny moment in it. That's not like life at all.

"Meh," I say to Evan.

He laughs. "Girls never like action movies."

"Not true," I say, even though, as I've just explained, it's incredibly true for me. But I can't help but bristle at broad generalizations about an entire gender. "Azadeh loves action movies."

170

Evan laughs again, and I'm about to defend Azadeh until I realize he's responding to a new trailer that just came on. This one's a comedy about a dude superhero. Ugh.

About halfway through it, Evan takes my hand as he guffaws at a woman superhero being thrown into a dumpster. His fingers rub the back of my hand in a way that is not unpleasant. I feel like I'm not entirely in my own body. It's strange that this boy doesn't know some very basic things about me—for example, that my dad is so ill he's had to start walking with a cane. I don't know how Evan would react, if he'd start to pity me, or, worse, not really care at all.

Now Evan has moved up from my hand to stroke my forearm. It's giving me tingles—like, the good kind—so I'm only half aware that the trailer now showing is for the five billionth *Transformers* sequel. Evan doesn't seem to care about it either, which is a turn-on. (I find it hard to trust anyone who's enthusiastic about *Transformers* movies.) As he's running his fingers up and down my arm, he inexplicably decides this is a good moment to open the Buncha Crunch, awkwardly attempting it with his free hand.

"Do you want me to help you with that?"

"I got it," he says, holding the box against his chest and pressing in the cardboard top with his thumb. He pours some out into his mouth, then holds the box toward me. "Crunch?" he asks.

"I'm good," I say. I do want some, but then my mouth is going to taste like chocolate when we kiss. Though I guess his is going to too, so it's probably a moot point. "Yeah, okay, I'll take some."

"Make up your mind already," he teases, tilting the box down to my open palm. "Geez."

171

The misshapen hunks of chocolate pile up in my hand, and I'm in the middle of contemplating whether I should peck them off one at a time or just hurl the whole lot of them into my mouth when suddenly Evan's negotiated his way over the recliner arm and his mouth is on mine.

It's happening.

I'm completely caught off guard, so for the first second or two I don't know how to respond. I don't pull away, but I don't kiss back, either.

"Oh," I finally say, laughing nervously.

He pulls his head back. "Was that okay? Sorry, I thought—"

"No, yeah, it was," I say. "Just surprised me. I was still thinking about the Buncha Crunch."

"Because you know I like you, right?"

"Yeah," I say. "I mean, I thought so."

"I really do," he says. "I think you're so cool and funny and pretty."

"Thanks," I say, sure I'm blushing.

"I mean it. But do you . . . you know, do you feel the same?"

Evan's hazel eyes peer into mine, vulnerable and inquisitive, and even though he seems calm, I can see he has a lot riding on my answer.

The chocolate is getting all melty in my hand.

"I do," I say, and the very nature of it being those two words, so classically connected to wedded bliss, makes it seem weightier than I'd intended it. Because, yes, I do like Evan, but I don't necessarily feel ready for whatever this is, this dramatic declaration of our feelings.

"Awesome," he says. "I thought so."

A new trailer has come on, and I hear Kate McKinnon's

voice. Seeing as she's one of those girls I'm trying to be like, I of course want to turn and look at the screen, but it seems rude.

I also want to get this gooey Buncha Crunch out of my hand, but it seems like an odd moment to cram them into my mouth.

"So, can I . . . ?" Evan moves his head toward mine. I answer the question by kissing him, which I'm happy to see catches *him* off guard. He tastes like chocolate. Or maybe I'm tasting myself.

"I've been wanting to do this for so long," he says between kisses. I'm into it, even though it's another line straight out of a movie. *So long?* He barely knew me until a few weeks ago.

"Mm," I say.

We make out through the next few trailers. I leave my glasses on, in case I'm able to sneak some peeks. Evan's kisses are a little sloppy but also nice. When the movie finally starts, I panic, as I immediately hear Tiffany Haddish saying something hilarious.

But then Evan, who still has one hand on my arm, puts his other on my cheek, and all I want to do is kiss him some more. I can see the movie again another time. It's no big deal, I'll just come back and see it again.

I take off my glasses and let my Buncha Crunch pitter-patter to the floor.

19

I'm scrolling through Instagram at the kitchen table as I tear through my second bowl of Life when a notification tells me I've been tagged. It's a selfie of me and Evan that he took while the credits were rolling last night, after we'd just made out for approximately two hours. He's squinting his eyes and sticking out his tongue. I'm smiling and looking dazed. The caption reads:

me and my gurl #moviesarekool #evenwhenyoubarelywatch them

His gurl.

He's telling the world I'm *his gurl*.

Kissing him for two hours *was* pretty kool. Sure, I wished I could have done that and also watched the movie, but at least I heard a lot of it. About halfway through, Evan slid his hands down to my chest, which was a little surprising, but I didn't actually stop him until he tried to go under my shirt. I whispered that I wasn't ready for that yet, and I thought maybe he'd get angry, but he didn't; he said he completely understood.

I'm not sure how I feel about his hashtags, broadcasting to everyone that we were too busy hooking up to watch the movie. Jess is going to hate this post in a profound way. And I hope Evan's parents aren't on Instagram. (Thank god mine aren't. Dad used to be, but now he just sticks to Facebook and Twitter, which he loves because it's "a great place to workshop jokes.")

"Everything okay?" Mom says as she walks in wearing an old ratty T-shirt of Dad's and purple pajama pants, making a beeline for the coffee machine.

"Oh yeah. Why?"

"You're staring at your phone so intensely."

"Oh no, just Instagram."

"I swear, those phones are going to be the end of civilization," Mom says. It's a regular refrain. "No one notices anything going on around them because they're looking at pictures of what's going on around other people."

"Not true," I say. "People do notice things . . . if those things will make for good Instagram photos."

"Blech," Mom says. The coffee machine gurgles behind her. I don't like coffee, but I'm comforted by the sound of its creation. "How was your date last night?"

"Pretty good," I say, trying to sound nonchalant.

"Was the movie worth seeing? It looks kinda stupid."

Mom thinks most comedies look stupid, so I know lying to her about how it was will be easy. I don't even have to fully lie: I just sort of shrug my shoulders and move my head side to side while saying, "Ehhh."

"Yeah, I figured," Mom says. "All those movies are the same after a while."

It was much harder to lie to Dad last night. He was the one who picked me and Evan up, which he was happy to do since it's an activity that didn't require his cane. I sat in the front seat because, unlike Evan's mom, Dad didn't "want to feel like a chauffeur." I also think it was sort of a power move for his first time meeting Evan.

"How was the movie?" Dad said moments after we pulled away from Bricktown Multiplex.

"Good," I answered quickly, sounding guilty. "Funny."

Dad knew immediately—I know he did from the way he smiled at my answer—so he proceeded to grill Evan instead. "What'd you think, Evan?" he asked into the rearview.

"Yeah, same," Evan answered, unfazed. "Some funny parts, but kind of a weak story."

"Right, yeah," Dad said, "that's what I've read in some reviews." I couldn't tell if this was meant to be confirmation that he thought Evan's opinion was legit or if he was suggesting that Evan had only read the reviews.

"Maybe I should be a movie critic," Evan said, smiling goofily, trying to share a gentle laugh with Dad, who wasn't having it.

"Well, Winnie already is," Dad said. "You think you'll review this one for the school paper, Win?"

"Oh," I said, not expecting to be back in the hot seat. "Uh, maybe. Probably. Yeah. Three stars out of five, I think."

Dad grinned. "Hey, Evan, what'd you think of the supporting cast?" He was truly enjoying this.

"Oh," Evan said. "Really solid."

"Who was your favorite?"

"Um . . ." Evan definitely had no idea who was in the movie besides Tiffany and Will. *Aidy Bryant,* I thought as loudly as I could, hoping he'd be able to pick up my brain waves. "I liked all of them, really."

"Great," Dad said, subtly sarcastic. "Great."

I was surprised by this protectiveness, but I've never had a boyfriend for him to meet before.

Is Evan my boyfriend?

That's a strange thought.

And Mom somehow has it at the exact same time. "So, is this Evan, like, your . . . boyfriend?" She sips her coffee right after, as if that makes it seem like a more casual question than it actually is.

"Mom, I don't know," I say, surprising myself with how annoyed I sound. "It was just one date."

"Okay, okay," Mom says, her hand in the air, "I'm not trying to pry. Just want to know if my little girl has a boyfriend or not."

No one wants to be referred to as *little girl*. Even actual little girls. "I'll let you know once I have official confirmation."

"Will you, though?" Mom says, almost to herself, as she slices a grapefruit in half and plops it onto a plate.

"Do you have a fax machine?" I ask.

"Hmm?"

"The official confirmation only comes through fax."

"Oh," Mom says, smiling. "That's funny, Win."

Mom gets most of my jokes, and I do think she appreciates them, but she never joins in the way Dad does. More often, it's what just happened, a kind acknowledgment that I've said something humorous.

"Hey, how's improv going, by the way?"

I'm somehow both happy and annoyed that she asked. "Um, it's good. I mean, I don't fully have the hang of it yet. Like, at all. But."

"Well, of course not, you just started. I remember doing a little improv in one of my acting classes. It was so much harder than I thought it would be."

"Yeah, right?"

177

Mom nods. "Definitely. I'd take sketch comedy over that any day. At least you know what you're going to say. You'd be really good at sketch, too, I think."

"Oh, maybe," I say, both flattered and secretly judging her for not being able to stick with improv the way Dad did.

"So . . ." Mom sits down across from me at the kitchen table, serrated grapefruit spoon in hand. "I wanted to talk to you about something."

It's impossible not to feel freaked out by that sentence. Doesn't even matter who says it; if it weren't intended to startle, upset, or destroy, they would have just said the thing instead of prefacing it like that.

"Okay," I say. I've finished all my cereal and now I'm sipping up the remaining milk (I don't wanna waste a single bit of my Life). I keep at it, my shoulders hunching the way they always do when I'm in an uncertain situation. It's like my body's involuntary defense mechanism.

Mom looks around, like she's worried the place is wiretapped, before leaning closer to me. "It's about Daddy."

I relax a little, knowing the something she wants to talk about isn't related to me, but a new thread of terror weaves into my body. Is Dad's ALS progressing faster than they realized?

"How do you think he's doing?" Mom continues, and, much to my surprise, I can instantly tell she's not asking as a test or anything. It's a genuine question.

I rest my spoon in the empty bowl. "I mean, not great. He has a cane."

"I mean more like his emotional state. Does he seem okay to you?"

"Oh," I say. Mom and I have been known to discuss our own

emotional states from time to time, but never my father's. "I guess. I'm always expecting him to seem more sad or down, but he still makes a lot of jokes. Which seems like a good thing."

"That's actually what I wanted to ask you about. You know how Daddy used to act and do comedy but then gave it up when we moved to Jersey?"

"Of course."

"I was just thinking . . ." Mom takes another look behind her to the stairs, I guess making sure Dad isn't about to walk into the room. "Maybe he'd want to do that again."

"Act?"

"Well, no, the comedy part. Like do stand-up." Mom is looking at me like she just pitched her invention on *Shark Tank*. "Do you think he would want to do that?" *Why are you asking me?* I want to shout.

But I also get it. As far as my dad and comedy go, I'm a knowledgeable source. Or I *should* be. "I don't know," I say. "Maybe."

"Just because," Mom tries to explain, "he may be running out of . . . If that's something he still wants, I just want him to know I support him doing it."

I stare down at the last drops of milk in my bowl. I blink a lot. In saying those three words—*running out of*—it was like Mom pointed at the elephant next to the breakfast table, the one I've been diligently ignoring every day.

"You could just ask him," I say without looking up. It comes out harsher than I intend.

"No, I know," Mom says. "But I don't want him to take it the wrong way, and I thought if he'd ever mentioned something like that, then—"

She's stopped short by the sound of Dad slowly coming down the steps. Mom walks over, grapefruit spoon in hand, to ask if he needs help.

"I'm good," he answers, his voice husky as usual. His new normal.

"Okeydoke." Mom comes back into the kitchen, holding the serrated spoon a little tighter than when she left. She grabs the Brita out of the fridge and pours herself and Dad glasses of water, not looking at me, leaving no bread crumbs of the conversation we had moments ago.

"Morning, Banana," Dad says as he walks into the room. *RUNNING OUT OF TIME.*

"Hey, Skipper," I say, and get up to take my bowl and spoon to the sink as Mom sits back down. I am overwhelmed.

"I hope you don't think you're excusing yourself right as we're about to have a family breakfast," Mom says.

I did think that, but only because I didn't want Dad to see my eyes all teary. "Chill out, lady," I say. "I'm just putting my stuff in the dishwasher."

"Don't call Mom *lady,* lady," Dad says.

"Don't call your lady *Mom,*" I say.

"Touché."

I grab a waffle from the freezer to stall a little more before I have to sit down. "Anybody want a waffle?"

"Sure, why not?" Dad says.

I grab another and pop them both into the toaster, hovering nearby while its orange-red coils make the waffles not cold.

"You know, it dings for a reason," Dad says.

"Yeah," I say, "but by the time I sit, it'll be ready, so I might as well just stay here."

"Suit yourself," he says.

Mom digs into the second half of her grapefruit.

Dad takes a big glug of water.

The toaster dings.

This isn't tense at all.

I bring the waffles and the maple syrup to the table, feeling good that I'm no longer on the verge of tears. Immediately after I sit, Mom says out of nowhere, "Russ, what was that bit you used to do in your stand-up routine about mannequins?"

"Ha, what?" Dad says.

"No, I was just trying to remember because it was so funny." I can tell Mom is nervous. She's testing the waters to see if she should bring up her idea. "Something about mannequins?"

"Oh yeah," Dad says, confused but flattered, "it was a bit where I wondered who decided to put nipples on mannequins. Like, what was the moment when someone thought, *You know what would help us sell even more clothes? Giving these plastic dummies nipples!*"

"Ah yes," Mom says, smiling.

"And then," Dad says, starting to get excited as the memory comes back to him, "I would talk about this time when I saw a nippled lady mannequin in a store window and felt very aroused. Even though she was headless. It made me question my entire existence. Like *Is my type actually women who are decapitated?*"

"Ha, that's right," Mom says, laughing in this way that isn't completely genuine, like maybe the bit isn't as funny as she remembered.

I, meanwhile, am thinking that it's kind of misogynistic.

"Yeah, I had some good material back then," Dad says, his

eyes sparkling with nostalgic pride. It makes me think Mom is even more of a genius than the mannequin nipple inventor because she's somehow managed to create the exact segue she was hoping for.

"You were so funny," Mom says.

"Thanks," Dad says, finally digging into his waffle.

"Do you ever think about . . . ?"

Dad chews as he looks at her. "What?"

"You know . . . Giving it another go?"

"Stand-up?"

"Yeah."

Dad looks to me then, like *Do you have any idea what she's talking about?* and I kind of lift my shoulders and eyebrows at the same time like *I've heard worse ideas.*

"Uh," he says. "I don't think someone who's literally having a hard time standing up should do stand-up."

Mom laughs, this time genuinely. "See? You already have the first joke of your set."

Dad can't help but smile at this, all skepticism suddenly draining away. It reminds me of myself when Evan—excuse me, *my boyfriend*—laughs at any of my jokes. "I see what you're doing," he says.

"You love stand-up so much," I say. Seeing the way Dad's gotten fired up talking about his old material, I'm fully on board with Mom's plan.

"Sure, I love *watching* it," Dad says. "But my days of doing it are way in the past."

"Only because I was born and you had to stop. If I didn't exist, maybe it would still be in your present."

"That's not even true," Dad says. "I also stopped because it was really hard and soul-crushing."

182

"But aren't you a little curious?" Mom asks. "You're older and wiser now."

"And sicker," Dad says in a way that's ten percent joke layered on top of ninety percent pain.

"That too," Mom says, her eyes locked on the table.

"So, wait." Dad looks from Mom to me, then back to Mom again. "Is this something you two have been planning for a while? To ambush me and get me to return to stand-up?"

"It's not an ambush," Mom says. "It was just an idea."

"I haven't heard about this till now," I say.

"Well," Dad says, staring past us at the oven. "I don't know. I'll think about it."

Considering I had zero investment in this plan as recently as ten minutes ago, I'm surprised to realize how excited I am that he hasn't outright rejected us.

20

So I'm someone's girlfriend. I got the official fax.

It's Monday, the first day back at school since my date with Evan, the first day interacting in person as *boyfriend and girlfriend*. It's kind of surreal. We talked for two hours last night. That's the longest I've ever spoken into a phone.

"So . . . ," I said. "I saw you called me your 'gurl.'"

"Hell yeah I did," he said. "Is that okay?"

I wished we'd talked about it first, but I didn't know how to say that without sounding like a downer. So instead I overcompensated with "Oh yeah, totally!" and sounded *really* into it. I'm not good at this.

"Sweet," he said. "I already told my mom you're my girlfriend. Hope that's all right."

"Oh sure," I said, even though I wasn't sure if it was sweet or disturbing. "I already told my stuffed turtle you're my boyfriend. Hope that's all right."

"Is he jealous?"

"Nah, we already worked through all that in third grade, when I was crushing on my teacher, Mr. Lee."

"TMI, girl."

As I get off the bus this morning, Evan is there to greet me, immediately taking my hand in his. I'm so used to finding Leili and Azadeh first thing, but they aren't here yet, and Evan is already walking into the school, which means I am too.

He walks me to my locker and makes jokes over my shoulder as I gather all the books I need.

"Hey, I had an idea," he says. "Why don't you do the announcements with me?"

My heartbeat quickens. I'm sure I've misheard him.

"That way we get to hang out longer." He flashes me one of his patented puppy dog grins. "And look, I'm even asking first!"

"Oh," I say. "Yeah, consent is important." I was trying to be funny, but it ended up sounding kind of serious.

"Right," Evan says, not really sure what to do with that. "So, you down?"

A river of classmates flows past us.

Of course I'm down. I couldn't be *more* down. I can't believe it took him this long to ask again.

"Sure," I say.

We hold hands as we walk to the office, the student population rapidly thinning as the clock ticks closer to homeroom.

"Oh, hello," white-haired Ms. DiMicelli says as we enter. "You brought the angry dog girl again, wonderful."

"Hi," I say. "It's actually Winnie." Really gotta put an end to this Dog Girl business.

"Hi, Ms. DiMicelli," Evan says, once again a sweet, all-American kiss-ass. "Winnie's doing the announcements with me today."

"You have approval from Mrs. Costa, I presume?"

"Of course!" Evan says, though I have no idea who Mrs. Costa is and I'm sure he hasn't asked for her approval.

"Then it's fine with me," Ms. DiMicelli says, her attention

already shifting elsewhere as she speaks into a phone at a fast, urgent clip.

"Welcome back," curly-haired Ms. Moore says from her desk without looking at us as we weave our way over to the PA system.

Evan takes down the sheet of paper with the announcements on it and examines it. "So, you want to just alternate every other one?"

"Uh, sure, whatever you want," I say. This time Evan's kindly informed me what's going to happen, but I still feel overwhelmed. Couldn't he have asked me about this during our epically long phone call last night?

"Should we make out between announcements?" he asks, I hope quietly enough that the secretaries haven't heard.

I just stare at him. I can't tell if he's kidding.

"That's totally a joke," he says three long seconds later. "Wow, would you have been down to do that?"

"Of course not, you maniac."

The homeroom bell rings. Evan gets the Ms. DiMicelli nod, then turns to me. "You want to be the one to do the Pledge?"

"Of Allegiance?" I ask.

"Do you know another one?"

"Okay, sure, I'll do it," I say. "Is it written on the paper?"

"You don't know the Pledge of Allegiance?"

"Time to get started," Ms. DiMicelli says, and now Ms. Moore is actually looking up from her work for once, to see what the holdup is.

"Sorry about the delay," Evan says, pushing the button and directing everyone to please stand for the Pledge. I assume this means he's going to do it, until he throws me a nod and an inquisitive look. I nod back. I got this. I can do this.

So what if I can't remember a single word of a pledge that I've recited every school day of my life?

My hands are shaking. My brain is a blank canvas. Evan is staring at me. I should have started by now.

Isn't Pledge the name of a cleaning spray?

I put my right hand on my chest, in the hopes that it will trigger my memory.

"I . . ." Pledge! It's a pledge! ". . . *pledge* allegiance to the flag of the United States of America." The sentence comes out in a garbled rush. Evan puts up a hand, like *Slow it down.* I nod and then realize I have no idea what comes next.

I will never again take the PA person's Pledge guidance for granted.

I give Evan my Panic Eyes. I can't tell if a few seconds have gone by or a whole minute, but he seems to be getting a huge kick out of it. He's trying not to laugh as he attempts to help me, mouthing the beginning of the next line. *Antu! Antu!*

"Antu?" I whisper.

And to, he mouths emphatically.

"And to!" I say. World's most atrocious game of charades.

Evan nods, and suddenly the rest of the Pledge is unspooling from my mouth, as if the knowledgeable brain cells have finally gained control of the ship's helm. Evan is silently applauding me, which feels earned, as it seems like a small miracle that I made it through.

Then he dives into the announcements and, as discussed, we alternate. Evan spices his up with his little jokes and asides, but I'm too nervous to do anything except dryly read the words in front of me. I sound boring even to myself.

Be funny, I think. *Be funny be funny be funny.*

But then we've made it down to the bottom of the paper,

and when I glance at the other side, it's blank. Evan concludes with a "Have a stupendous day, everyone!"

He pushes the button, and the school is no longer able to hear us.

I had my shot and I blew it.

I beefed the Pledge of Allegiance.

"I couldn't remember it," I say. "I couldn't remember the Pledge."

"Aw, I know," Evan says, wrapping me in a hug and kissing the top of my head. "That was pretty hilarious, but I bet nobody even noticed. I get it, you were nervous."

"Maybe next time you want to study up on the Pledge first, sweetie," Ms. Moore says. "Or print out a copy for yourself."

I'm too mortified to respond.

But then I realize: I *would* have been prepared if someone had thought to inform me it would be happening.

"It's not a big deal," Evan says. I can't begin to articulate the mix of shame and anger and sadness that's swirling inside me, so I put my head down and walk out of the office.

"Hey, wait." Evan catches up to me in the lobby, which is silent, since first period is about to start. "What's— Are you okay?"

"I'm great," I say without stopping.

Evan walks quickly to keep up with my pace. "Is this because of the Pledge? It really wasn't that big a deal!"

I shrug. I'm embarrassed that I'm so frustrated, and that he's seeing me so frustrated, and I just want to be in homeroom, no longer having this conversation.

"Can you at least tell me what's wrong?" Evan asks. "You seem kinda mad or something."

I stop in the middle of the hallway. I grip my backpack straps.

"I'm fine," I say.

"Okay . . . ," Evan says, one eyebrow up. "So what's the problem?"

Hmm. If we really are in a relationship, I should be able to tell him some version of the truth, right?

"I just . . ." Evan is giving me a wary look, like he's worried he's not going to like what I'm about to say. "I wish I had more time to— Like, I wish you'd told me about the Pledge last night so that I . . ."

"But it's the Pledge. I figured you would know it."

Well, I didn't, okay? I want to shout. *Because I guess I'm stupid about some stuff!*

"I know," I say. "I get . . . I get nervous sometimes."

"Aw, girl, I'm sorry," Evan says as he hugs me. He's trying to be sweet, but it's not what I need right now.

"So maybe . . . ," I say, the words sliding out almost involuntarily. "Maybe you don't always need to throw me into these situations. It always feels like you're testing me or something."

Evan pulls back from the hug, his arms still on my shoulders. "What does *that* mean?"

His surprised reaction makes me suddenly question if maybe *I'm* the one overreacting. "No, I don't know, like . . . last time we did the announcements. You didn't tell me I would be a part of it until a second before it happened."

Evan looks wounded, dropping his arms. "I already told you, I was trying to surprise you. I knew you'd be great."

"No, I know, but . . ." I've never had a boyfriend before, maybe this is just what it's like.

189

"Everybody loved what you did on the announcements that morning." I can't help but hear it as a contrast to *this* morning. "And I thought you felt good about it too."

"I did, yes, but—"

The homeroom bell rings. We're both late, but Evan gives no indication that he's going anywhere. "When else have I thrown you into a situation?" he asks, making finger quotes around *thrown you into a situation*.

I'm not a fan of finger quotes.

And at the moment, I can't think of other examples of him doing this, even though I'm quite sure there are some.

"If I'm just forcing you to do all this stuff, then say you don't want to do it."

"You're not forcing me," I say.

"Well, that's not what you just said." Why, hello there, Reason I Never Brought This Up Earlier. Part of me is annoyed that he's reacting this way, but another part wonders if some of the blame lies with me and wants to calm the situation down.

"I'm sorry," I say. "I didn't mean—"

"Do you two have somewhere to be?"

We turn to see our freakishly tall principal, Mr. Bettis, hands in his pockets, handsome and empty-headed as ever.

"Oh, uh, yessir," Evan says. "We just did the announcements, so we were discussing how it went."

"Oh, that was you?" Mr. Bettis leans his head back, like he's only now seeing us clearly. "You both did a wonderful job. Terrific diction."

"Thanks," I say, trying not to smile that he just complimented our diction.

"I'd say the only spot for improvement was the Pledge." My

stomach lurches. "Which of you did that?" He's asking to be polite, but obviously it was me, the female with the feminine voice.

I slowly raise a hand.

"Ah yes," Mr. Bettis says. "The rhythms were a little off. A bit glitchy."

Glitchy?

"She's still getting her sea legs," Evan says. I would have preferred *I asked her last-minute so she had no time to prep,* but it's better than nothing.

"Well, kudos to both of you. Now why don't you head on over to first period?"

"Absolutely, sir," Evan says.

"Thanks," I say again, not even sure what I'm thanking him for.

We stride down the hallway side by side. Evan's looking straight ahead, obviously still frustrated by our conversation. I am very good at being in a relationship. Only took me a day to completely eff it up.

As my homeroom comes into view, and we're out of sight of Mr. Bettis, I decide to speak, since Evan clearly isn't going to. "Hey, I'm sorry I said that stuff. That wasn't entirely fair."

"Did you think I was forcing you to go to the movies, too?" He's still not looking at me.

"No, of course not," I say. He's taking this harder than I would have expected. I'm actually starting to feel bad for him. "I think you misinterpreted what I said." I'm choosing my words very carefully. "I really like hanging out with you, and I'm so glad you asked me to do the announcements." Evan finally looks at me. "I would just love more of a heads-up next time."

Evan smiles. "So you're basically saying we had a fight because you couldn't remember the Pledge."

That's not how I would characterize the situation, but okay. At least he's not pouting anymore. "I'm saying we had a fight because our love triangle with Ms. DiMicelli is starting to stress me out."

Evan laughs. "I choose you, okay? Ms. DiMicelli is a thing of the past." He stops and takes my hands, and we're right back where we were first thing this morning, as if the fight never even happened. "So, Winnie Friedman, I would like to officially invite you to do the announcements again with me tomorrow. How's that for a heads-up?"

"Hey, that was really good. I'm proud of you," I say. "I would love to." I'm gonna get a chance to redeem myself after this morning's shit-show! Hallelujah.

"Awesome. Then I shall catch you later." Evan leans toward me, and I realize a second before his lips touch mine that he's about to kiss me. In school.

It's just a peck on the lips, but still. We're suddenly the couple fighting and kissing goodbye in the hallway. Who even am I?

"You're late," Mr. Novack says from his perch on the front of his desk as I step gingerly into class. I'm realizing I ran out of the office so fast I forgot to get a late pass.

"Yeah, sorry," I say, the entire class staring at me. "I was . . . doing the morning announcements."

"That was you who bungled the Pledge?"

A few of my classmates snicker. Of course I have homeroom with the most Pledge-obsessed teacher of all time. I look down. I want to cry.

"Okay," Mr. Novack says, moving on before I can answer,

a rare graceful gesture, "take your seat. We have a lot to get through this morning."

At my desk, I listen to Mr. Novack drone on about the way revenge functions in the plot of *Tess of the d'Urbervilles,* and my brain has chosen this moment to feel bad that I didn't get to see Leili and Azadeh this morning. I know they'll understand, but it's such a regular part of my routine, it feels like I left the house without getting dressed. I pretend to be reaching down into my bag for a pen and surreptitiously rattle off a text to them.

Someone clears his throat behind me.

I turn to see Fletcher at his desk wagging his finger back and forth like an old schoolmarm.

I narrow my eyes at him.

He slowly shakes his head, in this way that's so intense, I end up smiling.

An eternity later, Mr. Novack's voice is finally done filling the room, and I'm about to peek into my bag to see if Leili and Azadeh have texted back when Fletcher appears beside me.

"Flying close to the sun, Friedman," he says as we walk into the hallway.

"It's not what you think," I say.

"You weren't reaching into your bag to *text during class*?" He hasn't cracked a smile, still pretending to be angry.

"No, I was, uh, feeding my pet baby chick."

Fletcher's face finally relaxes. "Oh, why didn't you say so? I love baby chicks."

"Me too. How was your weekend?" Seamlessly shifting from a joke into actual conversation is one of my favorite things.

"Chill. Boring. Worked a lot." Fletcher takes a pack of Fruit

Stripe gum out of his pocket and unwraps a piece before folding it into his mouth. "You want?"

I stare at the zebra on the package. He's playing soccer. "I haven't had Fruit Stripe since I was, like, six. The flavor goes away so quickly."

"I know, but it's damn good while it lasts."

I shrug and take a piece. It's zigzagged with blue zebra stripes, and he's right, that first moment of chewing is pretty damn good.

"See?" Fletcher says, as enthusiastic as I've ever seen him. "That first burst is undeniable."

"I think I'm ready to spit it out now."

Fletcher laughs. "Thought maybe you and your dad would come into the store again."

"Oh. Yeah. No." Mom insisted on doing the food shopping this weekend. Dad wanted to, but she thought he needed another week to get the hang of walking with his cane. I can't say I disagreed; watching my father fall at Stop & Shop two weeks in a row is not my idea of a good time. "We didn't want my dad to fall again."

"Word. I get that."

"Yeah."

"Is he all right, by the way?"

I lift my shoulders. "Eh."

"I don't mean to get all in your business."

"No, it's fine." I actually mean that. And before I even know what I'm doing, I tell him. "He has ALS."

"Oh shit, seriously? That's, like, Lou Gehrig's disease, right?"

I nod.

"That's rough. I'm sorry."

He says it with so much genuine empathy that my eyes are suddenly wet. Damn you, Fletcher Handy.

"My uncle died from cancer," he says. "Two years ago."

It shouldn't make me feel better—cancer and ALS have nothing to do with each other, and why would I want to hear about someone dying right now—but for some reason, it's a calming reminder that everyone has pain.

"I'm sorry," I say. "That sucks."

Fletcher pops another piece of Fruit Stripe into his mouth as we walk in silence. I'm tempted to say something else to fill the dead air, but he doesn't seem bothered by it, so I don't.

Leili and Azadeh don't seem mad about me not seeing them this morning, but not to worry, there's tension at our table anyway.

Azadeh and Roxanne are doing their laughing thing again.

They're leaning into each other and nudging knees under the table. Leili is quietly eating her feta flatbread sandwich while Evan and I try to figure out what's so funny.

It came out of nowhere. We were all talking about how Principal Bettis's pants never seem to fit him right, and then Roxanne looked at Azadeh for a second, and they lost it. It's disorienting. I'm used to decoding Azadeh and Leili's nonverbal twinspeak, but this language I'm not fluent in.

"Wow, hard-core giggle fit," Evan says, which is like pouring gasoline onto a fire, the giggle flames climbing higher. Like last time, Azadeh and Roxanne are simultaneously cute—they clearly like being together—and annoying. Ol' Tattoo Shirt is absent today, but I almost wish he weren't. He could be an irritating counterbalance.

"Yeah," I say, trying and failing to make eye contact with

Leili, who's staring across the room. "Save some laughs for the rest of us."

"Sorry, sorry," Azadeh says, pulling herself together. "It's not even that funny."

"Is it about that thing Siobhan on the field hockey team does?" Leili asks while looking at the table. Her sarcasm levels are off the charts.

"Wait . . . what's up?" Azadeh asks, her love bubble momentarily pierced.

"Nothing's up," Leili says. "I'm great."

"Okay," Azadeh says, sharing a look with Roxanne like *Uh, she definitely doesn't seem great*. I feel a pang of jealousy, a small taste of what Leili might be feeling, as I'm usually the person Azadeh looks to in those moments. "Well, it's really not a big deal."

"Okay," Leili says. "I didn't say it was."

I want to jump in on her behalf, but again, taking sides with the twins has always come back to bite me in the butt.

"Great then," Azadeh says. "So. It's not a big deal."

We're all silent.

"Whatever, fine," Leili says, packing what's left of her lunch back in the sleek purple lunchbox she always uses. "I'm gonna go. I have yearbook stuff to do anyway."

I can't remember a single other time Leili has left lunch early.

"You're *leaving*?" Azadeh says. "Because we laughed?"

"I just feel bad for Siobhan," Leili says, even more sarcastic than last time, and man, she can really turn the knife when she wants to. I'm expecting Azadeh to say something else, to tell her to stay, but she just makes her offended face.

So I'll be the one. "Leili, stay."

Leili looks at me for the first time since the giggles. "What do you care?"

I stare back at her with an open mouth.

"See what I mean?" Leili says before swinging her backpack over her shoulders and walking away.

"What? Of course I care!" I shout at her back, too late.

I should follow her. I know I need to.

Across the table, Azadeh and Roxanne are speaking in hushed tones. Leili is almost at the far cafeteria door.

Maybe she needs the time alone. I mean, sure, the laughing was annoying, but I get the excitement of being in a new relationship, and maybe Leili could be a little more understanding. And furthermore, I've had a hard morning too, majorly beefing the announcements. I mean, I said *antu*! As if it were a real word!

So I don't follow.

When I turn my attention back to the table, Evan is cracking up at some video on his phone. "Yo, check this out," he says, "they're pranking this girl by replacing the frosting on her cupcake with wasabi."

I already regret my decision.

21

"You ready?" Evan asks, finger hovering over the PA button.

"Oh yeah," I say, patriotic words surging through my brain.

I spent most of last night in my room, reciting the Pledge approximately one thousand times in a row. Evan had finally given me advance notice on the announcements; I was going to make it count.

"Should we be worried?" Mom said, poking in her head to find me lying on my bed, right hand on heart, shouting the Pledge at the ceiling.

"Maybe," I said.

"Okay, great." She smiled and left me alone. Mom can be frustrating sometimes, but credit where it's due: she's usually good at staying out of my business.

The whole bus ride this morning, I stared out the window and mouthed the Pledge of Allegiance. Whatever, people already think I'm weird anyway.

I know I could save myself all this trouble by reading it off a piece of paper, but it feels like that would be admitting defeat.

Whether I can remember it or not will be made very clear within seconds, as Evan pushes the button and gestures to me to start. I see Ms. Moore and Ms. DiMicelli in my peripheral vision, both leaning forward slightly, anxious to see if I derail again. Bring it on, ladies. I got this.

"Please stand for the Pledge to the Flag," I say before launching into a bold, confident recitation.

It feels amazing. Like I'm finding the poetry in the words. Like I'm truly proud to be an American. Like I'm a goddamn superhero. As my tongue, teeth, and lips form the sounds, I picture my classmates, every student in school, all engaged in this same act at the same time, all of us connected by invisible strands, which web out to all the other high school students across the country also saying the Pledge at this exact moment.

". . . with liberty and justice . . . for all." I let the last words hang there, my chest puffed out with pride.

I did it. I nailed it. I nailed that Pledge.

I look to Evan, my eyes shining with tears. He seems concerned.

Are you okay? he mouths.

It immediately takes me out of my moment. I nod and glance over to Ms. Moore and Ms. DiMicelli, both of whom have stopped paying attention. Heathens.

Evan dives into the first announcement, which momentarily throws me off, as I sort of forgot there was anything beyond the Pledge. But along with my obsessive drilling last night, I was also prepping to be my best and funniest self during the rest of the announcements, mostly by YouTubing old "Weekend Update" segments from *SNL*. The Tina Fey–Amy Poehler years, obviously.

Evan finishes letting people know about some *Fall Sports Journal* thing, and it's my turn. "For all those on the MHS bowling team," I say, "there will be an informational meeting Thursday in Room B-44 immediately after school." That's what's written on the paper, but I push myself to go further. "Maybe you will learn why bowling is the only sport that forces you to share shoes with thousands of other people. Which is super-gross, no matter how much spray-in-a-can you use."

Evan is smiling, but in this shocked way, like he can't believe what I just said. I don't see what the big deal is. He riffs all the time.

Including now, as he reminds seniors that sign-ups for retakes of senior photos will start today outside Room 229. "So, if you blinked, or sneezed, or had mad crazy pimples when you took your photo, now's your big chance for a do-over." He looks over at me and smiles, like suddenly this is a competition, and I smile back. *Game on.*

"Join the MHS Travel Club," I read. "First meeting is Wednesday after school in Room 310 with Mrs. Winters." I add, completely straight-faced (er, straight-voiced), "And by *travel,* we mean time travel. Our first trip will be to prehistoric times, so please bring camouflage clothes that will keep you hidden from the dinosaurs."

Evan straight-up guffaws at this, and I look back, expecting Ms. Moore and Ms. DiMicelli to be glaring at us, but they're chuckling too.

I am invincible.

The rest of the announcements pass by in a joyous blur, with Evan and me trying to top each other with gags. Finally we get to the last one; it's my turn. I make a plea for anyone who finds two missing sequined Show Choir vests to please return them to Mrs. Zomro. "You obviously can't see us right now," I say, "but if you could, you would know that we are definitely not wearing stolen sequined vests. Again, I repeat: we are not wearing the vests that have been lost. Or at least, we won't be once these announcements end." I pause a moment, then shout "You'll never catch us!" straight into the microphone while laughing maniacally. I'm hoping to push the button because I can't think of a more perfect way to end the morning announcements, but Evan leans in front of me before I can.

"Thanks, everybody!" he says. "Have a delightful day!" Then he pushes the button and looks at me. "Whoa, you were on fire! Totally out of control but on fire."

"What do you mean 'totally out of control'? I was doing exactly what you do."

"I mean, yeah, I'll make a comment here and there, but you just went for full-on, like, comedy bits."

"I actually found that to be very humorous," Ms. DiMicelli says, and I once again want to kiss her.

"It was a little much for my taste," Ms. Moore says as she cuts a muffin with a plastic knife, "but you're definitely creative."

"Thanks." I'll take it! Evan, meanwhile, seems bewildered. "I figure the funnier it is," I say to him, "the more people will pay attention, right?"

"Yeah, yeah, of course," Evan says. "But, like, within reason. I mean, I don't want Mrs. Costa to get mad."

"Who even is Mrs. Costa?" I genuinely have no idea.

"Her," Ms. DiMicelli says, pointing into the lobby, where a wide woman with pinstriped black pants and dangly spiral earrings is striding toward us in the office.

"Oh boy," Evan says, a smug told-you-so quality to his voice, "here we go."

Mrs. Costa has an undeniably intense look on her face, but for some reason, I'm not afraid. I did what I came here to do: I absolutely killed. I don't even need outside validation to know that's true; I can feel it in my heart. So if I get in trouble, it was completely worth it.

"What is your name?" Mrs. Costa says after she opens the door, barely two steps into the office.

"Uh, Winnie," I say. "Winnie Friedman."

"I'm sorry I didn't ask first," Evan blurts out.

"What?" Mrs. Costa says with a sharp turn of her head to Evan and an annoyed look on her face.

"If Winnie could do the announcements with me."

"Oh, I don't care about that. She was incredible."

A warmth floods my body, beams of light shooting out from my hands, feet, and eyes.

"You were incredible," Mrs. Costa says to me, not even like she's trying to puff me up, just completely matter-of-fact, which is my favorite kind of compliment. "I want you to keep doing the announcements with Evan. You're a good team."

"Oh wow," Evan says.

"Great," I say, trying to seem calm and composed on the outside while inside I'm hurling chunks of birthday cake into the air as confetti rains down.

"But also . . ." Mrs. Costa narrows her eyes at me, the ring of keys she's inexplicably holding hovering in the air between us. "Have you ever thought about joining Speech and Debate?"

The short answer is: no. I know practically nothing about it, other than it exists and doesn't sound fun in the slightest.

"We could really use you," Mrs. Costa says. "In Impromptu. Or even CI. Maybe we'd actually start winning some tournaments again."

I don't understand the middle part of what she said, but the first and last parts deeply resonate.

"Okay," I say.

"Are you tied up in a lot of other extracurriculars? What else do you do?"

"Mainly just the improv troupe. I write for the newspaper sometimes."

"Oh, that's fine. Evan does Improv and S&D, and he doesn't have a problem, right?"

I had no idea he was on the Speech and Debate team. It's a reminder that there's still so much about Evan I don't know.

"No, not really," he says. "I mean, it can be overwhelming to juggle both at times, but—"

"Hush, hush," Mrs. Costa says. "We're trying to recruit her, not scare her off." She looks at me, very sincere. "We would make it work. You don't have to decide now, but definitely think it over. Our next meeting is tomorrow after school in my classroom, Room 226. Speaking of which, I've gotta get back there. My class has probably torn the walls down by now and used the refuse to start a bonfire."

She left her classroom to come ask me to do this. Wow.

"S'mores for everyone," I say, but Mrs. Costa is already out the door, hustling back to her classroom.

"Sounds like we'll be seeing a lot more of you," Ms. Di-Micelli says, giving me a quick impish smile as she organizes papers, plopping them into various trays.

"Sounds like," I say.

"We'll get you a permanent laminated late pass like Evan has," she says, scribbling on a piece of paper. A permanent late pass. That's, like, the VIP all-access badge of late passes. "Probably won't be necessary, since your homeroom teacher will hear where you are, but helpful in case there's ever a clueless sub."

"Right," I say, nodding my head like *Clueless subs are the worst, aren't they?*

"For today, take this." She hands over the nonpermanent late pass for ordinary people.

"Thanks, Ms. D," I say.

"Ooh, I like that," she says, as if I've just given her some startling new insight into who she is, as opposed to engaging in the common practice of shortening someone's last name down to one letter.

"This is so cool, right?" I say to Evan as we leave the office, my body practically humming with energy.

"It is," he says.

"We're gonna get to hang out and make jokes every morning! Like you wanted."

"Yeah. For sure, it's really cool." But he's not fully looking at me and doesn't seem particularly excited.

"I have no idea what those Speech and Debate words she said mean," I say.

"Yeah," he says. "If you end up joining, you'll learn." Or he could just tell me now?

We walk in a mysteriously tense silence until the tone sounds. "I'm gonna run to first period," Evan says, as if it's totally normal for him to be concerned about punctuality.

"Oh. All right," I say, wondering what exactly happened to so dramatically alter his mood. Maybe he's not feeling well.

"I was a little too late yesterday. I think Mr. Eng was pissed."

"No prob."

"Okay, cool." Evan's already a few steps ahead of me. I guess we're not kissing goodbye today? I wasn't totally comfortable when it happened yesterday, but now . . . "And again, good job this morning." He's so businesslike, it's actually alarming.

"See you at lunch?" I ask, wanting this interaction to end on a less unsettling note.

"Oh," he says, scratching his neck as he turns back to me, "I think so."

I think so? He's the one who got us eating lunch together in the first place!

"Might have to do some stuff in the library," he continues.

That's the first time I've ever heard Evan mention spending time in the library.

"Okay, so . . . Maybe see you later, I guess."

"Later," he says. I watch him walk away, my body's hum reduced to a purr, my triumphant moment all but vanished.

#Winning?

22

"Hey, what do you think of this?" Dad asks, seconds after I walk into the house.

He's sitting at the kitchen table, hunched over an index card with a pen, a dozen other chicken-scratched cards scattered in front of him.

"Hold on," he says, scribbling out one last thought, so expansive it requires him to write on the back. "Okay!" He looks up at me, a mad scientist fresh off an epiphany. "You ready?"

"Sure," I say, still standing in the exact spot where I stopped fifteen seconds ago.

"Maybe take your backpack off," Dad says, flicking his hand at my bag. "You're less likely to laugh if you're weighed down."

I finally understand what's happening here: Dad is *writing jokes*. I play it cool, not revealing how surprised and overjoyed I am.

"Is that a law of physics?" I ask.

"It is, actually," Dad says, frenetically arranging his cards. "Einstein discovered it. Any increase in gravitational pull leads to a proportionate decrease in comedic potential."

"Well, if *Einstein* said it . . ." I take off my backpack and chuck it near the front door, which Mom hates, but I'll move it before she gets home.

"I should really learn the names of some other physicists," Dad says. "Using Einstein for a physics joke is such a cliché at this point."

"I was going to say that, but I didn't want to hurt your feelings."

"I could have taken it."

"Sure you could have."

Dad now has all of his index cards in a stack, which he knocks against the table, like a dealer with his deck. "All right, so, okay, I, uh, have been writing some new material."

"That's awesome, Dad."

"Well, maybe wait till you hear the material first."

"No, just the fact that you're doing it is amazing. It's been a while, right?"

"How old are you again?" Dad asks.

"You know how old I am."

"Yeah, but it'll be more dramatic this way."

"Fine. I'm fifteen."

"It's been at least *fifteen years* since I wrote anything." Dad looks a little shocked, as if saying it out loud really drives home for him how long it's been.

"Wow. And now I know it's totally my fault, too."

"Not *totally*," Dad says. "Only partially."

"Dad!"

"I'm completely kidding. Obviously."

I guess I should be grateful he and I have as close a relationship as we do, considering I'm the one responsible for pulling his dreams out from under him.

"All right, so you want to hear this?"

"Yes! Just read your damn jokes!" I shout.

"I'm gonna stay seated," Dad says. "Hope that's all right."

"Well, I'm gonna stay standing," I say. "Hope that's all right."

"So, okay," Dad says, clearing his throat, "this first bit I wrote is something I've been thinking about for a couple years, but I think I finally—"

"I don't need an essay about your writing process, Dad. Just let the work speak for itself."

Dad looks stunned but also maybe impressed. I hope I haven't overstepped.

"I mean, I'd love to hear about process eventually," I say, "but isn't that what you always tell me?"

"It is. Yes. Good call." Dad reads over his card again. "I don't know, it might not be ready to share yet."

Seeing Dad so nervous about sharing his jokes with me is kind of a revelation. I always think of him as so confident, especially when it comes to comedy.

"Dad," I say. "Just read it. You're, like, my comedy hero."

"That's what scares me," Dad says. "I don't want to lose hero status in one fell swoop."

"That's ridiculous," I say, but now I'm feeling the weight of what's about to happen. The gravitational pull, if you will. The health of Dad's ego (and maybe also his health in general) requires that I produce some very genuine laughs in response to whatever he's written. No pressure.

"Okay, okay." Dad looks down at his card once more, then looks up, and I can tell he's about to begin. "So, Facebook," he says, speaking in a way I've never heard him speak in my life. Like he's an old-timey radio announcer having a bad day. "Anybody here like to use the Facebook?" He stares past me, first to the left, then to the right, then clarifies, in his normal voice, "That's me looking at different audience members."

"Gotcha," I say, now very worried that I've entangled myself in something that could tear the fabric of my entire existence.

"Here's my problem with Facebook," Dad says, back to the voice that sounds nothing like him. "I don't care about most of the stuff I read on there."

I force out a laugh, trying to make it sound as real as possible.

"Like, before Facebook ever existed, let's imagine this for a moment: if someone told you, 'Hey, I have an invention that lets you find out what's going on in the lives of dozens of people you only sort of know or met through a friend once or hung out with briefly at a birthday dinner,' would that be something you'd be interested in?"

I laugh, half because it's an actually funny idea, and half because I'm relieved that I am producing a laugh naturally.

"And you might say, 'Uh, I'm not interested in that, not even a little bit,' but then that someone would persist, 'But you can see what these people had for dinner! And amazing vacations they went on with their families! And hear their thoughts about our charged political climate! Doesn't that sound wonderful?'" Dad takes a pause, giving his trademark skeptic look, the one I've inherited, eyebrows furrowed, smirk in full force, before saying, "'No. No, that sounds like absolute hell to me.'"

And, thank you, sweet universe, it really does make me laugh.

Dad breaks character to look at me, his eyes lit up like a kid in an iPad store. It just about wrecks me. I had no idea my opinion would count for that much. "You really think that's funny?" he asks.

"I do," I say. "I totally do."

"Okay," he says, nodding. "Maybe this isn't all total trash."

"Of course it's not."

"I, uh, did a little research," he says, staring down at his cards. "And Ted's Roasters is doing an open mic night this Friday."

It takes me a few seconds to understand where he's going with this. "Ohmigod, you're gonna perform? *This* Friday?"

"I mean, I don't know," Dad says. "I was just thinking about what you and Mom said, and I figured Ted's could be good since it's a few towns away, less likely to be performing in front of anybody we know. But maybe it's a silly idea."

"Dad, it's not! It's an amazing idea!" I am astonished and delighted that he's done such a one-eighty on this. It makes me think I should trust my mom's intuition on things more often.

"It would just be a start," he says. "A place to get my feet wet before I dive back into gigs in the city. If I even decide to do that."

And suddenly a new vision of the future opens up before me, one where Mom and I are going to New York City comedy shows to watch Dad live out the dream he never got to pursue. It's beautiful. Exciting. Inspiring.

And then I, of course, remember that the reason we pushed him to do this in the first place is because his health is deteriorating. This past weekend Mom started replacing the buttons on his pants and on some of his shirts with Velcro because he was having too much trouble getting dressed. Who knows how long he has left before he's physically unable to perform any comedy at all?

"It's a great start, Dad. A perfect start."

"Yeah, yeah, we'll see. I might not be ready by Friday."

"You're doing it," I say. "Case closed."

Dad raises his eyebrows. "Oh wow, if the case is closed, I guess I have no choice."

"You don't."

"Well, in that case, I better get back to it, then." He spreads out his cards, picks up his pen, and returns to scrawling.

I walk over to the fridge and open it up, making it seem like I'm searching for a snack, but really I'm using it as cover so Dad won't see how hugely I'm smiling.

23

I can't stop looking at Evan's face.

I wish I meant that romantically.

We're at improv, and Mr. Martinez has all of us attempting an actual Harold for the first time. Here's (my limited understanding of) how a Harold works: It starts with a one-word suggestion, which inspires a group game, all of us onstage. In our case, we're doing a stream-of-consciousness word association as further inspiration for the scenes that will follow, each of us shouting a word brought to mind by what the person before us said.

After we've all said a word, a scene begins with two performers, everyone else moving to the back of the stage. The scene keeps going until a performer *not* in the scene ends it by running across the front of the stage (that's called an edit), after which an entirely different scene begins. Then another. Then another group game, after which we return to the stories and characters of those first three unrelated scenes, then another group game, then back to those three scenes to wrap them up and show how they're actually all connected in these unexpected ways (like maybe a character from the first scene turns out to be the brother of a character in the third scene) (I don't fully get what I'm talking about, that's just the example

Mr. Martinez gave). When done well, it's supposed to be really amazing, like you've taken the audience on this journey, almost like an improvised play, surprising them (and yourself) with the way everything's come together.

I don't think we're doing it well, though.

Since the entire Harold is inspired by one word (this rehearsal's suggestion, provided by the ever-inventive Shannon Niola, is *food*) and then flows from there, it's up to us to jump in instead of Mr. Martinez picking people scene by scene. Totally by coincidence, Evan and I both jumped out to start the second scene, which you'd think would be a fun thing, getting to do a scene with my boyfriend for the first time.

It wasn't.

Ever since Mrs. Costa fell in love with me on the announcements Tuesday morning, Evan's been super-weird, swinging from ooey-gooey-affectionate to pouty-mean, then back again. We've continued doing the announcements together, but it's clear that he wishes I weren't there. Which is bizarre since he's the one who invited me to do them in the first place. It's awkward enough that I decided not to go to the Speech and Debate meeting yesterday.

"I just feel like we should have some stuff that we, like, don't do together," Evan said right before the meeting as he walked me to the bus after eighth period.

"Fine," I said, even though *he's* the one who started sitting with me at lunch not thirty seconds after we started flirting with each other. "I don't even care about Speech and Debate!" And that's mainly the truth. I don't have any burning desire to give speeches or to debate things, but I figured I'd at least show my appreciation for Mrs. Costa's enthusiasm by showing up and seeing what the deal is. But nope, my new boyfriend doesn't want me there. Cool!

"Aight, I gotta run to practice so I'm not late," Evan said, leaning in to give me a half-hearted kiss I could have done without.

Then last night he called me, enthusiastic and flirtatious and goofy, and told me he did an impromptu speech at practice that went so well, everyone "lost their shit," with no acknowledgment whatsoever that I could have been at that practice, was in fact supposed to be, until he put the kibosh on it.

"What even is impromptu?" I asked, my voice inflected with just a hint of attitude. "I still have no idea."

"Oh," Evan said, suddenly sheepish. "It's like, you get a topic, and then you have seven minutes to come up with a speech inspired by it. Well, not even a speech, it's almost like a little one-man show. Or one-person show. Sometimes there are different characters and stuff."

"That's really cool," I said, suddenly struck by a powerful case of FOMO. Why didn't I go to that practice? Because it was going to make Evan all pouty? That's a terrible reason!

"It is," Evan said, going on to describe in detail what he did in his impromptu speech, which involved lightsabers, an asteroid headed toward Earth, a malfunctioning robot, and Pennywise, the clown from *It*. Maybe you had to be there.

When he finally finished, I lied and said I had to go help my parents with something. He was disappointed and said he couldn't wait to see me tomorrow. I agreed, but after I hung up, I stared at the ceiling and wondered what I was doing in this relationship. Did I even like Evan like that anymore? Had I ever?

Maybe I wasn't being entirely fair. I *had* stolen half of the announcements from him, which was probably a little jarring. And I definitely can relate to the feeling that things are moving too fast, becoming a bit suffocating. Plus, I still think Evan's cute, and we still make each other laugh sometimes. He's fun to text with. I figured I'd give it another week.

This morning, though, Evan started the announcements charming but, by the end, he was chilly at best. He spent lunch at the library again.

So, *of course,* the last thing I'd want to do is jump into a frigging scene with him. But once we were both standing there in the playing space, neither of us wanted to back down. I looked at him with my loving girlfriend eyes, trying desperately to make things right between us before the scene started. He looked away.

But his assholeishness was fuel for my fire. I dove into our scene, initiating with a character inspired by this guy Anthony who works at Luigi's Pizza (Dad and I do stupid impressions of him all the time), and I killed. Seriously, I was getting all the laughs.

And *that* is why I can't stop looking at Evan's face. During the scene, and even now that it's over, he's seemed a mix of broken and furious.

"Are you okay?" I asked him quietly as we walked to the back line after our scene.

"Yeah, totally," he said, barely glancing at me.

"Are *we* okay?"

He didn't answer, instead choosing to walk to a spot as far away from me as possible.

Not exactly a confidence booster.

And, like a terrible improviser, I've barely been able to pay attention to the scenes unfolding because I'm too busy sneaking glances at Evan, hoping to catch a smile or a wink or *anything* that might indicate he doesn't wish I were dead.

Naturally, as is the way of the Harold, our scene is about to return. Super. I step back into the space at the same time as Evan. He looks slightly possessed.

"Yo, welcome to Anthony's Pizza," I say in a huge voice with my probably offensive over-the-top Italian accent, my chest puffed out. "What can I get for you?" People crack up as much as they did the first time around.

"Uh," Evan says. "We're not actually in a pizza place, you know. You're just a homeless person."

This gets a huge laugh, even though I can tell a lot of people also recognize that Evan has violated the key principle of *Yes, and*. Leili looks pissed. Fletcher, too. I refuse to sink to Evan's level, though.

"I prefer the term *street dweller,* but thank you." I wish he hadn't put me in a position where I have to make light of homeless people. "But I am the best street pizza maker in the city! Look! I got a little oven over here and everything."

"That's just a box," Evan says. More laughs.

Well, fine, I can be an asshole, too.

"No!" I shout, throwing one expressive hand in the air the way Anthony does when he's making a point. "It's an oven! *Mamma mia,* maybe you need some new glasses or something. Thinking an oven is a box. Either that or you got spaghetti for brains!" This gets a large laugh, winning everyone back over to my side.

"Nope, it's definitely a box," Evan says. This time not so

many people laugh, as it's a fairly blatant improv block. "And that's not pizza in there, it's a soggy magazine."

"Heyyy!" I say, the way Dad and I have said many, many times, mimicking this moment when Anthony watched a delivery guy accidentally drop a pizza on his way out the door. "Why you come to my restaurant if you don't like the pizza?"

"Because it's actually a gross magazine."

"It's delicious pizza!"

Our peers' heads snap back and forth between us, like they're watching a tennis match.

"Magazine."

"Pizza!"

"Magazine."

"Pizza!"

"Magazine."

We've now been reduced to a Bugs Bunny, Daffy Duck–style confrontation, and I don't know how to get out of it. I'm still in mild shock that Evan's being such a dick to me in front of everybody.

Mr. Martinez seems like he's on the verge of stopping the scene, but since he hasn't yet, I will.

"Hey, hey, you know what?" I say. "You're right, it's a gross magazine." I do some impeccable object work to mime picking it up by one corner. "*Stupid Jerk Weekly.* This'll be a great read for you."

Everyone gasps, some letting out a quiet "Ohhhh!"

I probably shouldn't have said that.

Evan's keeping up his apathetic façade, but I can tell I made a direct hit.

"Okay, okay," Mr. Martinez says, and it's immediately obvious he doesn't know how to deal with this situation. "This, uh, scene has gotten a bit out of hand. What, uh— Let's, uh, try and track back and see where we went off the rails."

"Probably when she called me a stupid jerk," Evan mutters, not looking at me.

"Right, sure, that was inappropriate, Winnie—"

"It was a character choice!" I say, knowing that's very untrue but feeling compelled to defend myself.

"Okay, let me turn this question over to all of you." Mr. Martinez looks out at the rest of the troupe. "Does anyone—"

"From the second this scene started, Evan wasn't supporting any of Winnie's choices," Jess Yang says, her strong voice booming across the stage. It's so unexpected, I have to squint to make sure the words aren't coming from someone else.

"Right, yes!" Mr. Martinez says, as if Jess has knocked his circuitry back into working order. "Say more about that."

"What's there to say?" Jess rolls her eyes. "Winnie began with a strong, interesting character and Evan kept denying the reality of her choices. *No, but* instead of *Yes, and.*"

Did Jess just say I did something *strong and interesting*?

"Totally," Leili says. "Like, it was funny, but *cheap* funny." Leili, oh Leili, love of my life Leili.

"Like, for real," Rashanda says. "I think lots of us were just laughing because we were shocked he was playing it like that."

"Never heard of shock humor?" Evan says in a quiet voice only I can hear.

"What was that?" Mr. Martinez asks.

"Nothing." Evan bites his thumbnail.

"I thought Winnie's character was actually kind of obvious," Mahesh says. "Like, we've all seen that Italian stereotype before. So when Evan was saying all that stuff, I thought it subverted the scene in a great way."

Evan's spirits are up for the first time all afternoon, and he's nodding along with Mahesh's point. Stupid jerk.

Sure, maybe my Italian guy character could have used some more nuance, but that is not why the scene sucked. And Mahesh and Evan and Tim and Dan do annoying stereotypical characters all the damn time.

"All right," Mr. Martinez says. "I think there are insights to be drawn from all of those comments, so let's see if we can learn from them as we continue with this."

Oh man, he did not just end the discussion like that. *Insights from all of those comments?* But Leili and Fletcher are already coming onstage for the third scene, so I march back to my spot, seeing flames the whole time.

Leili and Fletcher do a scene where they're ants in the process of moving to a new anthill, and it's, of course, incredible. They listen to each other. They make discoveries. They *collaborate*. I'm very jealous.

I know that somewhere buried under my anger, I'm sad, too. I don't know why Evan suddenly hates me so much, but it sucks. I don't want to be mad at him. I wouldn't even be here at improv practice, or doing the morning announcements, if it weren't for him.

When our scene comes back around, I step out, but Evan doesn't, so Rashanda jumps in, playing Evan's sister. Our scene goes okay, but I'm barely thinking about it.

"And let's black out there!" Mr. Martinez says. "Well, there you have it. You all just completed your first Harold." Everyone cheers and whoops. I only sorta do, as I don't feel very cheery.

"Not bad at all! Some bumpy parts, but that could have been much worse. Bravo. This week please think about moments where you could have made stronger, more helpful choices, so we can learn from this and get better. Because reminder: our first performance of the year, the Homecoming week show, is just two weeks from tomorrow!" More cheering. More whooping. "Again, this should be very low stress: one Harold, about thirty minutes long, and I will let the audience know we are still new at this. But also don't slack off—we need to be as good as we possibly can. If we do well, they might allot us more money in the budget! But don't even worry about that—we're just gonna have fun." Mr. Martinez seems suddenly exhausted. "Okay, see you next week, everybody."

As we're all filing offstage, I'm still pissed, but I know that if I don't go talk to Evan right now, I'm gonna feel crappy about it all night.

"Hey," I say, touching his back. He flinches away. "Can we talk?"

"Oh. Sure. I actually was gonna ask you the same thing."

Thank god. I can't explain what a relief it is to hear him say that. He nods at Tim, who heads out. "Great," I say, "because I want to make sure—"

"You know, you're not really doing improv," Evan interrupts.

"Excuse me?"

"Like, you have all these prebaked characters with all these catchphrases and lines you've thought about beforehand. That's not improv. I mean, it's fine and funny and whatever, but just so you know."

"Oh." My eyes are thick with shocked, angry tears.

"Anyway, I gotta roll." He walks up the aisle and out of the auditorium before I'm even able to think the words *Fuck you,* let alone say them.

That's what he wanted to talk about?

What a supreme douche. My boyfriend is a supreme douche.

It's all very disorienting. I barely know where I am.

"Hey," a voice behind me says, and I'm assuming it's Leili, but it's not. It's Jess Yang.

"Oh, hi," I say.

"Are you okay?"

"I . . . don't even know."

"Well, whatever he said to you, you should ignore him. It's not worth it."

I'm not sure why or when Jess has become my guardian angel, but I'm not entirely minding it. She looks down at her hands, pulling at her own fingers. "Also . . . I wanted to say sorry. For being such a bitch to you this past month."

"Oh."

"Evan and I broke up before school started, and I hated that you were his new person. But it was awful of me to take it out on you. And . . ." Jess looks away, possibly fighting back tears. "When I did that scene with you"—she's whispering now— "I was trying to come up with something emotional and mean to say, but I didn't know . . . I didn't know about . . ."

Leili must have told Jess about my father. "Oh, it's okay," I say. "I mean, it sucked, but I figured you didn't know."

Jess nods. We sit in a mildly awkward silence until it's interrupted by Leili.

"Hey, Winner," she says. "I have to run, my mom is here."

"I thought we were giving you a ride home," I say.

"No, because I have a thing to go to." Leili looks vaguely sheepish. Usually I know about all the things she would be going to, but she seems like she's in a hurry, so I don't press her.

"All right, I'll catch you later, then."

"I have to run too," my new friend Jess says, which is how I find myself putting my jacket on alone in the empty auditorium.

24

I haven't been in Dad's car for more than two minutes when my phone yodels.

It's a text from Evan:

I think we should take a break. Agree?

In light of what just went down at rehearsal, it's the most nonshocking message of all time. Yet I'm shocked.

"Everything okay?" Dad asks.

It takes me a moment to process what he's said.

"Eh," I say. "Evan dumped me. In a text."

"Aw, Banana. I'm sorry." But I can tell he's kind of not.

"He was only my boyfriend five days. I feel like I'm defective or something."

"You? Win, you're not defective, he's a huge asshole." I laugh. "That's not a joke," Dad says. "It's the truth. I'm sorry you feel bad. But you deserve someone so much better."

When I get home, I head straight to my room and take out my phone.

"That's atrocious," Azadeh says, her voice on speaker as I lie in bed on my back.

"Really, he saved you a lot of trouble," Leili says, and I can tell that she's knitting. "You would have agonized over whether or not to break up with him till at least next year." I want to argue, but I know she's probably right. "Did you respond yet?"

"You should write AGREE in all caps," Azadeh says.

"Yeah, or write the same exact message back to him," Leili says. "Mess with his head."

"Ha, maybe I will," I say. "Hey, at least Oz and Roxanne are still going strong."

"Oh," Azadeh says. "Yeah, we're good. But what's not good is I gotta go write a paper about the Revolutionary War. Love you, Winner! Screw him!"

"Love you, Oz!"

Azadeh mumbles something to Leili as she leaves the room. I notice Enya playing softly in the background.

"Oh, hey," I say to Leili. "Do you know what Evan said to me before he left rehearsal?"

"Uh-uh." She's still knitting.

"I thought we were gonna talk about how awful our scene was, but instead he said I'm not doing improv right! He said I'm showing up with characters in advance, so it doesn't count. What the hell?"

Leili hesitates a little too long before responding. "Well, yeah, that's annoying."

"Wait, do you agree with him?"

"No. Like, obviously he's a dick for saying that, but . . ."

I sit up. "But what?"

"It doesn't matter, Win."

There's a vibe I've been picking up from Leili all week. I can't figure out what it is, but it's unsettling. "No, what?"

"Just that . . . there's some truth to what he's saying. Like, improv is supposed to be about starting with nothing and leaping into the unknown. Which isn't exactly what you're doing. But whatever, it's fine."

I can't even believe what I'm hearing. "You're seriously agreeing with the asshole who dumped me?"

"I mean, not completely, just . . . Forget it."

"What is up with you this week?" I ask. I'm feeling fiery.

"Ha!" It's a sarcastic laugh. "This is the first time it occurs to you to ask that, when I say something you don't like?"

I'm not sure what's happening. Leili and I aren't friends who fight. At least not since the epic blowout we had in fifth grade after I copied off her math quiz. (I'm not proud, but I'll own it.) "Well, yeah, when the something I don't like is you insulting the way I do improv, yes."

Leili sighs. "Has it not even occurred to you to ask how *I'm* doing after I left during lunch Monday?"

"I . . ." My mind scans back through the days since that happened. "What're you talking about, I texted you after." I think I did. Didn't I?

"I literally said to you 'What do you care?' before I left, and you completely proved my point by actually not caring."

"I care! I care a lot! You're my best friend!"

"Yeah. Words, words."

Ohmigod. She's completely serious. I have somehow hurt my best friend without having any idea I was doing it. "They're not just words," I say, "I mean it."

And anyway, she was having a fight that day with Azadeh! Why is this *my* fault?

"I know you have a lot going on with your dad and everything," Leili says, "but lately, it feels like you're so wrapped up in Evan stuff, and obsessing over how improv is going, and how funny everyone thinks you are, and whatever else, that I'm just an afterthought."

"What? That is so not—"

"I'm always telling you how well you're doing, and trying to be supportive, and I feel like you rarely do that for me."

"You are so not an afterthought!"

"Well, that's how it *feels,* okay? And Connie says—"

"You've freaking talked about this with *Connie*?"

"Uh, yeah, she's my therapist. That's what you do at therapy. Not that you would know."

Now she's taking a dig at me for not going to therapy? What the hell is happening? "Look," I say, standing up from bed and pacing around wildly. "I'm sorry for whatever you're feeling, but it's been a hard month for me. My dad needs a cane to walk."

"Winner, I know, and that's awful, but no offense, sometimes you act like you're the only one with any problems."

"What?" I got dumped literally forty-five minutes ago, and now I'm receiving a surprise lecture from my best friend on all the ways I'm a subpar human.

"I'm well aware it's been hard for you," Leili continues. "That's why I haven't brought this up sooner. But it's not like I have zero problems—"

"I know that!"

"You do? What are my problems?"

"Like, you know, not getting to see Oz as much because she's with Roxanne. And, you know . . . being so busy with everything you do I'm sure is hard." I pause to see if I'm right or not. "Are there other ones?"

Leili hits me again with her sarcastic laugh.

"Are there?" I ask again, searching for ground beneath my feet and finding nothing.

"I actually should get going," Leili says.

Get going? She can't get going! We haven't figured anything out at all, and I'm gonna be left with this horrifying feeling all night.

"Connie says that if people can't make me feel seen, I have every right to step away. Otherwise I'm only enabling them."

It takes me a moment to chew over that one. "Wait, do you think you're enabling *me?*"

Leili doesn't say anything.

"Do you?"

"I don't know," she says finally. "Maybe."

"Okay, so let me get this straight: I'm doing improv wrong, I'm a terrible friend, I only care about myself—have I covered everything?"

"I really should go, Win," Leili says, unnervingly composed.

"First tell me—"

But she's already hung up.

I call back. It goes straight to voice mail.

I grit my teeth and quietly scream as I push my Lisa Simpson piggy bank off the dresser. There's a clangy thud as it hits the floor, at least five years' worth of change shifting around.

I call again. Voice mail.

I am angry. But I also can't shake the feeling that I am a terrible friend. And a terrible person. And a terrible improviser. Definitely didn't *Yes, and* that conversation.

How has everything gone so wrong, so quickly?

I scroll back through all my texts with Leili from the past few weeks, desperately searching for confirmation that I'm in the right, that I'm an okay friend, that I *did* text her that day she stormed out of the cafeteria. (I didn't.)

An old text from her stops me in my tracks:

Are you making prudent decisions?

I stare at the words.

"Doesn't seem like it!" I want to shout at my phone.

It's only when I see my actual response that I remember Leili was jokingly quoting Mrs. Tanaka. It was the night I found out about Dad.

And Leili was there for me. Like she always is.

I sink down on my bed and cry. For a long time.

25

As Mom and I sit listening to a woman playing guitar and singing a sad song with lyrics about flowers and knives and blood, I realize I'm very nervous. It's as if the person about to perform is me and not Dad.

He's standing in the back with his cane, too anxious to sit. I keep throwing glances his way to make sure he's all right. He's nodding his head to the music, which, to an outsider, might seem like he's in a very mellow mood, but I know that's not the case.

Cory and Ed are here too, at a table right behind us. Dad made a point of not inviting anyone except the two of them, since he so values and trusts their opinions and feels like they "have a good sense of the industry." And, somewhat incredibly, they were both available to come.

I've only been to Ted's Roasters a couple of times before this. It's your standard-issue coffeehouse, a bunch of square tables spread around the room, with a small, crudely constructed stage about a foot off the ground at the front. Mom is drinking a chai latte (she's obsessed with anything chai), while I got a large hot chocolate (extra whipped cream), which I've barely touched.

It's pretty crowded tonight, almost all the tables in use.

There are a few people my parents' age, a bunch my age, but most look like they're in their early twenties. I know they'll laugh, because Dad is hilarious, but I want them to laugh *a lot*.

I did the announcements by myself this morning, which was very surreal. I was anxious when I got to school, ready for Evan to be every bit as awful to me on the announcements as he was at rehearsal yesterday, but he wasn't there. Ms. DiMicelli had heard from Mrs. Costa that he no longer wanted to do the announcements, though she wasn't sure why. I had an idea.

A ripple of nausea passed through me as I thought of doing them alone for the entire school, but once I started, I was somehow able to get in the flow.

"Guess you didn't need that Evan after all," Ms. DiMicelli said with a playful wink once I'd finished. "Just dead weight."

Truer words, Ms. D.

I couldn't feel that great, though, because I'd never gotten in touch with Leili. Still haven't. She spent lunch today working on Yearbook. Azadeh said Leili was pissed at her, too, for a while and eventually came around, so I shouldn't be too worried. BUT OBVIOUSLY I AM. My best friend and I aren't talking! It's a nightmare.

A bouncy, bearded guy named Micah is the host of the open mic, calling the acts to the stage in the order they signed up. We showed up a little late, so Dad is further down the list. But we've already watched at least seven (mainly excruciating) acts, so he might be soon.

Micah pats the sad guitar girl on the back and gets ready to introduce the next performer. Oh, please, let it be Dad so I can stop feeling such horrendous jitters. It's not. A guy named Rex is called up to the stage. No last name, just Rex. As soon as I see that he's not holding an instrument, I get concerned.

And it's warranted, because Rex steps onto the stage, literally puts his mouth on the microphone to say "Hi. I'm Rex" in a deadpan voice, and then starts telling jokes.

This is not the hugest disaster, but so far, no other comedians have performed, and it seems like it would have been helpful if Dad could have been the first. Oh well.

Rex is probably in his late twenties, wearing a plaid shirt and skinny jeans, with shaggy hair not dissimilar to Evan's, and he gets big laughs right away. Not from me or Mom, but from most of the other people in the room. I can tell from Mom's expression that she's also desperate for Rex to crash and burn so that Dad will have a higher likelihood of success. No such luck.

"My girlfriend is always telling me I'm too negative," Rex says, "and I'm like 'Shut up, I hate you, I have no idea what you're talking about!'" This gets a huge laugh, and my stomach sinks. It's not the cleverest joke, but he really sells it by shouting the second part in a demonic voice. I start to turn back to Dad to give him a reassuring look or something, but the thought of seeing him in the midst of anxiously comparing himself to another comedian overwhelms me, so I don't.

The laughs, meanwhile, keep rolling. Rex talks mainly about his girlfriend, but also about how boring his office job is, which gets people roaring. Most of his jokes have previously been made on *The Office,* but no one else seems to mind.

"And that's my time, folks!" Rex says to conclude, like this is some huge comedy club and not a local coffeehouse with bad air circulation. (It's so hot in here, my god.)

"All right, everybody, let's give one more hand for Rex!" Micah says, chuckling as he says it, as if the mere mention of Rex's name is making him laugh at his jokes all over again.

Please don't let Dad be next. Please. Let's have at least one act in between, a palate cleanser before he has to go up there. If there is any sort of Benevolent Force in this universe, let there be a name underneath Rex's on the sign-up sheet, one that isn't Russ Friedman.

"Next we have Russ Friedman!" Micah shouts. "Come on up here!"

Farts.

Dad slowly makes his way from the back of the room, and it's taking long enough that the applause dies down before he's even halfway to the stage. Why did Dad have to stand back there? Or why didn't he memorize who was before him so he would be able to anticipate his entrance?

It's not his fault. I just feel bad that the whole room is watching him. And, of course, we're only here in the first place because Mom and I put the idea in Dad's head, so if anything, it's our fault.

On a different day, Dad would make a joke right now to put everyone at ease, something witty and self-deprecating, like "Nothing to see here, folks. Talk amongst yourselves." Instead, he tries to speed up a little, which, since I've now been present for two separate falls, makes me tense. Sure enough, his cane catches on the base of one of the tables, and he wobbles forward.

My heart shoots into my mouth.

Mom gasps.

He can't fall right now. He can't. That would most definitely be evidence of a Malevolent Force in the world.

Dad is able to balance himself, and we breathe a sigh of relief. Mom makes eye contact with me, like *Thank fucking god,* and I look back like *Yeah, no shit.*

Micah puts a hand out to help Dad onto the stage, and, finally, Dad is up at the mic. He takes it out of its stand, and I shout "Woo!" to give him a boost of encouragement.

It backfires horribly, though, as my *Woo!* startles Dad, causing him to drop the mic, which lands with a huge thudding pop that makes the entire audience flinch, followed by screechy feedback.

This is going really well.

Micah kindly scurries onto the stage to pick up the mic and hand it back to Dad, but not before saying, "You're supposed to save the mic drop for the end of your set," which gets a huge laugh. Shit.

I know he was trying to defuse the tension and give the audience permission to laugh at a man with a cane who has accidentally dropped something, but I wish he'd let Dad make the joke himself. Because he definitely would have.

"Uh, yeah, I'll remember that for the future," Dad says. "Mic drop at the end. Very good." Some people lightly chuckle. "So, uh, hi, everybody. My name is Russ, like he said, and I, uh . . ." Now Dad is not only nervous but also a bit shaken by the dropped-mic incident. I'm sure most people can't see that, but I do. "It's a little presumptuous of me to try to do stand-up comedy when I struggle just to do the standing-up part."

This gets a solid laugh. Mom and I look at each other again, relieved but still on edge. We're not out of the woods yet. Far from it.

Dad catapults straight from that joke into his Facebook material, which instantly seems like a mistake. After sharing those jokes with me earlier in the week, Dad decided he wasn't going to run anything else past me or Mom ahead of time. He said he wanted it to be a surprise and to get our genuine reactions live with an audience rather than in our family room.

It made sense at the time, but now I'm deeply regretting it. If I had seen this in advance, I would have told him to do at least a few more jokes about why he has the cane, what it's like to walk around with one all the time, something where he further invites the audience in instead of just being like "Hey, I can't stand well! Now here're some completely unrelated jokes!"

I would have thought he would have known to do that. He's the one who first played Tig Notaro's classic stand-up set for me, the one where she'd had a string of terrible things happen to her, including being diagnosed with cancer *earlier that day,* and somehow spun it into confessional comedic gold. I'm kicking myself for not pushing Dad to go in that direction.

His jokes about Facebook are going over fine, some scattered chuckles, but he's hitting that strange announcer persona even harder than he did with me. I wish he would just talk like himself.

Much to my dismay, the jabs at Facebook make up his strongest material. He transitions into bits about online shopping ("I miss having a checkout person to flirt with! Siri doesn't quite cut it"), gardening ("I ended up with tons of weeds, which, if you took away the *s,* would actually be okay with me"), and, sadly, that old bit about mannequin nipples that he did years ago. It sounds less like my father and more like what he *thinks* a stand-up comedian should sound like.

That said, he's still getting some laughs (along with the ones coming from me, Mom, Cory, and Ed), but it's nothing close to the kind of response I was imagining for him.

Was he ever actually good at this? I want to shout at Mom.

I know she's feeling as guilty and mortified as I do. What have we subjected Dad to? The whole point of this was to build him up, to remind him that he is more than his disease, to send him on a journey of self-fulfillment, and it feels like we have very much done the opposite.

"Well, this has been a lot of fun," Dad says, mercifully wrapping things up.

Has it, though?

He slowly and carefully maneuvers the mic back into the stand, making sure not to drop it again, even though I feel like doing that would, in fact, be the *perfect* way to call back to the beginning of his set and bring everything full circle.

Alas, it's not that kind of night.

"Thanks, everyone." Dad throws up a hand and takes steady but determined steps off the stage to the sound of gentle applause. I'm so happy it's over. After watching helplessly as he drowned for seven minutes, I'm glad he's finally made it to dry land. I want to *Woo!* again but I'm too scared. Doesn't matter anyway because astute open mic host Micah, not wanting to invite yet more dead air, is already introducing the next act as Dad totters to the back of the room. I assumed he would join us at our table—there's a seat for him and everything—but then again, wading into a mass of people who thought I was mediocre wouldn't be my first choice either.

As luck would have it, the next act is YET ANOTHER CO-MEDIAN, this time a woman named Liddy Ramani who kills from the moment she steps onto the stage. She's really funny, and even as my insides are melting, knowing that Dad has to experience the profound pain of being sandwiched in between two performers with objectively more successful sets than his,

I'm thinking I want to see her perform again sometime when I can actually concentrate on what she's doing.

It's a fleeting thought, though, because Mom and I simultaneously notice that Dad isn't in the back of the room; he's walked out of the coffeehouse altogether. After a rapid-fire nonverbal conversation, we decide to follow him.

He's not hard to find, standing outside on the sidewalk, one hand on his cane, the other holding a cigarette. It's a very shocking sight. I've always known he used to smoke when he was younger, but I've never actually seen him do it.

My first instinct is, of course, to say, "Gross, Dad, why are you doing that?" but the look on his face—eyes staring into the distance, muddied with pain and disappointment—stops me. It's a look I only remember seeing one other time in my life, at Grandpa Harvey's funeral.

"Hey, Friedo," Mom says. That's one of her nicknames for him, the one reserved for the most tender/desperate moments.

"Hey," Dad says, blowing a bunch of smoke out the side of his mouth. It's so unsettling, seeing him do something I usually associate with dirtbags and losers. Smoking is the worst.

"Is that the best idea?" Mom asks, gesturing to the cigarette.

"Probably not." He still hasn't looked at us. It's a very rare thing when my dad can be mistaken for one of those people who never smile. But that's where we're at. "Don't worry, I didn't buy a pack or anything. I got it from the guy behind the counter."

I want to say something helpful, but I can't figure out what. Thankfully, Dad takes the lead.

"Well, that sucked," he says.

"No," I say, unconvincingly.

"It was all right," Mom says, one hand on his shoulder.

Dad turns and looks at us for the first time, the angriest deadpan I've ever seen.

"No, it did suck," Mom says.

"Yeah, it really did," I agree. "I'm sorry."

Dad gives a rueful shake of his head. "I forgot that part, you know? How hard it is. It was like I knew it wasn't going great as it was happening, but there was nothing I could do to stop it."

"It's been a while," Mom says in her most sympathetic voice. "You're rusty."

"Every comic has stories like this," I say.

"That's true." Mom jumps onto my point, grateful for evidence that maybe this is all part of a trajectory toward triumph.

"It is," Dad says. "But I'm donezo, baby. You just witnessed the epilogue of my comedy career."

"Oh, come on, the first set was always going to suck. It just was," Mom says, taking up the role of Tireless Cheerleader, which impresses me because, really, I never thought Mom cared about comedy one way or the other. Then again, she'd probably be just as tireless if his old passion were kicking puppies. *Come on, these puppies* need *to be kicked!* "And you got some very genuine laughs in there."

"Eh." Dad exhales again. The cigarette smell is so gross. "So much of doing stand-up is exactly what just happened. You go out there, and you're bad."

"But you'll get better every time you go onstage!" Mom says. "You just will."

"For sure," I say, joining in.

"Please stop!" Dad says, his voice rising enough so that two people walking to their car turn and look back at us. It sends ice down my spine, curving around to my stomach. Dad isn't usually a shouter. "Please. I'm not saying I'm done because I want this to be a cute moment when you rally me back onto my feet. I'm saying I'm done because I don't want to do this anymore."

Mom and I are both quiet then, looking in any direction but at Dad. It feels like we've been scolded.

"Hey," we hear from behind us as Cory and Ed walk out of the coffeehouse, the open door letting out cheers and hooting and applause, which makes Dad cringe. Guess Liddy Ramani's set is done. The door mercifully closes.

"I'm sorry that went the way it did," Cory says, instantly reading the situation and matching his energy to my dad's.

"Yeah," Dad says. "Well."

"I didn't know you started smoking again," Ed says.

Cory shoots him a look, very easily interpreted as *Shut it, sweetie.* "There was some really funny stuff in your set," he says, not giving Dad a chance to respond to Ed. "It was great to see you up there again."

"Glad you were here for it," Dad says, "because it was my grand finale. I was just telling them: I'm done."

"Oh." Cory is genuinely bummed. "That's a shame."

Dad flicks what's left of his cigarette onto the street, which is a disappointment. A smoker *and* a litterer. "I know," he says, "you guys are saying I'll get better and better, but life is too short, you know?" The question hangs there as we all think about his probably abbreviated life span. "Especially mine," Dad adds, with perfect comedic timing. I can't laugh because it's too sad, but *that's* the funny father I know. I wish he could have brought that to his performance.

"I hear you, man," Cory says.

"I'm in enough pain as it is," Dad says. "I don't need to spend whatever time I have left making it worse."

Well, when he puts it like that.

"Of course," Mom says. I can tell she feels bad that we dragged him into this, but there's something else in her face I don't recognize. Sadness, maybe. Or defeat.

I peek through the front window back into Ted's, where a woman is playing a violin like her life depends on it. You can't really hear the music out here, and it's hard to tell from this angle whether or not there's anyone else onstage. Her hair bounces as she ferociously moves the bow back and forth.

Ed notices my staring and joins me, followed by Cory, then Mom, and finally Dad, all of us captivated by this mad violinist.

Cory walks over to the door and cracks it open. Much to our surprise, the sound of a full bluegrass band blasts out at us, not just the violin but also drums, guitar, and upright bass, with a man's lively tenor bouncing over all of it.

"Huh," Dad says.

We stand and listen until the song ends.

26

"Awesome, thanks," Dad says to our server, a bright-eyed twenty-something named Shauna (according to her name tag, anyway), as she places waters in front of each of us.

Mom keeps her eyes on her menu the whole time. She can be very rude at restaurants sometimes, and it's always a little embarrassing.

This is supposed to be "a fun Sunday night family dinner" at Chili's, one of our favorite spots, but for some reason, everything is incredibly tense. It's been sort of a strange weekend. By Saturday morning, Dad had already miraculously bounced back from the profound disappointment of Ted's the night before, greeting Mom and me in the kitchen with chocolate chip pancakes and jokes about the bags under our eyes.

I was beyond relieved, as I'd been irrationally worried all night that he might veer into being suicidal. I expected Mom to feel a similar lightness, but no. Instead, she returned to a more heightened version of the tired and high-strung human she's been in recent weeks. Sometimes I just want to shake her and be like "Dad's body is failing! Don't be mean to him on top of that!"

"So, how's school going?" Dad asks now, powering through the thick tension with his good mood. The dinner table is where he seems most comfortable these days. I think it's because it's one of the few places where he can pretend his life is what it always was. Table as time machine.

"Okay," I say, though, three days out from getting dumped by Evan and then having a horrendous fight with Leili, *terrible* would be a more apt response. "Getting nervous for the improv show."

"When is that again?" Mom says, closing her menu with so much force it makes a loud smack on the table.

"Not this Friday, but the next one."

"Oh shoot, that's right." Mom's eyes go into faraway planning mode.

"You can't come?"

"No, it's okay. It'll be fine. Yeah, I can come, I just have— I'll have to switch around this client dinner, but it's—"

"It's fine if you can't make it," I say, trying to give her an out. "There will be more—"

"I'll be there, Win," Mom says, her voice raised, surprising her as much as it does me.

"Calm down, Dane," Dad says, and I immediately know that's not gonna go over well.

Mom smiles an unhappy smile, rolling her eyes up toward the TV behind Dad, on which a large-bellied man in a uniform is getting ready to swing a bat at a ball. "Please don't say that to me," she says quietly.

"Sorry," Dad says. "But you're practically shouting at Win."

Mom turns to me. "I'm sorry, Winnie. I didn't mean to shout." On the apology scale, it falls somewhere near Four-Year-Old Forced to Apologize After Stealing Friend's Toy. "And, Russ, I'm sorry I'm not living up to your standards of behavior."

"Oh, come on, that's not—"

"Are we all set to order here?"

Shauna's back. Bouncier than ever.

"Ooh," Dad says, looking down at his menu. "Ooh ooh ooh ooh ooh, I think . . ." He flings his head back up. "Yes! I do believe we're all set."

His antics elicit some gentle laughter from Shauna. "Excellent," she says.

I, of course, have no idea what I want. I surrender and get what I always get, a cup of soup and a Quesadilla Explosion Salad.

Dad orders a Guacamole Burger.

Mom orders a California Turkey Club Sandwich.

We're all very predictable.

"Any appetizers?" Shauna asks as she collects our menus. "Boneless Wings? Crispy Cheddar Bites?"

"Crispy cheddar?" Dad says. "That sounds hazardous."

Shauna guffaws as if this is the most hilarious thing anyone has ever said about the Chili's menu. "They're actually really good," she says.

Dad looks to us. "Should we . . . ?" I shake my head. Mom is tuned out, watching the baseball game (even though I know for a fact it's the sport she cares about the least). "Nah, we'll pass, but thanks."

"No prob!" Shauna says.

I'm excited for her to walk away, as I don't think their exchange is going to be particularly helpful for the family dynamic, and she's about to when Dad says, "Has it been busy tonight?"

He does this sometimes, randomly engages strangers in

conversation, like he's incredibly fascinated by their lives. Or, in this case, by the traffic patterns of this Chili's location.

"Not really," Shauna says, suddenly looking a little nervous, like maybe we're secret shoppers or restaurant critics or something. "I mean, it was a little busier earlier, but it's quieter now. I'm sure it'll pick up, though."

"Gotcha," Dad says, as if he's going to log that in his ledger later. "Guess we'll have to get a bit rowdy to make up for it."

Rowdy? What is happening?

"Ha, right," Shauna says, not laughing nearly as much as she did a moment ago. Now she just looks concerned she might be fired. "Okay, I'll go get this order in for you guys."

"Superduper," Dad says. "You do that."

"Thanks," I say, less to Shauna and more to the universe for finally ending that excruciating chapter of my life. I don't blame Dad for wanting to make conversation—he doesn't get out these days as much as he used to—but I also don't understand why it was necessary to do so right at that particular juncture, with Mom already fuming across the table. Like, pick up the cues, Daddy-o.

"*Superduper,* huh?" Mom says, her gaze still on the television.

"I can't say *superduper*?" Dad asks.

My shoulders tense, my stomach wobbles. I want this to end as quickly as possible.

"No, say whatever you want. I know you will either way." Now Mom's looking straight at Dad. "I mean, you just said more to Shauna than you have to me all week, but who's counting?"

"That's— It's called being nice to your server. You should try it sometime."

243

"Screw you, Russ. Seriously."

Oh god, I hate this so much. I don't know where to aim my eyes, so I take out my phone under the table. Even though Leili still isn't talking to me, I desperately want to text her and Azadeh. So I do.

My parents are having a fight at Chili's. So fun.

I stare into my lap and send them a deadpan selfie.

"May I remind you I'm the one with ALS?" Dad whisper-shouts. "I'm the one walking with a goddamn cane!"

"I'm well aware of that, Russ," Mom says. "I think *you're* the one who needs reminding. I have no clue what you're thinking about any of this. You don't tell me anything!"

"That's not true."

"Okay!" Shauna says, appearing at our table like a hologram flipping on. "I have the broccoli-cheese soup." As I shove my phone back in my bag, Shauna places the soup in front of me with great precision and care, nimbly dropping two bags of crackers next to it. She definitely thinks we're secret shoppers.

"Thanks," Dad says without looking, underplaying it this time. Thank god.

"Of course," Shauna says, in total professional mode, before walking away.

"Aw," Mom says. "Are you sad you didn't get to chat more with your close friend Shauna?" She's not usually this sarcastic. If I didn't feel so anxious, I would find it really funny.

"You're being ridiculous," Dad says.

I want to chime in, I want to help the situation, but I have no idea how, so I stay mute.

"Am I?" Mom asks, and I can tell everything that's already gone down at this table has been but mere prologue to what's about to unspool. "Look, I understand how intense this is, how horrible this diagnosis is, so I've been trying to support you in every way I can, giving you the space to handle it however you need to."

People around us are starting to stare. There's a couple of women Grandma's age that keep glancing over. *Mind your own beeswax, Grandmas!* There's also a family behind Dad, two moms with their two elementary schoolers. "Are they in a fight?" I hear the son ask.

Oh, how I wish I were anywhere but here.

Dad's obviously thinking the same thing because he says, "Let's not do this here, Dana."

"Where should we do it?" Mom asks. "Home? 'Cause that never happens!"

"Yes, but maybe our daughter—not to mention every single Chili's patron—doesn't need to hear us work out all our shit."

"At some point we have to talk about this, Russ! You're always dodge, dodge, joke, joke, but if I don't know what you're thinking, I can't help you! So I look up information about an ALS support group, thinking maybe that will be a better, you know, way for you to open up. Do you follow up on it? Of course not! I don't know what else to do. But I do know eventually I won't *want* to help anymore because this is so . . . fucking . . . lonely. You can be all la-di-da with ol' Shauna over there, but when it comes to your own wife, you've got nothing."

I'm taking all of this in, even though I wish I weren't, and matching it against my own experience with Dad. I mean, he definitely talks. Maybe not always about serious stuff, but he's dealing with his situation by, like, making jokes and stuff, which I think is pretty heroic.

Right?

Dad is chuckling in this nervous way like he's stalling because he doesn't know what to say. "That seems a little hyperbolic, but okay," he says finally.

I remember that my soup has arrived and decide to start eating it, even though I have zero appetite. I crumble the crackers in the package before dumping them in. Dad's method.

"Russ," Mom says, taking her voice down several notches, her eyes wet with tears. "At some point, we need to talk about the future. Whether we're going to need in-home assistance or whether I should take a leave from my job—"

"You won't have to take a leave from your job," Dad says.

"I might! I feel like I'm the only one taking this seriously!"

I wonder if Mom thinks *I'm* not taking it seriously. I think I am.

Though the idea of in-home assistance for Dad had never even occurred to me. So maybe I'm not.

"Of course I'm taking it seriously!" Dad nearly shouts. The eyes of the girl elementary schooler behind him are open really wide. "Look how serious I am." He furrows his brow and makes a solemn face, and even I know it's a bad move.

"Stop," Mom says. "It's not funny!"

"I'm sorry," Dad says. "I'm sorry. Everything you're mentioning, we'll have time to talk about all that."

"Oh good, great. Let's just put it off until you're in *really* bad shape, good thinking."

I think Mom's overreacting, but I also see the merit to some of her arguments.

"That's not what I'm saying," Dad says. "I'm just . . . getting used to my situation."

Mom snorts and looks away, shaking her head.

"What?" Dad asks.

"That's exactly what you used to say when we first moved out here, in the first couple years after Winnie was born. And we all know how well *that* went."

Wait, what? Not *all* of us know. What is she talking about?

Dad's whole body goes rigid. "All right, let's not— We don't have to go there."

"No, no, you're right," Mom says, eyes back on the TV, which is showing a gross beer commercial with women in tight white T-shirts. "Let's not talk about anything, just like we did back then, and you can go cheat on me again to get your confidence back. Great plan."

The color drains from Dad's face.

Did she just say *go cheat on me again*?

Again?

"Are you out of your mind, Dana? Why are you—"

"What are you talking about?" I ask.

"Nothing, Win," Dad says.

"You cheated on Mom?"

He pauses a moment, puts both hands on the table, as if he's trying to ground himself so he doesn't fly away. Mom isn't saying anything, watching to see how he responds. "No, of course not," he says.

"Okay, forget it," Mom says, standing up from the table and grabbing her jacket.

I gasp. It's not like Mom is some dramatic person who walks out of restaurants all the time. I've *never* seen her do that.

"What are you— Where are you going?" Dad asks.

"I can't be here right now. You know, you and Winnie

have your whole little comedy thing anyway—why do you even need me?"

"Of course we need you," Dad says.

"Nah. You'll be fine. Why don't you go ask Shauna to be your caregiver?" And Mom walks out the door of the restaurant.

"Dana!" Dad says in his husky way, reaching his maximum volume these days, which is nowhere close to the booming voice he used to be able to summon. He starts to get up to follow her, but it's a slow process, and I know he can feel people watching him, and it's clear he'd never be able to catch up to her anyway, so he gives up and sits back down.

There are too many devastating things happening at once, and my brain shuts down. I think I'm in shock.

"Is she taking the car?" I ask. It's a pretty stupid response to what's gone down, but it's all I can manage.

"No," Dad says, patting his pocket. "I have the keys."

I think he's in shock too.

"So she's just gonna walk?"

"I don't know, Win."

"Or maybe she'll call for a cab? Maybe I should run out and see if she's still outside?"

"I think . . . I think maybe Mom needs some time alone." Dad awkwardly shifts his body to take his phone out of his back pocket. "I'll text her."

Dad looks down at his phone and slowly moves his thumbs.

I sit there for a moment before shooting out of my seat so I can check if Mom is waiting in front. I don't care what Dad says, *someone* has to run after her.

"BRB," I say, not giving him a chance to respond.

But out front there's just a guy in a white button-down shirt smoking a gross cigarette and talking on the phone. I check both sides of the building.

She's gone.

When I arrive back at the table, Shauna is dropping off our food. Dad just nods as his burger is set down in front of him.

"Need anything else?" Shauna is asking Dad as I sit down.

"We're good," I say. "Thanks."

Dad is staring ahead of him. He's not crying, but he looks like he could.

"Did Mom text back?"

"Not yet," he says.

I want to ask again about the cheating, but I just can't.

I never would have thought Dad cheating on Mom was a possibility in a million years.

I mean, he said it wasn't true, but why would Mom make that up?

Which would mean it is true.

Which would mean maybe my dad, who I think I'm so close to, is actually someone I don't know at all.

Dad takes a bite of his Guacamole Burger.

I peer down at my exploded quesadilla situation. It looks like vomit.

I still haven't touched my soup. Fragments of cracker float in the coagulated yellow, green broccoli dots shimmering around them.

I know nothing about anything.

Except that I'll never be ordering this soup again.

27

"You really bring such wonderful levity to these announcements," Ms. DiMicelli says moments after I flick off the switch and grab my backpack from the floor to head to English.

"Thanks so much," I say. I wasn't entirely sure if the bits I'd broadcast minutes ago to the whole school were funny or just weird and confusing and sad. Because the latter three are where my head is at.

Mom never came home last night. Dad and I barely talked the rest of dinner or even once we got home, other than me continually asking, "Are you worried?" and him saying, "No, Mom's a strong, independent woman, she's able to take care of herself. She'll reach out when she's ready." To which I wanted to respond, *Yes, but what if she NEVER DOES? What if she's gone FOREVER?* When she finally texted at nine-thirty that she was staying at Paige's, it was such a relief, replaced a minute later by a suffocating sadness. My mother and my (very ill) father are in such a huge fight that she can't even be in the same house as him.

I wanted to reach out to someone, but I was astonished to realize there was no one. Leili and Azadeh hadn't responded to my text from Chili's, and I had too much dignity to pathetically text again. Evan obviously wasn't an option. And though

I was starting to feel closer to improv people like Molly and Rashanda, even Jess, I didn't feel text-them-with-my-problems close.

What was wrong with me? How could there be *no one*?

I lay in bed, put on an episode of *2 Dope Queens,* and tried to imagine myself on it, cracking up Jessica and Phoebe with my edgy, honest material. "Lemme tell you, if your dad ever gets diagnosed with ALS, get ready for the shit storm. Because it. Is. Coming."

That's not even a good joke. I don't know what it is. That's how much of a rudderless clusterfuck my life has become.

Though I didn't want to think about what had happened at dinner, one definite conclusion to be drawn was that Dad was keeping things from me. And, from Mom's reaction, it was fair to assume that one of those things was the truth about what was happening to him. Banter no longer seemed like a solution, and I couldn't feel worse than I already did. And since I couldn't trust Dad anymore, I no longer had to keep my stupid promise.

I googled ALS.

Turns out I could feel worse than I already did.

Though ALS does manifest in many different ways, most of them involve a very bad ending. And the speedy progression of Dad's symptoms thus far did not inspire confidence about the way his was manifesting.

The average life expectancy of a person with ALS is two to five years from the time of diagnosis.

In two years, I'll be seventeen. In five years, I'll be twenty.

Riluzole, the drug Dad is on, can extend life by approximately two to three months. *Months.*

So I'll *still* be seventeen or twenty, and my dad will be dead.

As ALS progresses, driving will be discontinued. (So: my dad will be home a lot.)

Weakness in the muscles used to swallow may cause choking. (So: my dad may need a feeding tube.)

Weakness in the muscles used to breathe may cause "respiratory insufficiency." (So: my dad may need something called a BiPAP.)

Eventually, speech may no longer be possible. (So: my dad may need a communication device.)

May cause.

May be.

May need.

(So:

(So:

(So:

I read and read and read and fell asleep with a wet face.

Now, walking down the hall to Mr. Novack's class, I'm a shell of myself. A teacher I don't recognize is giving me a suspicious look, so I flash my permanent late pass at her. That's right: VIP, bitch!

I ghost past Mr. Novack's desk and head to my seat. I accidentally make eye contact with Fletcher, who gives me a genuinely sympathetic look. I turn away because I'm worried I'll start to feel even worse for myself than I already do.

I get through about ten minutes of arrogant, vaguely misogynistic yammering about *Tess of the d'Urbervilles* before my hand shoots up into the air.

"In a moment, Ms. Friedman," Mr. Novack says.

"No, I'm sorry, I have to— You're not talking about this book right."

"Excuse me?" Mr. Novack peers at me over his glasses. "How should I be talking about it?"

"I don't know, not the way you are!" I'm as surprised that I'm speaking as he is, but I can't stop. "Like, all these horrible things happen to Tess, and then she's *blamed* for those horrible things, leading to more horrible things. To the point where she's so desperate she has to murder the dude who's been abusing her the whole book! Sorry, spoiler alert for anybody who didn't finish, but, you know, do your homework on time. And then it ends with her being executed! And you're going on about the way the themes tie into the Industrial Revolution, but like, obviously, it's about how stupid and unfair it is to be a woman! Are you ever gonna talk about *that*?"

The classroom is silent as Mr. Novack continues to stare at me. I kind of hope he sends me to the office. "Well, Ms. Friedman, I believe I *have* talked about that—"

"You haven't. You definitely haven't. I would remember."

He stares a beat longer before raising his eyebrows and cocking his head to the side. "Fair enough," he says. He picks up exactly where he left off.

It's a victory, I guess, but it doesn't feel like one. Nothing means anything. Class eventually ends, and I'm out the door, ready to zombie-hoof it through my day, when Fletcher appears next to me, pack extended. "Fruit Stripe?"

"Nah," I say. "Thanks."

"Enjoyed the rant. You aight?"

Unlike much of the school, Fletcher knows my dad has ALS, so it's easier to be around him than most. Still, though, not feeling very chatty. "Oh yeah," I say. "Don't I look it? I'm fantastic."

"Not everything has to be a joke," he says.

I can't help but hear it as a reprimand. He didn't even say it like that, but either way, it's not helpful. "Well. Whatever, I gotta go." I pick up my pace down the hall, trying to shake him.

Fletcher is unshakable. "I didn't mean that in a dick way," he says, somehow catching up to me without breaking into a slow jog, let alone a run. "I mean it's okay to say you feel shitty if you feel shitty."

"I know that." I'm on the verge of tears. "So I feel shitty. Okay? Happy?"

"Do you wanna take a minute and come with me?"

Good god, not this again. What's with guys needing to whisk girls off to surprise places?

"It's not a surprise or anything," Fletcher says as people pass us in the hallway. Weirdly, Evan walks by at that exact moment. He pretends not to see me. "There's this spot off the A Wing that's usually empty. My boy Terrence showed it to me last year before he moved. I chill out there sometimes."

Hmm. "Chilling out" in some random spot in school doesn't exactly sound tempting, but the alternative is spending gym class trying not to cry. "Yeah. Okay."

"Cool," Fletcher says. "This way." We walk side by side toward the A Wing. Once there, he looks around a few times, then, with a decent amount of force, backs through a door I've passed hundreds of times without a clue what it led to. I follow, and it's a random school closet, drab gray metal shelves stacked with textbooks that look like they're from 1995.

The tone for second period sounds. I've never straight-up skipped a class before.

Fletcher walks farther into the narrow closet, then steps to the right and disappears. The closet is L-shaped, with a whole section you can't see when you first walk in. This part has no shelves, so there's slightly more space to move around in. Fletcher bends down and picks up a hardcover book called *Devil in a Blue Dress* from the floor. He flips the top of it toward me, so I can see a bookmark sticking out. "Almost halfway done," he says.

"You come here so much you leave your books?"

"Just blends in with all the other shit," Fletcher says, smiling. "I think this is mainly a dumping ground for supplies teachers are getting rid of. And no other students seem to know about it. It feels like a locked door until you push hard enough."

"Wow."

"Yeah." Fletcher kicks one foot up onto the cinder block wall, almost like a nervous habit.

Bizarrely enough, standing here with him does make me feel calmer. And, at the same time, part of me is buzzing with the thrill of knowing we are definitely not supposed to be here.

"So what's your deal?" I ask.

"What do you mean?" Fletcher takes his foot down from the wall.

"I don't know. Like, I know you work at Stop & Shop, and I know you're in Improv Troupe, and your thing is physical comedy, which you're totally a genius at, but . . ." Fletcher looks down at the floor in this almost childlike way, which is unexpectedly endearing. "Oh, and I know your uncle died two years ago. Which I'm sorry about. But that's all I know. Do you have other friends?"

Fletcher's head snaps up, now wearing an expression like *What the hell?*

"Well, I don't know!" I say.

"You think 'cause you see me in English class and improv and the supermarket, you know my whole deal?"

"No, that's what I'm saying!" I'm backpedaling madly. "I *don't* know! I—as you would say—didn't mean that in a dick way."

"I'm just playin' with you," Fletcher says, a little too proud of himself as he half smiles at me. "But yeah, I have friends. You just don't see 'em."

"Oh. So, imaginary friends."

"You need me to take out my phone and show you pictures?" Fletcher starts thumbing through his phone. "I got some of my boy Chris, here's some of Nicky—"

"Which Chris?" I ask.

"Bryant."

"You're friends with Chris Bryant?" I've never been more aware of my limited vantage point on the world than the past week. "Chris Bryant is great. I've known him since first grade."

"Yeah. Well, I've been tight with him since eighth grade. So I know he's great."

"Wow. I seriously don't know anything about anything." And just like that, I'm thinking about my parents again. I sit down cross-legged on the dusty floor.

"It's really all good," Fletcher says. "I don't know who *your* friends are. Besides Leili."

"No," I say. "My mom and dad got in this huge fight last night. And my mom left dinner and didn't come back."

"Oh shit." Fletcher slinks down, back against the wall, and sits across from me. "And with your dad, like, and his ALS situation, that's pretty intense. He must have really pissed her off."

"Yeah," I say, openly crying now. "I think he— She said he cheated on her."

"Whoa!" Fletcher runs one disbelieving hand over his hair. "In his condition, that's . . ."

"No, it was a long time ago."

"Oh."

"If it even happened." I wipe my face, but I can't stop the tears. "I'm sorry I'm such a mess right now."

"Nah," Fletcher says. "That's what this closet is for."

He's being so sweet about it, but I actually would prefer to not be crying. So I change the subject. "Why did you join Improv Troupe?"

Fletcher blinks a few times, like I've splashed him with water, before staring thoughtfully at the ceiling. "To get better," he says finally.

"At physical comedy?"

"At all comedy. At any comedy."

"Okay."

Fletcher senses that I want more of an answer than that. "My main thing was always dancing."

Once again, I think he's messing with me. Which is actually completely sexist—why couldn't he be a dancer?—but it does seem out of left field.

"No, for real. That's how I first learned to move. I've been dancing since I was, like, a baby. My mom used to be a professional dancer, and now she teaches, so I would go to her classes. And I was good at it, you know?"

Fletcher's got my brain spinning like whoa. He's a *dancer*. It simultaneously makes complete sense and no sense at all. "Yeah."

"Anyway, after a while, being the only guy in my dance classes got played out, so I took a break from all that. But it was still in me, you know? And my dad knew that, so when I was eleven, right before he and my mom got divorced, he forced me to watch a couple of movies that changed my life."

The way Fletcher casually mentions that his parents are divorced makes me feel like a wuss, unable to handle my mom being away from the house for even one night. "What movies?" I ask once I realize he's waiting on me to continue.

"You heard of *Breakin'*?"

"Uh. No."

"Aw man, seriously? Or *Breakin' 2: Electric Boogaloo*?"

"Oh yes! I've heard that title before, but I have no idea what it is. Are they good movies?"

"I just said they changed my life, so yeah, they're *incredible*. They're the best movies ever made."

The way Fletcher is lighting up about this makes me genuinely smile for the first time all day. "What are they about?"

"Here." Fletcher stands up, digs his phone out of his back pocket, and sits down next to me. "I'll show you." He pulls up a YouTube video labeled "*Breakin'*—Turbo (broom scene)." "This is gonna blow your mind. Are you ready?"

I nod.

Fletcher hits play. We watch a very 1980s-looking guy in red pants and white Nikes sweeping the sidewalk in front of a convenience store, underscored by an amazing instrumental track that sounds like it was played on Dad's old keyboard. "That's Turbo," Fletcher says. "Actually Michael 'Boogaloo Shrimp' Chambers."

But Turbo's not actually sweeping. He's dancing. Like, gliding along the sidewalk and moving his body in all these unreal ways, spinning the broom around, doing some incredible version of the Robot. And then he makes the broom levitate.

It's hilarious and beautiful at the same time. And it actually is blowing my mind. "Is this what the whole movie is?"

"Kinda. I mean, there's a plot, with one break-dancing gang facing off against another, but it's all just, like, so stupid it's magic."

"Ohmigod, is that why you wanted to work at Stop & Shop? So you could be like Turbo?"

"Whoa, shit," Fletcher says, leaning his head back. "Now you're blowing my mind. That's truly never occurred to me." He shakes his head back and forth, like it's a thought too profound to fully engage with at the moment. "But check this." He pulls up another video, this one from *Breakin' 2*. In this one, Turbo is wearing all red, and a headband, and a studded belt, and showing a little midriff, and we watch as he climbs the freakin' wall and starts literally dancing on the ceiling. It is a delight. I am delighted.

"I really love this," I say. "I'm not just saying that." I am also highly aware of how close our bodies are to each other. I feel a little tingly.

Fletcher shows me another clip.

And another.

And another.

And another.

"You gotta see the whole movies," he says after we've exhausted the Internet's supply of *Breakin'* footage. "I've seen 'em literally hundreds of times. It was the moment I realized dancing could be funny." He says it with this reverence I completely understand. "And then I spent months going down the Internet rabbit hole of what else is out there. You know, Gregory Hines, Cab Calloway from *way* back in the day, this dude

Donald O'Connor wrestling with a mannequin and walking up walls in *Singin' in the Rain*."

"'Make 'Em Laugh'! That's so amazing, I love that too!"

"Yeah, of course you know *that* one."

It takes me a second to get that he's saying the one clip I know has a white person in it, and then I start blushing.

"Oh. I—"

The door opens, and Fletcher and I freeze.

We hear footsteps, then a stack of books placed with a grunt on one of the shelves. The door closes again.

I am terrified. Fletcher seems chill. "They never walk all the way in," he laughs.

"You don't understand," I say. "This might be the most rebellious thing I've ever done."

"See, that's funny, because onstage you're, like, fearless."

"I am *not* fearless. Trust me."

"But it seems like you are. Which means you are." This might be my favorite compliment I've ever gotten. Even more than being called funny. "Anyway, to answer your question, I joined Improv because I wanted to see if maybe I could learn how to do comedy that's not just, you know, physical. And I'm not there yet." Fletcher laughs at himself.

"You kidding? You're doing so well!"

"Nah, nah," Fletcher says, flicking a hand in my direction.

I like him.

The thought descends suddenly and undeniably. I like his deep brown eyes. I like his beanpole arms. I like the way he rescued my father in the supermarket. I like his white Nikes, and I like that I now know they're obviously inspired by Turbo. And it's not, like, the he-likes-me-so-I-like-him-back Evan style of liking. I just like him.

And maybe he likes me. I mean, he brought me to his spot.

"What?" Fletcher says.

I was staring. "Oh, nothing, I just—"

The tone sounds.

"We should jet," Fletcher says, already up on his feet and extending a hand down to me.

"Oh yeah, for sure." I take his hand. He lifts me to my feet.

The rest of the day I don't find myself thinking about Mom and Dad nearly as much as I would have expected.

28

"When are you coming home?" I ask.

"I don't know," Mom says.

We're sitting at a bright pink table at Forever FroYo, the name of which has always made me slightly skeptical. What about two hundred years from now, when dessert technology has significantly evolved? Might be singing a different tune then!

"I miss you," I say, spooning a glob of Reese's Pieces–covered vanilla into my mouth. "Dad misses you."

"Thanks, Win," Mom says. "I miss you, too. I just need to . . . take some time. You understand that, right?"

"Sure. I mean, I guess."

Mom's staying at Paige's again tonight, but she picked me up after dinner at home with Dad so we could talk. The whole thing is still shocking to me. It feels like this is someone else's life. It can't be mine.

Mom and I used to come to Forever Fro Yo all the time when I was younger. It was our Saturday afternoon tradition while Dad was teaching classes. But then at some point we stopped. Maybe once Dad's schedule changed.

Mom smiles, a bite of chocolate and blueberries in her mouth. I want to cry.

But instead I force myself to spit out the words that haven't left my brain since she left Chili's.

"Did— Did Dad really cheat on you?"

Mom grimaces, like she feels worse about the pain it's causing me than for herself. "That's actually why I wanted to see you," she sighs. "So I could say sorry. I shouldn't have said that in front of you."

Wait, so maybe she made that up? Is that what she's saying? "So . . . Dad didn't cheat on you?"

Mom goes totally still, her eyes looking to one side, then back at me. "No, he did."

And even though I'd thought it had to be true, the entire room tips on its side. I almost fall out of my seat.

"But we worked through it," she says. "I understood why it happened. I forgave him."

"Why did it— What did you do to make Dad cheat on you?"

Mom's head jerks back a little, as if my words have slapped her. She quickly recovers, though. "Come on, Win. You know it's not that simple."

I do, and I'm embarrassed that I phrased it the way I did. It's just . . . My dad wouldn't be a cheater for no reason, would he? My funny dad. A cheating fucking liar.

"Who was it?"

"What?"

"Who did he cheat on you with?"

"Oh, it doesn't even matter now, it was so many years ago."

"I want to know," I say.

She opens and closes her mouth a few times before finally saying, "Stella. She taught with him at Tumble 'n' Play."

I don't remember any Stella. But the idea of Dad cheating on Mom with some chirpy coworker at Tumble 'n' Play makes me want to punch a froyo machine. Demolish it.

"You wouldn't remember her," Mom says, as if she's reading

263

my mind. "She stopped working there after it all came out. You weren't even two yet."

"This is so fucked up," I say, really hitting the word *fucked*. We're the only people in here, but the girl at the counter glances my way for a second. "I don't— How could Dad do that to you?"

Mom gives me another sympathetic grimace. "That's exactly how I felt back then, too. It was awful. We came really close to getting a divorce."

WHAT THE HELL? My parents almost got a divorce and I never knew about it?

"But I understand it differently now," Mom says. "I still wish it hadn't happened, but I get it. And that's part of why I left dinner the other night. And why I'm at Paige's now. Because I see the same things happening again, and I can't live like that a second time."

"You think Dad's cheating on you again?" My heart beats triple time.

"No. I don't." Thank god. "But when your dad gets nervous or scared, he hides those feelings away and doesn't talk about them. Not even with me. And it's infuriating. So instead, he ends up acting on his fear in unproductive ways."

"Like by skanking it up with Stella?"

"Don't say *skanking it up,* Win. That's offensive."

"Mom, who cares if I offend Stella by calling her a skank."

"Stella wasn't a skank. She was a confused girl in her twenties who made some bad choices."

"That's far too generous."

"I'm just saying, that makes Stella the villain here, when really it's your father. Call him whatever you want. But calling Stella a skank is unnecessarily demeaning to her. And all women."

Whoa, geez. When did Mom become such a feminist?

264

I'm suddenly reminded of all the times Evan called Jess crazy, which turned out not to be true at all. Maybe that's what I'm doing by skank-labeling Stella, a woman I've never even met.

I hate when Mom is right about things.

Wait, maybe that's sexist, too. Because I don't hate when Dad is right about things. Why is that? What's wrong with me?

"Okay. I won't call her a skank. Dad is a skank, though."

"Much better," Mom says, totally straight-faced.

"So why *didn't* you divorce Dad? I would have. I want to divorce him as a dad."

"Ha, don't do that." I don't understand how Mom can find any of this funny.

"But really," I say. "I always thought—" I'm trying to finish my sentence, but the lump in my throat wins. I sob.

"Oh, Win," Mom says.

"I always thought Dad was one of the good guys." I can't wipe my face fast enough. The tears keep coming. I really wish this wasn't happening at Forever Fro Yo. Better than Chili's, I guess.

"He is, Win. He really is. People are complicated, though."

"You mean people are sucky."

"Sure. That, too." The counter girl drops something. A zillion tiny somethings, actually. Miniature M&M's, maybe.

Mom comes around the table and hugs me. "Aw, my sweet girl," she says. It makes me cry harder.

"Come home," I say.

"I know," Mom says, which isn't a valid response.

"I picked such weird toppings," I cry, staring at my bowl, which is overflowing with Reese's Pieces, blackberries, and Sour Patch Kids.

"I didn't want to say anything, but yeah," Mom says. She

holds me for a minute more before sitting back down. "You have to understand what that time was like for Daddy, Win. He gave up his acting career, his comedy dreams, to stay at home with you and to support me in my career. And we'd left the city to come to Jersey just a few months before you were born. So even though he loved being a father to you, it was a tough transition for him. His confidence took a serious hit."

"Well, he shouldn't have agreed to do it if it was gonna lead to him cheating on you." I blow my nose into a flimsy napkin.

"Definitely. But I don't think he knew it *was* gonna lead to that. He just missed being around people, making people laugh. And I wasn't always helpful with that."

"What do you mean?"

"Well, by the time you were one, we were able to socialize more, see some of our friends from the city, meet people in our neighborhood. And for Dad, that was such precious time because he was rarely around adults—this was right before he started working at Tumble 'n' Play—and I was *always* around adults."

I don't really get where Mom is going with this, but I am rapt.

"There was this one dinner party, I remember this so well, at our friends Seth and Tanya's house—they moved to Colorado soon after—and there were like fifteen people there, and Dad was so psyched to be going out, to be around people his own age. And I actually didn't even want to go. Work was exhausting as always, but I could tell how much it meant to Daddy, so we got a babysitter for you and went."

"Was Stella there?"

"Oh no, there's no cheating in this story. At least not in this

266

part. I'll cut to the chase: once dinner started, I said something dry about the helicopter parents in the neighborhood, and everyone at the table thought I was hilarious. And somehow, over the course of the meal, I became the funniest person at the table. And I knew it was destroying your father."

Mom, the funniest person at the table? Those friends must have been a bunch of duds. No offense.

"So I would try to set him up for jokes, you know," Mom continues, "try and steer the spotlight back onto him, but nothing worked. I was the funny one that night. And Daddy hated it."

I am so confused by this story.

"When I asked him about it, he pretended everything was fine. Looking back later, that was where things turned, but at the time, I just kind of shrugged it off. Which was a mistake. I should have pressed him harder, talked it out."

"I don't fully get how this relates to Dad cheating."

"His confidence, Win. He'd lost it. And I . . . I wasn't around much. And when I was, I was getting the laughs, so he ended up cheating on me with someone who *would* laugh at his jokes, who made him feel confident again."

"Oh," I say.

"Like I said, I didn't figure all this out until later, once I'd found out he was cheating on me, once I'd bawled my eyes out, once I'd stopped talking to Daddy for a week. When he and I finally talked it all out and, you know, decided we would move forward, I privately made a decision: I was never going to be the funny one. If your dad could make the huge sacrifice he did so that I could have a career, I could make that sacrifice for him. And I still get to be funny at work, anyway, so I'm good."

Wait, what?

267

What the hell is my mom telling me? That she intentionally stopped being funny around Dad so that he could feel good about himself?

And suddenly moments are popping into my head, little glimmers when I'd thought, *Hey, Mom actually has a sense of humor.*

The time she backed her car into a tree in front of our house and told Dad not to worry because the tree's insurance would probably cover it.

The time she packed my school lunches while Dad was on a road trip with Uncle Noah, including messily written notes like *Please don't actually eat us* and *If you let us live, we can be helpful to you.*

The time the airline lost our luggage and she demanded that the man behind the counter give us someone else's.

But I thought that's all they were. Glimmers. Tiny flashes of potential. What an idiot.

"You stopped being funny around Dad? And me?"

"Well, not entirely," she says. "Just pulled back a bit. Played the straight man. And you ended up giving him what he needed most: an audience. He hasn't cheated again because he hasn't needed to."

"Ew, Mom! Because he's cheating on you with me?"

"Ha, no, Winnie, of course not. But you look up to your father and you love his jokes, and that makes him feel good."

I don't know what to make of any of this. I feel like I've been duped or something.

Ohmigod.

The realization dawns on me like a ton of bricks.

"That kind of happened with Evan. He didn't like that I was funnier on the announcements than he was, so he quit. And

268

he told me not to do Speech and Debate, even though the club supervisor specifically asked me to. So I didn't."

"Oh." Mom sounds surprised. "Wow. Yeah."

"But I think Evan's actually an asshole. Is Dad an asshole?"

"No, Winnie, Daddy's not an asshole. And Evan probably isn't either. Like I said, people are complicated."

"I just like to smile," my phone says. "Smiling's my favorite." It's Will Ferrell as Buddy the elf, my text tone for Dad. I don't want to check it, but I feel compelled, in case he fell or something.

Hey Banana. Hope the talk is going all right. Heart emoji.

Feeling guilty much?

It's jarring to be reminded that the person we're talking about is a real human being who I'm living with. A human being who I no longer have any idea how to feel about.

I don't text back. This insecure cheater doesn't deserve a response.

"Sorry," I say. "It was Dad."

"You don't have to hate him," Mom says, again reading my mind.

"Yeah, but you do," I say. "You can't even stay in the same house as him."

"I don't hate Daddy. I love him. A lot. I just needed to take a moment. And I needed him to know that I'm not messing around." Mom's voice gets wavery. "He's very sick, Winnie. And he doesn't seem to want to acknowledge that."

I have no response to that. I wipe my face again.

"I don't want to bring him down. But if he can't talk this out with me, I can't just hang around and watch. I'd rather repeatedly bash myself over the head with a hammer."

Hey. That's something I'd say.

Did I get that line from *her*?

I am overwhelmed. I've seen Mom and Dad in one particular way my whole life, a way that turns out to not even be accurate. How can you so completely misread the two people who you're supposed to know better than anybody?

"I'm . . . I'm sorry, Mom."

"Why?"

"For not, like, understanding how funny you are. For being shitty to you with my inside jokes with Dad when really you were being strong and incredible. I just . . . I didn't know all of that."

"Oh, Win, you don't have anything to be sorry about. But thank you."

"I think you should come home and start letting yourself be funny again."

"Well, we'll see," Mom says. "I'm actually thinking of quitting my job and giving the stand-up thing a shot."

"What?" My entire world is imploding.

"That's a joke, Win."

"Ohhhh." I laugh. "You really are funny."

29

I'm not talking to Dad.

I can't. I'm too disgusted with him.

Unlike Mom, I can't find somewhere else to stay for the week. If I weren't still on terrible terms with Leili, maybe I could stay with her and Azadeh, but that seems like a lot to ask.

Plus, no matter how pissed I am, I wouldn't want to leave Dad solo in this house. What if he fell and couldn't get to his phone?

So I'm staying put at home. But I'm not talking to him. When we'd usually be watching *Marvelous Mrs. Maisel* or whatever else, I've been in my room. Dad cooks dinner for two, we just don't eat at the same time.

Last night after dinner, though, I watched *Breakin'* on my laptop in the family room because why should I be the one who has to hide out in my room every night?

"Ohmigod, I haven't seen this in forever," Dad said. "How'd you hear about this?" I shrugged. "I didn't know teenagers knew this existed. Is it . . . Do you mind if I sit and watch with you?"

I didn't respond, which Dad took to mean it would be all right. Which is kind of what I meant. As furious as I am, it felt nice to have some company. I never directly spoke to him, though. Not even during the broom scene.

Mom didn't talk to Dad for a week after she found out he cheated, so I figure I can at least match that. It was officially confirmed Monday night, and it's now Thursday afternoon, so what is that . . . two and a half days? Geez. I kind of thought it had been longer.

But whatever, I'm not talking to him for at least another five days.

Unfortunately, Leili has been using a similar strategy with me. Not that I've tried that hard to reach out to *her*. I mean, I'm still pissed. But it feels like I'm walking around without some vital organ, like my liver or something. Leili's conveniently had yearbook work to do every day during lunch, and I somehow never see her in the halls.

And Evan's back to sitting with Tim Stabisch and some other dodos at a table as far from us as possible, so it's been me, Azadeh, and Roxanne at lunch every day. Which has been surprisingly nice. I hate to admit that Leili's right, but I have sort of been in my own bubble for the past few weeks, and it's cool to have some substantial conversations with Azadeh and get to know Roxanne better.

"They all know?" I ask.

"Yup," Azadeh says, sticking her fork into a cucumber-and-tomato salad. "All of 'em."

One of the girls on the field hockey team figured out their fairly obvious secret, and now everyone knows.

"I'm so glad," Roxanne says. "Doing the Monica and Chandler thing was fun for a minute, but then it just felt stressful."

I look to Azadeh, mouth agape, like *Is she saying that because you told her? Or because she had the same thought Leili and I did?*

272

Azadeh shakes her head, smirks, and rolls her eyes, like *I didn't tell her. She independently made the same imperfect reference you did.*

"I totally hear that," I say, beaming at Roxanne. "I'm mainly just glad Siobhan knows."

Azadeh lets out one of her trademark loud laughs.

"Well played," Roxanne says before glancing at her phone. "Oh shoot, I'm supposed to go meet Mrs. Okin for extra help before the test tomorrow. Gotta jet."

"Don't goooooooo," Azadeh says, grabbing Roxanne's arm as she gets up from the table.

"I gotta, I gotta," Roxanne says, giggling.

"Okaaaaaaaaay." Azadeh makes a pouty face.

"I'll see you at practice. That's, like, really soon."

"Fiiiiiiiiine."

I should probably be annoyed, shouting "Get a room!" but it actually makes me really happy.

"So," Azadeh says as soon as Roxanne is gone. "Today's the day, right?"

"Improv rehearsal?"

"Well, yeah, that, but no, I mean today's the day you and Leili make up."

"I want to," I say, "but she's avoiding me!"

Azadeh gives me a deadpan stare, like *Come on.* Even I heard how defensive I sounded.

"Yes. Today's the day."

"Good," Azadeh says, forking some salad into her mouth.

"I really miss her."

"And she misses you! This is so stupid!"

"Yeah, but—"

"I'm done talking about this."

"Okay, but—"

"New topic: Did you see *SNL* last weekend?"

"I did, but—"

"Today. Is. The. Day."

I sigh. "Today's the day."

I can't stop looking at Leili's face.

We're doing a couple of practice Harolds this afternoon at improv, and I've been trying to get Leili's attention all rehearsal—I really do want this to be the day—but it hasn't worked. Evan's not here—he's clearly avoiding me at every turn, which makes me feel simultaneously terrible and powerful— but I'm still so in my head after his and Leili's comments.

Thus far in rehearsal I've been trying to stick with what's worked, using my go-to characters and bits, like I need to prove to Leili that she's wrong. But it hasn't felt exactly right. It's like I'm trying too hard to be funny instead of living in the moments of what's happening.

Leili gets up to do a scene, and I realize if I want my best friend's attention so badly, there's an easy way to get it.

I jump up into the playing space. It's the third beat of the Harold, so Leili's already established her character in two earlier scenes: a park ranger with the supernatural ability to talk to trees, which confounds all her coworkers. I decide I'll play a loudmouthed tree. It's not a character I've ever done before, so it will count as real improv.

As I make my arms into branches and stare at Leili, about to speak, it occurs to me that this is the first scene we've done together since I joined Improv Troupe. How is that possible? She's my best friend and we haven't even performed together in a single scene? "Hey, lady," I say, in my most gregarious tree voice.

"Oh, hello," Leili says. She looks right at me, and it's with none of the baggage of our past week. I don't know how she does that. She's just so in it, as if we're meeting for the first time. As if I'm actually a tree.

"I'm lonely," I say, the thought forming and leaving my mouth simultaneously. "I'm the loneliest tree in the forest."

"I've heard about you," Leili says, without missing a beat. "The other trees are worried about you."

It feels so nice to be talking to Leili again, even though it's in this supremely weird way. "If they're so worried," I say, "why don't they come talk to me directly?"

"Well, I guess maybe . . . It's because they're rooted to the ground."

Everyone laughs, and I pout and say, "Well, they could *try*," and I am, for the billionth time, in awe of my best friend. How does she come up with lines like that? I want to do what she does, and I can't!

Oh man.

The scene continues, and I try to respond in cogent ways, but the truth is, I can barely focus. Because I'm seeing it now:

I am jealous of Leili.

I've been jealous of her since the first day of rehearsal. Has some part of me been shutting her out the same way Evan shut me out? Because she's better at improv? Is it so hard to let her be the funny one sometimes?

Finally, the Harold ends and so does rehearsal. Leili speeds

275

toward her backpack as soon as Mr. Martinez dismisses us, but I'm ready for it. I jump off the stage into the aisle to block her. I kind of twist my ankle in the process, but I don't care.

"Lay, wait," I say, grimacing.

She doesn't.

"I'm so sorry, Leili."

She stops walking and looks at me. I'm glad because my last resort was to start blasting Enya from my phone.

People are all around us getting their stuff, but I don't even care. I want them to hear this. "I've been a shitty friend, and I'm so sorry."

Leili looks at our feet. "You haven't been a shi—",

"I totally have. Just let me say it."

"Okay."

"I'm not going to be a shitty friend anymore."

"Well, I was shitty to you on the phone, so—"

"Yeah, but I deserved it! You're so amazing, Leili. You're the most amazing. Honestly, I think, like . . ." It's hard to get the words out. "I'm jealous of you."

"What?" Leili looks confused, like this never would have occurred to her in a million years. "Why?"

"Uh . . . Because you're good at everything, including improv. And I think of myself as so funny, so I thought this would be the one area where I could, like . . . But you're way better than me at this, too."

"I'm not—"

"You *are*. You're smart and funny in every scene you do, and you're so good at listening, and I just think you're incredible. And I don't know why I don't tell you that more. I know that everything . . . like, Azadeh being with Roxanne, and me with what's-his-face, has been hard. And I'm sorry I haven't been better about being there for you."

Now people *are* kind of staring and listening, which feels more awkward than triumphant. "Thank you for that," Leili says. "But here, let's . . ." She gestures to the far wall of the auditorium.

"Yeah, good idea."

We walk over there. I sort of limp, actually.

"Is your ankle okay?" Leili asks.

"I dunno. But we're talking again, and not just in an improv scene, so yes, definitely. This feels really good."

"It does." Leili smiles.

"What's going on? Are you all right?"

Leili sighs. "Not yet. But I will be. It's really not your fault. It was mainly the stuff with Azadeh, how she's, you know, got a new person now. And how she's been around so much less. But also . . ."

"Also what?"

"I don't know." Leili looks at her Chuck Taylors again. Almost everyone has filed out of the auditorium. "You think I'm good at everything, but I'm not."

"What do you mean?"

"Like, people just gravitate to Azadeh in every room she's in. It's always been that way. We're almost identical, yet people never want to . . ."

"You are so gravitational," I say. "You totally are."

"You know what I mean, though. She's the fun one. So she attracts people, like Roxanne, and then you're so funny, and you attract Ev— I mean what's-his-face, and I'm like . . ." She starts to quietly cry. "The closest thing I have to anything like that is my pathetic crush." She side-glances at Mr. Martinez, who's trying to untangle the strap on his messenger bag. "And obviously I'm so happy for Oz, and I was for you, too, but what about me? Will I ever have that? So I threw myself even more into everything else I have going on. Because that's my thing. I'm the driven one. But, ohmigod, Winnie, it's so exhausting."

Now I'm crying too. "I'm really, really sorry. I want you to know: you are so fun and so pretty and so smart and so wonderful, and people are and will be attracted to you. And I won't ever drop the friendship ball again. Can I hug you?"

"Of course." We hug. It's such a relief.

"Can we keep hugging forever?"

"No. But I could probably go for a few more minutes."

"Deal!" I shout.

Our laughter fills the auditorium, which we now have all to ourselves.

30

I'm home from school, running the same drill I've run every day—scouring the cupboards for a snack to bring up to my room so I can avoid seeing Dad—when I hear him behind me.

"We're gonna have to talk sometime, Banana." He somehow managed to sneak up behind me, which is notable, as his aggressive cane maneuvering usually announces him half a minute before he appears.

"I know," I say, my back still to him as I snatch a bag of Goldfish.

"Please," he says. "This is killing me. Pun completely intended."

I turn around, careful not to display anything resembling a smile. He got my laughs for fifteen years. He doesn't get them now.

At the same time, though, I'm tired of avoiding him, of running from this. It's painful. He's still my dad. And in a few hours we'll have hit the one-week mark. So.

"Well, it really kills *me* that you cheated on Mom."

He winces. "I know."

"And then lied to me about it at dinner."

"I'm sorry, I was completely caught off guard. I didn't know what to say."

"The truth is generally a good response."

"I can't tell you how sorry I am, Winnie. I wish I could take it all back."

It might be the most sincere I've ever seen him, and it crushes me. I hate this, and I'm probably ready to forgive him, but I figure I'll make him squirm on the line a bit longer.

"Well, you can't," I say.

"Yeah," he says, staring at the kitchen counter, where his bottle of Riluzole is lined up next to his various supplements and vitamins. "I know."

"If quitting comedy was going to be so devastating for you that you had to have sex with some other woman, you shouldn't have quit." I suddenly understand why Mom wanted to push Dad back into comedy. It was her final attempt at getting him to open up, at trying to save him. And it didn't work. Nothing had. So she left.

"It was— That's not exactly right."

"Oh no? You guys had me, and you had to stop doing what you loved. I ruined your life."

"You did not r—" He wobbles back and forth, and my heart skips a beat. "Hey," he says once he's regained his balance, "can we sit down at the table? It's tiring for me to stand this long."

"Oh, of course," I say, the angry daughter act sloughing off me like skin off a snake as I walk my father over to the table and help him into one of the chairs.

"Thanks," he says. If I were him, I'd totally be using my condition to gain sympathy/forgiveness, but the heartbreaking part is, I don't think that's what he's doing.

I sit next to him, our chairs angled toward each other. Our knees are nearly touching.

"So?" I ask. "You were saying?" I'm trying to get my infuri-ated skin back on, but it doesn't quite fit anymore.

He smiles at me, like he's experiencing some inside joke I'm not privy to.

"What?"

"It's good to be talking to you," he says.

And then his smile wavers and crumples, and my father is crying in front of me.

"I miss you and Mom," he says, rubbing his thumb in one eye, index finger in the other.

It's a shocking sight. I think maybe he's doing a bit.

But it keeps going, and pretty soon my eyes are swelling too.

"I really . . . I screwed up back then," he says. "And again now. I don't do well with fear."

"It's okay, Dad." I wish Mom were here for this.

"I'm just— This is scary. What's happening."

I don't know what to do, but I want to do something, so I stand and give Dad a hug in his chair, like Mom did to me. I think part of me is still waiting for him to look up at me with a smile and say, "Gotcha, sucker." But it doesn't happen.

"I'm not going anywhere," I say. "And Mom isn't either." I don't know that for sure, but I say it anyway.

"Thanks, Win," Dad says, patting my arm before giving his face one final wipe with his whole hand. "I hate for you to see me like this."

I don't say anything as I sit back down in my chair, though I realize I *don't* hate it. I mean, I don't want to see Dad cry on, like, a daily basis or anything, but it feels . . . real.

"What happened with . . . ," Dad says. "It was such a mis-take. I won't ever forgive myself."

Not sure how to respond, so, again, I say nothing.

"And yes, it was a tough transition for me, but that doesn't mean it wasn't the right transition." Dad's looking at the table, gliding the pepper shaker around. "You have to know, Win, you absolutely didn't ruin my life. I don't care that I never had a comedy career. Cory tells me all the time how hard it still is, even with the success he's had. The constant uncertainty, going gig to gig, always auditioning, having to prove yourself over and over again. I hated that.

"It really hit home at that open mic. You know, after my ego took a day to recover. I realized, I *have* been able to spend my life doing the thing I love more than anything."

I try to form the words *What's that?* but I can't, so I ask with my eyes.

"Raising you."

I'm a mess again.

"Being your dad has brought me a billion times more joy than standing on a stage ever did." Dad finally finds the nerve to look up from the table, straight at me. "I really believe it's what I was meant to do. Which is why that thing in my past has always haunted me. I almost threw it all away."

"I'm glad Mom forgave you," I whisper.

"Oh man, me too. She's . . . She's the best person I know." Dad is crying again. "So, look, Win, if . . . I know I said we don't know how my ALS will manifest, but . . ."

"Please don't—"

"I know, but we have to start talking like this, Mom is right. And I definitely am getting worse. So . . . when I'm . . . less capable, you have to be there for Mom as much as you can."

I was not prepared for this, and I don't feel quite up to the task of handling it. I don't know how to talk to this vulnerable version of my father.

"Really, the thing that bums me out the most is the idea that . . . that I might not get to see the rest of what happens to you." Dad's making no attempt to hold back his tears, like rain on a windowpane. "You know that Aerosmith song? 'I don't want to close my eyes, I don't want to fall asleep'?" He sings the lyric. He really isn't a singer.

"I don't know, but you sound very bad," I say through sniffles.

"'And I don't want to miss a thi-ing.' That really is how I feel."

"You're not going anywhere yet, Dad," I say, though it sounds more like "Yernahgoonennewehyeh, Dah."

"I know, which is why you have to tell me about your life while I'm still here. Like, all the details, the stupid details. I've felt you holding back sometimes, and I don't like it."

"Well, I don't want to burden you with my . . . You're dealing with way more important stuff."

"Your life *is* the important stuff!" Dad gracelessly lowers his face to wipe it on the collar of his T-shirt. "It's the most important. Promise me you'll keep talking to me about every mundane thing, Win. Like if you're frustrated because your shirt gets a hole in it from the dryer. Or you lose one of your favorite socks. Or, I don't know . . . For some reason I can only think of clothing-related examples. You get what I'm saying. I want to hear it all. Even when I'm getting worse and the shit's hitting the fan. Especially then."

I wipe my nose. "I promise."

"Good." Dad takes a deep breath. "You are an amazing

person, Winifred. And a hilarious person. And a smart person. And whatever it is you go on to do, whether it's comedy or something else, you're going to kick serious ass. And if it is comedy, promise me you won't let the miserable, lonely guys get in your head. There's a lot of them out there. There's good ones, too, but . . . And if any comedian masturbates in front of you, you call the cops, you tell the papers, you shout it from the freaking rooftops—"

"Dad, Dad, okay, I get it," I say.

"Sorry. Went off the rails a bit there. My point is, you're a force, Winnie. Remember that."

I nod. "I will."

"Good."

I grab my phone off the kitchen counter and quickly text Mom, *Dad crying, misses you.*

The three dots pop up instantly, followed by *Leaving work now, see you in a bit.*

"I think Mom's coming home tonight," I say.

"What?" Dad looks like a five-year-old who's just been informed Santa's showing up early this year.

Dad insists we make dinner for Mom, but there's no time to go out for groceries, so we throw together this stir-fry with chicken and peppers and onions and some white rice and some brown rice. Dad is adorably nervous, and he keeps dropping things. I keep scolding him to be more careful, but in a funny way. I just don't want him to fall before Mom shows up.

When she finally does, it's less triumphant and more awkward and tentative. It's like we temporarily forgot how to speak

284

to each other in a natural way. But as the meal progresses, it gets better.

It's only later that evening, once I've said good night to them both, that I eavesdrop on them talking in the bedroom and know they're going to be all right. They're both crying, and Dad is saying he thinks Mom is right, that he should start going to the ALS support group, and he'll call first thing in the morning, and it's all so moving that I start crying too, out there in the hallway.

I didn't know my parents were capable of speaking to each other that way, but then I remember there's a lot I don't know about them.

31

"My hands are literally shaking," I say as my mascara under-shoots my eye by about an inch. "I'm so nervous."

"Leaving it like that could be a cool statement," Leili says.

We're side by side at the harshly lit mirrors in the girls' bath-room, frantically putting on makeup before the performance. Both of us were sporting almost none when we got here, but then we saw that Jess, Rashanda, Nicole, and Molly were all rocking smoky eye shadow, striking red lipstick, and other stuff I don't know the name of.

"Should we be wearing more makeup?" I asked Leili.

"I don't know," she said. "I have some in my bag if you want."

"None of the guys are wearing any—we shouldn't have to either."

"For sure," Leili said. "We can do whatever we want."

"I want people to see me up there and think I'm funny," I said, "not focus on how I look."

"Well. It can probably be both."

It was such a relief to hear her say that. "It can, right? Be-cause those other girls look so freaking badass. Like, I don't even see them as sexy, they just seem, like, powerful."

"I know! I was thinking that too!"

So that's why, while the rest of the group is in the band room hanging out after all our warm-up games, we ducked out to the bathroom.

Leili wipes the stray mark below my eye with a wet paper towel, then proceeds to do my mascara for me, working with a precision that surprises me until I remember she's Leili, innately skilled at everything.

We stare at ourselves, and even though Leili only had mascara and some light pink lip gloss, we look pretty cool. I almost don't recognize us.

But I'm still nervous. I can't put a finger on what's most responsible for my acute jitters. Probably that my parents are going to watch me perform for the first time since my bat mitzvah, and I want it to go better than it did then. Or maybe it's that the past two weeks have been the most intense of my life, leaving me with residual nerves, like aftershocks.

"FYI," Leili says, making one last adjustment to her purple hijab, "I was super-nervous for every one of our shows last year, but it mostly goes away once it starts."

"Mostly?"

Leili shrugs.

"That was mostly helpful," I say.

"You're mostly welcome."

Tim Stabisch greets us as we walk back into the band room. "Did you just put on makeup?"

"Shut up, Tim," Leili says, an uncharacteristic response for her, and way better than the one I was coming up with.

He nods and goes back to pushing both arms against the wall, his body stretched out behind him, as if he intends to get so physical during the performance he's worried he might pull a hamstring.

"Circle back up, everybody," Mr. Martinez says, and he

seems almost as nervous as me. He's wearing a blue suit and a black tie with white vertical letters that say *YES AND*. Pretty dorky. But endearing, too. I can tell Leili definitely thinks so.

As we all form a circle, I try to make eye contact with Evan across the way, as a peace offering or something, like if I flash a quick smile, it won't be awkward if we end up in a scene together. He either doesn't see me or pretends not to. And who am I kidding, we haven't talked since he dumped me in a text. No smile's gonna save us from that.

"The three most important things to remember tonight," Mr. Martinez says, "are to *listen* to each other, to play the scenes as honestly as you can, and . . . to *have fun*. We've obviously never performed a Harold for an audience before, but the good part is, there are no mistakes in improv. They're all opportunities for you to support each other as a group and spin what could have been a mistake into a brilliant scene. Because, look, Steph Curry may be one of the stars of the Warriors, but the real star is the way they work together as a team."

Man, he sure is obsessed with Steph Curry.

His words remind me, though: I'm not going to do any of my characters tonight. Evan's not my favorite person, but Leili is, and they're both right. I haven't really been improvising. But I want to. I'm going to come in with an open mind and listen and respond honestly and hilariously, thereby spinning an inspiring web of improvisational magic.

"And, uh," Mr. Martinez continues, "Principal Bettis is in the audience tonight. He told me he's never seen an improv show before, so you get to be his first. But no pressure!"

Oh geez, that's probably why Mr. Martinez is so nervous. I don't know if that adds to my nerves or calms them. Mr. Bettis is such an airhead, it's unlikely he'll understand what's happening.

"All right, team," Mr. Martinez says, looking at his phone for the fourth time in the past minute, "we still have at least five minutes till showtime, but let's walk down to the backstage area."

I'm the kind of nervous where my mind is whirling on its own axis while my body works on autopilot, so when I snap back into the present moment, I'm walking down the hall with Leili on one side and Fletcher on the other. I have no idea how long he's been there, but he seems incredibly calm.

"Oh, hey," I say.

"Hey," he says, staring forward, hands in his pockets. I realize what I interpreted as chillness is actually his version of butterflies.

"You're nervous," I say.

"Me? Nah."

"When in doubt, just think: *What would Turbo do?*"

Fletcher cracks up. "That's what I'm worried about. Gonna freeze up and spend ten minutes pretending to sweep."

We cross the threshold to backstage, our eyes adjusting to the darkness as the din of audience chatter hits us. My stomach somersaults. The curtain's already open, since it's not like we have a set or anything, just a few chairs and a couple of black cubes to sit on. I'm tempted to peek out at the crowd, though I still have the psychic scars from when Lacey Rengle scolded me before one of our middle school *Annie* performances.

"Don't look out there, Winnie," she hissed at me. "That's bad luck!"

"What is?" I said.

"Peeking out at the audience before the performance!" She shook her head and clucked her tongue, like I was a server who'd screwed up her order. "If we have a bad show, I know who to blame."

We did, in fact, have a bad show—the musical director had a migraine and inadvertently conducted the band a few beats slower than usual on every song ("Tomorrow" was a confusing, messy dirge)—and Lacey did, in fact, blame me.

But screw that. That rule probably doesn't apply to improv. I inch over to the curtain bunched up to the side and peek out.

The auditorium is about two-thirds full, which is more people than I was expecting. I gulp like a cartoon character.

Azadeh is the first familiar face I see. Roxanne is next to her, with Ramin and her parents on her other side. I wonder if they know yet. Roxanne seems to be telling them all a funny story, leaning forward in her seat and gesturing. Mr. and Dr. Kazemi aren't cracking up like Azadeh and Ramin are, but they're definitely into it.

Evan's mom is the next person I notice, sitting with a man who looks like a balder, older version of Evan and two of Evan's older siblings, a guy and a girl staring intently at something on the girl's phone. I wonder if they know anything about me.

And I wonder if Evan's mom knows her son and I aren't going out anymore. I wonder if she thinks it's my fault. I hope not. She was nice.

I continue scanning the crowd, and I'm mildly panicked to not see my parents anywhere. What if something happened? What if Dad fell?

Not a second after I have this thought, Mom appears in the auditorium doorway, stepping forward and looking around for the best place to sit. I see Dad leaning on his cane in the shadows outside the auditorium. They discuss something, and then Mom scans the crowd again, calculating, strategizing, and finally settling on some seats that aren't too far off the aisle, thereby reducing the number of people who will have to get up as my dad slowly shuffles past.

I wish they'd gotten here earlier.

Mom walks back into the shadows, and she and Dad emerge a moment later, his arm linked through hers as he navigates down the aisle with his cane, white streamers and all. It's a slow, choppy walk.

Undeniable proof that he's getting worse.

As they slowly move forward, I can tell how hard he's trying to seem like this is a normal situation, like *Oh, what, a cane? No big deal!* when actually, for many people here, this will be their first awareness that something is Wrong with Russ Friedman. It's his ALS coming-out moment. And he's having it because he wants to be here for me.

"Hey, quit peekin'," Leili says from behind me.

I jump.

"Sorry, sorry," she says. "We're about to get started, so." I must look fairly shaken up because she says, "You're gonna be great, Winner."

"You too," I say.

Before I can find Mr. Martinez, he's appeared onstage, starting his opening spiel, about this being the second year of Improv Troupe, about attempting something called long-form improv, about this being "a low-pressure experiment," seeing as long-form is very advanced and not something high schoolers usually take on, about being really proud of the great progress we've all made, and a lot of other things I can't take in because I'm still thinking about Dad. Hopefully he and Mom are seated by now.

Everyone around me in the wings starts moving onto the stage—I guess Mr. Martinez officially introduced us—as our troupe theme song plays (the majority voted, in spite of Leili's and my heated protestations, for "Uptown Funk") (she, Rashanda, Jess, and I voted for Enya's "Book of Days," which is actually an awesome song that gives me chills and would make hilarious entrance music, but oh well). Most of the group does these self-conscious, trying-to-be-ironic dance moves, like *Look at us, we're very funny people and this is gonna be so much fun!* Even Leili is doing this dorky bounce thing I've never seen her do in real life. And Evan does a cartwheel, for crying out loud. I try to focus on the task at hand. Gotta get my mind back in the game.

We form a line across the back of the stage, and I breathe easy seeing that Mom and Dad are both seated, seeming relaxed and happy.

Don't worry about being funny. Just listen and be honest. No recurring characters. Don't try so hard. Be present, and the funny will happen. Let it happen.

"Can I get a word from the audience?" Mr. Martinez asks.

Leili grasps my hand and gives it a quick squeeze. Here we go.

"Filibuster!" a pretentious-looking dude with glasses shouts.

Oh please, let Mr. Martinez choose a different word from someone else.

"Filibuster," he says. "Perfect."

I don't even remember what a filibuster is exactly. I know

it has to do with government, I remember Mrs. Howard going over that last year.

"Okay, here we go!"

We start our stream-of-consciousness word association based on the suggestion. My one contribution is "Cheese!" which came on the heels of Mahesh shouting "Senator!" and I'm immediately kicking myself because in what world is the word *cheese* at all connected to the word *senator*? It puts me so deep in my head that the first scene quickly comes and goes, followed by a second that features Leili and Shannon as senators, without me even attempting to jump in.

This is my problem. I'm so worried about failing that I can't enter a scene until I know I'm fully prepared. That changes *now*.

Well, maybe not *now,* as Fletcher and Jess both beat me to it. In their scene, Fletcher is a guy named Phil, and Jess is his girlfriend (which immediately makes me jealous) (which is its own can of worms I can't begin to think about now), who has just discovered that he's cheated on her. Thus, *Phil* is *busted*. *Filibuster.* Genius. I know improv isn't really about how well you connect your scene to the suggestion word, but I'm still impressed.

And, of course, I'm also reminded of my own father's indiscretions. Fun!

Fletcher and Jess's scene is the first of the night to get bona fide laughs. They end up in a slow-motion battle, with Fletcher bending backward *Matrix*-style as Jess throws a punch in his direction, and the crowd is so on board with what's happening, there are nonstop waves of laughter crashing our way. Principal Bettis is clapping and cheering like a child at the circus. I'm so happy to see Fletcher kill it, but I also wish I had already killed it myself, so I can get to that mostly-not-nervous place Leili alluded to.

Mahesh runs out in front of them, ending the scene, and we move on to the next part of the Harold, another group game. This one is a sound symphony. It starts with an improviser repeating some kind of sound or word, and one at a time, everyone else joins in, building up to a chaotic yet harmonious wall of sound. As I give a ghostly howl over and over again, I think about what's happened in the show so far, trying to get ideas for what I can do when I go out for a scene right after this.

I'm still deep in thought when Evan breaks out from the sound symphony, immediately transitioning into a new scene, with Mahesh and Tim jumping out to join him. Argh! Missed my chance *again*!

Leili gives my shoulder a gentle pat.

Evan, Mahesh, and Tim's scene is loud and nonsensical and involves them being Ghostbusters. (Not even the new awesome Ghostbusters. The old Ghostbusters.) Evan's pretending he just got slimed and shouting really loud, and it's all spectacularly stupid.

I can't believe he was my boyfriend.

I'm laser-focused now, ready to make my move. There's a big laugh, so I run across to end the scene. Evan gives me a hard stare—he thinks I've cut it off too quickly, which is probably true, but, frankly, I don't give a shit—and now it's my moment.

The stage is empty, and Rashanda walks out with me.

My brain is thinking of all these different characters I could do—Sandy the Dog! Sue the Super-Talkative Hygienist! Anthony the Pizza Guy!—but I shut it down.

We're not doing that, Brain, remember?

Instead, I stand onstage and stare at Rashanda, completely at sea, my mind a blank canvas. I think back to what the second scene of the show was, since this is technically supposed to connect to that. I wasn't paying attention as much as I should have been, but I know it was a smart scene with Leili and Shannon as senators. I guess maybe I'll be a senator too?

"Hello," I say, in my normal non-charactery voice.

"Hey," Rashanda says, walking past me like there's something interesting to look at on the wall. "You have anything to eat in here?"

It catches me off guard since I thought I was being a senator.

"What?" I ask. Maybe we're in my office.

"Do you have anything to eat?" Rashanda repeats.

"Oh, here?" I ask. I am adding approximately nothing to this scene. "We do have some things to eat. In that fridge over there." I point across the stage.

"Cool, thanks, Mom," Rashanda says.

Oh shoot, now I'm also her mom. Okay. I can roll with that.

Rashanda mimes opening a fridge and leaning in to examine its contents. I have no idea what to say next. If I'm not going to be a character, I at least want to say the right thing.

"You got weird food in here," Rashanda says.

"Like what?" I ask, regretting it as soon as it's out of my mouth. *Don't ask questions.* "Like apple juice!" I shout, trying to amend my own mistake.

"Yeah," Rashanda says. "There's *nothing but* apple juice in here. That's what's weird." We get our first laugh, thank god. Or, I should say, Rashanda gets it.

"Yeah, I guess you're right." And again, I can't think of a

single other thing to say. I don't know what's wrong with me. I turn my head to make it look like my character is thinking, but really I'm taking a peek at my parents. They look like they're concentrating hard, trying desperately to lock into the frequency of my subpar improv.

"So can I have some of this apple juice?" Rashanda asks.

"I don't think so," I say. *Yes, and,* Winnie, for god's sake! "I mean, have as much as you want."

"Cool," Rashanda says, then mimes pouring apple juice into a glass and taking a big gulp.

"I like being in the Senate," I say finally, trying to tie our scene back in with the earlier one, even though it makes no sense.

"We know, Mom," Rashanda says, getting another laugh.

Evan runs across the stage, ending our scene.

Total dick move.

We were barely getting started. And, yes, I know, maybe I edited his scene early too, but not *that* early. As he and Fletcher begin a new scene, I want to punch something. I did *nothing* in that scene. Like, almost literally nothing. Nothing funny, no smart choices, a total embarrassment.

In the scene now, Evan has called back to Fletcher's earlier scene by initiating that he was another guy named Phil, and they were both at a support group for guys named Phil who cheat on their girlfriends. It's a funny idea, I'll give him that.

Another group game goes by, and I get myself amped up for another chance in the ring, another opportunity to prove to my parents and myself that joining Improv Troupe is one of the best life decisions I've ever made.

Evan, Mahesh, and Tim jump out for another Ghostbusters

scene. Mahesh immediately establishes that many years have gone by, and now they're old men, so fighting ghosts is harder for them (bad back, achy joints, terrible eyesight). I glance out at the crowd, and Dad is one of the few people not laughing at the old men Ghostbusters. At first I'm very moved, as if he's taken a no-laugh stance against Evan on my behalf, but then I see his faraway contemplative look, and I think I understand.

He probably won't live to be an old man.

I look at my feet, blinking my tears away, pretending there's something in my eyes so I can quickly wipe them.

I'll never see what Dad is like as an old man.

"Your grandpa Russ was amazing," I'll have to tell my future kids. "He's the reason I'm so funny, and thereby the reason you're so funny too." (Because of course I'm going to have funny kids.) (Unless I marry someone unfunny, in which case we won't have kids at all because I'll have killed myself first.) (Sorry, I shouldn't joke about suicide. I was just trying to make a point.) "But here, why don't you ask your funny grandma Dana about him?"

Ohmigod, is Mom going to marry someone else?

WHY HAVE I NOT THOUGHT ABOUT ANY OF THIS? AND WHY AM I THINKING ABOUT IT *NOW*?

I realize how skilled my brain has been at hiding details I don't want to acknowledge. The weight of everything clamps down on my chest, steals my breath.

I'm literally pulled out of these thoughts as someone tugs at my arm and drags me onto the stage. It's Rashanda, returning us to the immensely unsatisfying scene from earlier. I hadn't even realized Evan, Tim, and Mahesh's scene had ended.

"I drank all your apple juice," Rashanda says.

"All of it?" I ask. *Be funny, Winnie. Listen and be funny.*

"I think so," Rashanda says. "Unless you've got a secret stash I don't know about." A nice laugh from the audience.

"But, sweetie, I was saving all that apple juice. For a party."

"What party, Mom?"

And again, my slow-moving brain can't come up with anything. Well, that's not entirely true. It's more like my brain can't *decide* on anything. I'm trying to think three steps, four steps ahead to what would make the perfect sense for this scene. A birthday party? A retirement party? What other kinds of parties *are* there?

"I hope the Democratic Party," Rashanda says, and she gets a hearty approving laugh. She connected it back to my comment about the Senate from the last scene. So smart.

"Yes," I say. "It's apple juice for the Democrats. Because they are the best."

Silence from the audience. Which I get, seeing as I didn't really make a joke. Rashanda is about to speak, but I cut her off in an effort to redeem myself. "I'm excited for the big election," I say, trying to introduce something new to spice up the scene a bit.

"Oh yeah," Rashanda says, rolling with it, "I think we can win. Especially if we run on our Apple Juice for Everyone platform." All of Rashanda's apple juice material is killing, yet rather than building on that, I go with an idea I was thinking of before she mentioned the apple juice, as if it were too late for me to course-correct.

"I've been knocking on a lot of doors," I say. "For the campaign."

"I hope you brought apple juice." Rashanda crosses her

arms and nods her head as she says it. Another big laugh. "I mean, that would definitely persuade *me* to vote for whoever."

"More like apple-juice-ever," I say, trying to get in on the apple juice humor.

The audience is silent. That was very bad.

Not even a pun, really.

Rashanda, meanwhile, rolls her eyes, which gets a real laugh.

"Hey!" I shout, fueled by genuine rage at myself. "Don't ever drink my apple juice again, okay? Just . . . don't."

Rashanda raises her eyebrows, looking a little shocked, as perhaps I've come off a little more intense than I'd intended.

The audience seems a little shocked too.

At this point, I'm ready to surrender, hoping desperately that Leili or someone will edit the scene and put me out of my misery.

Before that happens, though, Evan jumps onto the stage, not to end our scene, but to join it. "Hey, I heard a horrible screeching, shouting sound!" he says, yet again in Ghostbuster pose, pretending to hold his imaginary ghost gun, or whatever it is. "Is there an unfunny ghost here?"

It takes me a moment to realize he's referring to me, at which point I become too enraged to speak.

"Hell no," Rashanda says, immediately getting what Evan's doing and nobly ditching *Yes, and* and all other rules of improv to defend me.

"Are you sure?" Evan says, now straight-up pointing at me. "Right over there. I see a screechy, boring ghost."

"Knock knock knock," Fletcher says, surprising all three of us onstage as he knocks on an invisible door.

"Uh . . . who is it?" Rashanda asks.

"Police." Fletcher uses a gruff, low voice I've never heard from him before.

"Okay, be right there." Rashanda walks toward the door, and at this point, I'm watching like an audience member, like *What's gonna happen?* As she lets Fletcher in, Leili comes forward from the back and walks through the imaginary threshold with him.

Fletcher doesn't miss a beat. "I'm Officer Jones," he says, "and this is Officer Bones." He gestures to Leili, who nods. "We've been searching for a Ghostbuster impersonator."

"Yeah," Leili says. "He's been going around with a vacuum cleaner, claiming he's a Ghostbuster."

The improv police, here to save me. My heart.

Evan stares at them, like *You can't do this,* but Leili and Fletcher are unfazed.

"There he is!" Leili says.

"Yup, that's him, all right," Fletcher says.

I'm not really sure what the audience is making of all this, but I am freaking loving it.

And I love it even more when Jess joins the scene. "I'm sorry," she says as she walks in, "I couldn't help overhearing what you were saying, and I wanted to confirm that yes, that man is a fraud." She points at Evan, and I can tell she's enjoying this as much as I am. "He's not even qualified to be in the same room with ghosts, let alone bust them."

"I'm not a fraud," Evan says. "I'm a real Ghostbuster!"

"Of course you are," Leili says in a very soothing voice. "Of course you are."

I feel a little bad that Evan's getting ganged up on like this, but not *that* bad. So it's disappointing when Dan Blern runs across the stage to end the scene, though I understand it's probably for the best.

I fall back into line, and even though my performance thus far has been a disaster, I feel okay. Good, even. As the next scene returns to the support group for guys named Phil who have cheated on their girlfriends, I have a huge smile on my face.

I watch as, one by one, each of my improv teammates walks onstage as a guy named Phil, and I'm still smiling as I become an unfaithful Phil myself and enter the scene to join them.

32

"Hell yeah! We killed it," Rashanda says as we leave the stage to robust applause.

"What what!" Mahesh says.

Mr. Martinez is waiting in the wings to give each of us a high five as we pass through the stage door into the hallway.

"Nice work, Winnie," he says, though I feel like it's implicitly understood that I beefed it.

"Thanks, Mr. Martinez," I say. "That was fun."

"It was, right? Awesome job, Leili!" She's behind me. It's obvious from the contrast in tone and word choice that I am one billion percent correct about my beefing it, but I'm actually okay with that. And I'm happy for Leili, who will be able to ride this compliment from her illicit crush for at least the rest of the month.

"You really were great, Leili," I say once we're heading to the band room to get our things. "I want to be you when I grow up."

"That's stupid," Leili says as she puts an arm around me. "You're great."

"Maybe, but my improv wasn't. That was so terrible."

Leili laughs. Because she knows I'm right.

"I tried to not do all my usual bits," I say, "and I tried to listen, but then . . . I don't know. Maybe improv isn't my thing. Just like stand-up wasn't my thing."

"Ugh!" She literally pronounces the word *ugh*. "Don't you hear how ridiculous you sound? You've tried each of those things exactly once! Your bat mitzvah was *one set*. Under very weird and specific circumstances! No one's good after doing something once!"

"Yeah, but—"

"You mean *Yes, and*?"

"Touché." Evan, Mahesh, and Tim are up ahead of us, howling as they literally jump off the walls like skateboarders without skateboards. I scan the group for Fletcher, but I don't see him. "Seriously, though, I just feel like—"

"Winner, I love you, *and* I'm right about this. There will be lots of bad shows. Because all this stuff takes practice. Steph Curry, remember?"

Is it possible I've spent all this time making a huge deal of my bat mitzvah set for no reason? I'm embarrassed as I remember what Mom told Dad after the open mic show. *The first set was always going to suck. It just was.* And I agreed with her! So how come I haven't applied that same logic to myself?

"Okay," I say. "You may be right."

"I definitely am."

Only Leili can make declaring herself right seem endearing. "Fine," I say. "I'm willing to keep sucking it up at improv. But it would be— I mean *AND* it would be cool if our school had a sketch comedy group. I feel like I could do better if I know what's happening before it happens."

"Well, why don't you start one?" Leili says, like it's no big deal.

I stare at her, the words sounding impossible and foreign.

"People do that all the time. All you need is a faculty super-visor."

"Nah," I say. "I would have no idea how to go about—"

"Didn't you say Mrs. Costa is, like, begging you to join Speech and Debate? Maybe she'd supervise for you."

"Yeah, but I didn't even go to Speech and Debate."

"So what? If you start a sketch group, I'll join."

This is vintage Leili, getting a ball rolling before I've even acknowledged the existence of the ball. I see how it's a good idea, but it's also overwhelming, and I have no business creating a sketch comedy group.

"Or if you think you can't handle it, don't do it," she says. "It was just a suggestion."

Can't handle it? Of course I— Damn Leili. I see what she's doing.

"Okay, fine," I say, "maybe I'll start a sketch comedy group. If you'll be in it too. Which might be impossible because you're already in so many—"

"Great! I'll make it work."

"Wait, did you just say you're starting a sketch group?" Rashanda says, poking her head in between us. "I want in."

"Yeah, me too," Jess says, appearing to my right.

"And me," Molly says. "Totally."

"Maybe it should be an all-female group," Leili says.

"Is that allowed?" I ask.

"Shit yes," Rashanda says as we walk into the band room, which is crackling with postshow energy. "And if it's not, we'll just intimidate any guys who show up so they won't want to come back."

"Wow, okay," I say. "We're doing it, then. Our own sketch group."

"Wait, what?" Evan says from across the room, holding a huge mallet he'd just been using to bang on a bass drum someone left out. "Who's starting a sketch group?"

"Me," I say. My voice shakes a little. "It's gonna be an all-female sketch comedy group."

"Ha," Evan says. "Good luck with that."

"You don't have to be jealous."

"I'm not. Why would I want to be in a group that's not funny?" Tim and Mahesh laugh.

"Yo," Rashanda says, getting fired up.

"You have no idea what funny is," Jess says.

"Hold up," I tell them, throwing a hand in the air. "I got this." I stride across the room toward Evan. Mahesh and Tim stop laughing, taking a few steps back. The whole room is suddenly quiet.

Evan stands tall, still holding the mallet, but I know that look in his eyes. He's feeling insecure.

"You don't have to be threatened by me," I say.

Evan scoffs. "I'm not. Especially after that performance today."

"Yeah, it's true. I beefed it. Big-time. But I'm still funny. And I know you know that."

He opens his mouth, but I interrupt before he can say something else stupid. "It doesn't even matter. There's room in the world for both of us to be hilarious," I say. "You seemed to know that when you wanted to date me. And when you wanted to date Jess. But once we got *too* funny or too cool or too whatever, you forgot, I guess."

Evan looks confused, maybe on the verge of tears. "I don't even know what you're talking about."

"I think maybe you do." I pick up my backpack and walk out of the room before anyone can say another word.

It is incredibly badass.

I stop about ten steps outside the door because I don't want Leili to think I was ditching her. The band room is vibrating with energy again, a cacophony of voices as people try to understand what exactly they just witnessed.

"Well, that was interesting," Leili says a minute later, as she walks out of the room toward me.

"Was I too intense?"

"What?"

"To Evan."

"Oh. Considering he's been a total jerk to you, probably not. But I think you made him cry a little."

"Yeesh," I say. "I'll apologize later."

"I think Tim Stabisch just asked me out," Leili says.

"Wait, what?"

"Yeah, just now." Leili's speaking slowly, like she doesn't fully believe it happened. "He walked over to me after you left and said he's sorry Evan was such a dick to you and would I maybe want to go out with him sometime. He said I'm obviously the hotter twin."

"Holy bajoly! That's . . . Are you gonna do it?"

"Uh, absolutely not," Leili says. "Tim's a doofus. But it's nice to be crushed on." She smiles.

"Toldja you were gravitational."

In the lobby, there's a sea of family and friends, of bouquets and balloons. Azadeh bounds into our path.

"Yeah!" she says, wrapping up Leili and me in a hug. "That was so good!"

"Thanks, Oz," I say.

"You really made all that up on the spot?" Azadeh asks. "That was ridiculous!"

I'm tempted to call out some of my bad scenes—that if those had been written ahead of time, it was some truly terrible writing—but I resist the urge.

"Yup, that's why it's called improv," Leili says with a healthy layer of sarcasm.

"Oh, shut up, Lay," Azadeh says, getting her in a solo hug and squeezing tight before kissing her on the cheek. "I'm trying to compliment you, sister."

"Good show," Roxanne says, appearing from behind Azadeh, followed by Ramin and the Kazemis, who wrap Leili in a hug. "That was dope."

"Thanks," I say. I wonder if she's nervous being around Azadeh's parents. Probably not. She's so cool. But I'm trying to remember that everybody's always dealing with something, usually with a lot of somethings we have no idea about. Even the most together-seeming people are just figuring it out as they go.

I notice my parents off to the side near the trophy case. I'm sure Dad doesn't want to be positioned with his cane in the center of everyone.

I gallop over to them.

"Yay!" they both shout.

"These are for you," Dad says, gesturing to a bunch of fruit cut into flower shapes that Mom is holding. "It's a chocolate banana bouquet."

I'm moved, and it catches me off guard. "Thanks, Mom and Dad." I've never been moved by fruit before.

"That was a lot of fun," Mom says.

"It really was," Dad says.

I know they know I sucked and are being polite parents.

"We were thinking we could go get some ice cream or something," Mom says.

I feel an arm wrap around me. "Yo yo," Rashanda says. "These your parents?"

"Yeah," I say. I see her eyes flick to Dad's cane, but only for an instant. "Mom and Dad, this is Rashanda."

"You did an awesome job," Mom says.

"Yeah, great show," Dad says.

"Thanks, Friedmans," Rashanda says. "You have a badass daughter. There's talk of hitting up IHOP. Want to come with me and Jess? I'm driving."

A warm feeling floods my insides. I have new friends.

But then I look at Mom and Dad. Of course they'd be fine with me going to IHOP, but the limited nature of opportunities like this one, of getting ice cream with Mom and Dad, of being a complete family, crashes down on me.

"Oh, thanks," I say. "I'm actually going out with my parents."

"Honey, you don't have to—" Mom says.

"Yeah, it's fine if—" Dad says.

"No, no, I want to," I say.

"Cool cool." Rashanda gets it. "In that case, see you at school, Win. Nice to meet you, Mr. and Mrs. Friedman."

"You too," Dad says.

"Eat some pancakes in my honor," I say as Rashanda walks away into the crowd.

"Nah," she shouts without turning around, "I'm really hungry, so I gotta eat 'em in my own honor!"

"I respect that," I shout.

"Didn't you wear a jacket tonight?" Mom asks.

I look down and immediately realize that, in my badass haste, I left my new awesome denim jacket lying on a folding chair in the band room.

"D'oh! Lemme run and grab it. I'll meet you outside."

I skirt the edges of the already thinning lobby mob and head down the hallway toward the band room. Everyone should be out by now, but I'm remaining cautious in case Evan is for some reason still in there.

My whole body unclenches as I step into the empty room. I'll obviously have to see Evan again soon, but I'm glad it's not right now. As I bound up the risers and grab my jacket, I realize the room isn't as vacant as I thought.

Fletcher is hunched over in a folding chair on the top level, so what looked from the door like a coat is actually a human being. He's got earbuds in, his elbows balanced on his thighs, super-focused. He has no idea there's another person in the room.

For a moment, I consider scaring him by shouting "Boo!" but then I think better of it. I've moved on to more sophisticated comedic fare. I lean my body in front of his face and wave.

It totally scares the shit out of him anyway, his shoulders jolting up to his ears.

"Hi, sorry!" I say.

"No, no, it's all good," he says, pausing whatever's in his ears. "Just glad you didn't say 'Boo.'"

Man, my instincts are spot-on. "You're just hanging out back here?"

"Yeah. I mean, my mom and stepdad are waiting out in the lobby, but crowds trip me out. Thought I'd give it a minute."

"What are you listening to?"

Fletcher gets a little sheepish. "Actually? Tonight's show."

"Seriously?"

"Figured if I could listen back and hear what worked and what didn't, it might make me better. Nerd alert."

He's misreading the look on my face because I don't think he's a nerd *at all*. I'm kicking myself because the idea of doing that didn't even *occur* to me.

"What? No! Lots of big comics do that. I feel like an idiot that I didn't think to."

"Oh well, I can send you this file if you want."

I stare at Fletcher, at his sincere eyes, his strong chin, his kind offer to give me a recording of the show, and I desperately want to kiss him.

"Or not," he says, trying to read my likely inscrutable expression. I don't know how to get a kiss going. Do I just lean in? Should I ask first? I think he likes me, but maybe he's just a nice guy, and if I kiss him, he'll have to gently extricate himself and explain he's never liked me like that. That would be worse than the worst. But my spot-on instincts are saying I should kiss Fletcher Handy!

So I should probably ask. Consent works both ways.

"You all right?" Fletcher asks. "It's really not a big deal for me to send it to—"

"Can I . . ." I can't do it. "Ask you something?"

"Sure." Fletcher's eyebrows rise slightly in this adorable way, and I don't know what to say next. Suddenly everything he's doing, every slight gesture, every half-formed utterance, is adorable.

"Um . . . do you think they're going to make *Breakin' 3*?"

Dammit, Winnie!

Fletcher's eyebrows drop back down, a small smirk on his face. "Uh, I'd say that's highly unlikely."

"Yeah."

"Though I'd be lying if I said I didn't hopefully google it from time to time."

We laugh, and then the room is silent again. I stare at a lonely tuba on its side under the whiteboard. I think I missed my moment.

"I *would* like for you to send me that file," I say. "That was really nice of you to offer."

"Oh, cool," Fletcher says, and his eyes light up in this irresistible way that makes him look like a boy and a man at the same time, and that's it for me, I'm like a rubber band snapping, the laws of physics dictating there's nowhere for me to go but forward.

But as I go in for the kiss, Fletcher leans down to push buttons that will transmit the audio recording through the air from his phone to mine, and I end up kissing the top of his head.

"Oh," Fletcher says, flinching back.

"I tripped, I tripped," I say, in some kind of shock, even though his hair felt nice on my lips and smelled like honey. "Sorry."

"No, it's cool, it's cool," Fletcher says, but he seems like he might be in shock too, frozen in place with his phone in the air. My heart is running circles in my chest, shrieking in embarrassment.

"Anyway, thanks for sending that," I say, racing through my words so I can end this interaction and have my parents whisk me away from all the cringing. Fletcher starts to get up because

311

I'm sure he feels the same. "I really do appreciate it, and next time I'll—"

Fletcher's lips are on mine.

We are kissing.

It takes me a full five seconds for my body to stop flipping out and catch up to the reality of what's happening.

And the reality of what's happening is really great.

"I told you it's cool," Fletcher says as we pull apart.

"I didn't realize you knew I was, you know, trying to kiss you."

"Your lips were on my head."

I smile and look away, my face flaming up. "Yeah. That's true."

"I'm glad you did," Fletcher says, one side of his mouth grinning at me, and I'm about to rubber-band all over again when Mr. Martinez walks into the band room. Fletcher and I separate as if vacuum cleaners on either side of us had turned on.

"Oh, hey, guys," Mr. Martinez says, the hint of a smile in his voice but otherwise no recognition that he just caught us about to make out. Very kind man. "About to shut this room down, so . . ."

"No prob," Fletcher says.

"I just came in to get my jacket," I say, awkwardly thrusting it into the air.

Mr. Martinez laughs. "Super. And again, great show tonight. Everyone seemed to really love it. Including Principal Bettis. Who didn't understand that it was improvised until I just told him."

Fletcher and I laugh as we head to the door.

"Have a good night," Mr. Martinez says.

"You too," I say.

Neither of us says much as we walk down the hall back to the lobby. It feels like we might be dreaming.

"So, maybe I'll, like, text you this weekend," Fletcher says finally, right before we reemerge into real life. "Or call you."

"Yeah, that, or maybe my dad and I will come surprise you at Stop & Shop."

"Oh, cool."

"I'm kidding, you should definitely call me."

"Aight, good. I will."

"Good."

"Just know that if you get more laughs than me, I'll have to end this."

"Too soon," I say as we round the corner and other people come back into view.

33

"Hey, look, everybody," Dad says. "It's geriatric Spider-Man!"

Having placed his cane next to me on the backseat, he's leaning on the car and, as if it's a sideways climbing wall, making his way to the driver's seat. Dr. Yu says he'll probably have to stop driving sometime within the next six months, as his feet and hands continue to get stiffer, but for now he's fine.

"So, where to?" Dad asks once we pull out of the school parking lot.

"Winnie's choice," Mom says.

"Let's do Indigo," I say. It's a no-brainer. We've been going to the Indigo Diner as long as I can remember. Their ice cream sundaes are kind of boring (they only have three flavors) (guess which ones) (you're right), but the ambience more than makes up for it.

"Indigo it is," Dad says.

I haven't mentioned anything to my parents about what happened with Fletcher. What am I gonna say? *Mom and Dad, I just made out with Fletcher, and it was awesome!* I like that it's my little secret, to delicately cup in my hands and then store away to look at again later.

I mean, it's not a total secret. Obviously, I texted Leili and

314

Azadeh about it on the way to the parking lot. By the time I'd come up for air, so to speak, they'd already left for IHOP.

Kissed Fletcher, I wrote. *It was very great.*

OMG WHAT, Leili wrote, followed by the shocked-face emoji.

YAY! Azadeh wrote. *Which one is Fletcher?*

The Indigo Diner is a couple of towns away, so it's a bit of a drive. I'm glad. For the first few minutes after we leave, we're silent, lost in our own thoughts, I guess. This view, staring at the backs of my parents' heads, always whisks me right back to being a kid.

At some point, maybe a year from now, maybe four, I'll be the one sitting in the front seat for family trips.

"So I'm thinking we should go to Hawaii," Dad says.

"What?" Mom and I think he's joking. He's not generally much of a planner.

"I'm serious," he says. "During Winnie's holiday break."

"Uh . . . yes, please," Mom says, looking stunned.

"Same," I say, also stunned.

"Awesome," Dad says.

We all know the subtext here, that we only have so much time together to do things like this. Thankfully, it stays subtext. We're silent again.

"So, Win," Mom says after a few minutes, "I promise I'm not bringing this up to make you feel bad, but . . . what exactly was going on for you during some of those scenes?"

"Mom!" I can't believe she's bringing up the show.

"No, no, I'm only asking because I know how funny and sharp you are, and that Winnie . . . was not up there." Something about the way she says it—maybe the compliment part up top—softens me and makes me less annoyed. Part of me also appreciates the honesty. "Look, I used to be a performer too. I know how hard it can be to bring what's in your head onto the stage, in front of tons of people."

"And god knows *I* know," Dad says.

Mom and I laugh.

"I know, I know," I say. "I got in my head, I guess. At other rehearsals, I was always doing characters I'd already developed with Dad. Like, you know, Sandy the Dog, or Anthony from the pizza place—"

"Aw, I love your Anthony impression," Dad says. "You should have done that in the show."

"Well, I know, I would have, but Evan said that didn't really count as improv."

"Ew," Mom says.

"I hated how he totally sold you out during the show," Dad says. "I wanted to flick him in the ear."

"Me too!" Mom says.

"Thanks, guys," I say, genuinely touched.

"I get why he's no longer your boyfriend," Mom says. "And anyway, why wouldn't doing characters count?"

"Just 'cause, like, they were bits I'd planned in advance," I say. "Leili sorta agreed with that, too."

"Bullshit," Dad says, in that way where you make it sound like you're coughing. I love it when Mom and Dad curse in front of me.

"No offense, Russ, but you're not the world's foremost improv expert . . ."

"I know some things," Dad says.

"Right, sure you do," Mom says. "So, Win, instead of doing a character, you decided to do . . . nothing?"

She's not trying to be funny, but the description is so accurate and so ridiculous, we both start laughing.

"Oh god, I don't know." My face is buried in my hands. "Is that what it seemed like?"

"'Hello,'" Mom says through her laughter, imitating my dull-as-grass delivery. "'Don't drink my apple juice. Okay, never mind, you can.' I felt like I was watching your brain melt."

"I was trying to do good improv!" I say, loving her impression of me and the unbelievable relief of laughing at myself.

"Remember when . . . ," Dad says, stopping midsentence to silently laugh, maybe my favorite quality of his. "Remember when—I'm sorry—when you shouted intensely at her about the apple juice?"

Mom really loses it now. "You seemed so angry . . . There was a grandmother a few seats down from me who flinched so hard after you said it. You really scared her." Mom imitates the grandmother, flailing her hands. "'Yaaggh!'"

"Oh no!" It's a hilarious impression. Mom is so funny.

"Or remember when you randomly declared that you loved being in the Senate?" Dad asks.

"I wanted to call back to the last scene!" I shout, pretending to be angry when really this is the happiest I've felt in a long time.

"We don't mean to gang up on you, Winnie," Dad says, still riding the tail end of the laugh rush. "Thanks for being a good sport about it."

"Don't worry," Mom says, "there's enough to go around for everyone, Mic-Drop Boy."

"Oh no no no, this is Winnie's night," Dad says, but he's smiling. "Let's not make this about me."

"No, please, let's." I'm literally bouncing in my seat. "I shouldn't suffer alone."

"And anyway," Dad says, "I can't help it if I dropped the mic. Someone shouted 'Woo!' and startled me."

"*Someone?*" I ask. "That was me!"

"What?" Dad says, staring into the rearview, mouth agape in shock. "Are you serious?"

"Who did you think was *Woo!*ing you?" Mom asks, the giggles bubbling up all over again. "Some random fan?"

"I mean, maybe, yeah!"

"Like your fans have come out of hibernation after fifteen years to catch your act at a coffeehouse open mic night?"

"Possibly!"

We're all cracking up so hard.

"Some of those jokes, Russ," Mom says. "What was that one about flirting with Siri?"

"Oh, I don't know! I was rusty, okay?"

"RUSS-ty," I say, and Mom and I are completely gone.

"That's legitimately awful," Dad says.

"How have we never made that pun before?"

"Speak for yourself," Mom says. "I used to call your dad that all the time before you were born. But then he forced me to stop."

"Because it's a stupid name pun, and I don't like it."

"Siri thinks it's cute, though," Mom says, wiping away laugh tears.

"Oh god, was my Siri material really that bad? You should have told me."

"I think the audience did, sweetheart."

"It really was a horrendous set," Dad says, getting the words out between silent laughs.

A loud horn honks out of nowhere.

"Oh shit!" Dad says as he swerves our car to the right.

"You were swerving into the other lane, Russ!" Mom says, stone-cold serious. "You can't laugh and drive. How many times do I have to tell you that? Don't. Laugh. And. Drive."

There's a brief sober silence, then we all bust out laughing again.

"So sorry, Officer," Dad says, "you're absolutely right. I'm so ashamed." He for real pulls the car to the side of the road, maybe as part of the bit and maybe because he's truly shaken up by the near accident we just had.

"Oh, okay, wow, you're actually pulling over," Mom says.

"Just don't tell my family, Officer. They'd never let me live it down," Dad says.

"Of course," Mom says. "I'll probably let you go with a warning. That is, as long as you don't have any gardening weeds in the car."

Dad looks at Mom, confused.

"That's another reference to your bad stand-up comedy," she says.

"Hey, come on, that was funny. *Weeds* and *weed,* they sound alike."

"Yeah, we got it, Dad," I say from the backseat.

"I AM A FUNNY PERSON!" Dad shouts in his husky way. "Nipples on mannequins are funny!"

"Nope," Mom says.

"Definitely not," I agree, and by this point, we're all in hysterics again, losing it on the side of Route 34 as car after car whizzes by us.

I know our future isn't pretty. I can barely think about it without wanting to sob.

But right now, I don't have to.

Right now, we are a family of three, sitting in a parked car on the side of the road, making fun of my father's terrible attempt at stand-up comedy. And my terrible attempt at improv.

And we are hilarious.

We laugh for a very long time.

Acknowledgments

This book is so close to my heart that I'm tempted to individually thank everyone I've ever known. But that's not realistic. So, a general thank-you to everyone I've ever known, and some more specific gratitude to:

Kathy Valentino, who works with the Joan Dancy & PALS Foundation in New Jersey, which is dedicated to improving the lives of ALS patients and their families. Kathy's incredibly thoughtful and specific read helped make the book truer and better. I'm also grateful to everyone who was at Kathy's ALS support group the night I visited; those with ALS, their families, and their caregivers were all gracious, vulnerable, funny, and inspiring. ALS is a brutal disease for which there's still no cure, and if you'd like to learn more or donate, please visit Joan Dancy & PALS (joandancyandpals.org) or the ALS Association (alsa.org).

The late Susan Spencer-Wendel, whose huge-hearted memoir, *Until I Say Good-Bye,* was helpful and beautiful and hilarious, and also wrecked me.

Nancy Siscoe, my brilliant editor, who is directly responsible for this book existing, as she generously rejected it in its previous, very different form (definitely didn't seem generous at the time) and helped me find a better way to tell that story.

Also, thanks to Marisa DiNovis, Ray Shappell (for the beautiful, eye-catching cover), Artie Bennett, Barbara Marcus, and the entire Random House family.

Superb agent Mollie Glick and everyone else at CAA, including Julie Flanagan and Dana Spector.

My insightful, honest, and encouraging first readers: Katie Schorr, Zack Wagman, Ray Muñoz, Mariel Hull, Dustin Rubin, Kathryn Holmes, Greg Andree, Jillian Tucker, Leah Pearlman, Sarvenaz Tash, Leah Henoch, and Natasha Razi. Added thanks to Kathryn and Greg for being fantastic writing buddies (one in person, one online) and for talking with me about this book. A lot.

All my other author peeps. You know who you are.

The librarians, booksellers, teachers, festival organizers, bloggers, and READERS who make the YA world such a warm and wonderful place to be. Extra-special shout-out to the fearless, delightful students who did improv during one of my school visits, further inspiring this book.

French Woods, where I first experienced the magic of improv theater games.

Mike O'Keefe and Pete Capella, who welcomed me into ImprovJam!—a short-form improv comedy group that performed at the now-defunct Internet Café in Red Bank, New Jersey—when I was a senior in high school and were, in effect, my Mr. Martinezes. Much love also to Andy, Carl, Cate, Dimitry, Lauren, Rich, Kevyn, Lisa, Keith, Sadecki, Bobby, Alice, Andrew, Bart, Gary, Francis, Darren, and anyone else whose name I accidentally left out.

The cast of *The NYC*, the long-form improv teen drama that I started with Pete Capella in a gross dive bar basement in

2005. Hey, Samara, Alan, Dave, Jenny, Ray, Krystal, Phil, Ali, Andy, and Katie! That was fun.

The Rubins, Schorrs, Smiths, and Hulls, all of whom I feel very lucky to call family.

Minna Rubin, whose hilarity and heart and brusqueness I tried to memorialize in Grandma Mitzie. Miss you, Grandma.

Sly and Roger Rubin, the funniest little dudes around.

Jeff and Halice Rubin, my wonderful parents. In 2001, my dad was diagnosed with ALS. It's been a long, up-and-down journey for him since then, but he was ultimately diagnosed with a subset of ALS called PLS (primary lateral sclerosis), which is slower-progressing. Russ and Dana's story is not the story of my parents, but it's still a vulnerable thing to have your son write a book even sort of inspired by something you went through, so I'm thankful in advance for that. And I'm also appreciative that they gamely agreed to be interviewed about their memories of when my dad was first diagnosed. Love you, Mom and Dad.

And Katie Schorr, my favorite person to laugh and cry with, who I was in a pretend relationship with in an improv show before we ever started our real relationship in life. (A relationship we at first hid from the rest of the cast. Just like Monica and Chandler on *Friends*!) She makes all my books better, but especially this one, seeing as I was only able to write Winnie Friedman because of how well I know Katie Schorr. She is funny, wise, fearless, and supportive, and I am very grateful.

TOMORROW IS THE DAY
I'M GOING TO DIE. I DON'T MEAN
TO BE DRAMATIC ABOUT IT.

DENTON LITTLE'S DEATHDATE

"Highly original,
fantastically entertaining,
and laugh-out-loud funny."
—Jennifer E. Smith, author of
*The Statistical Probability
of Love at First Sight*

LANCE RUBIN

"Wildly funny, brilliantly
weird, and achingly
heartfelt."

—BECKY ALBERTALLI,
New York Times bestselling
author of *Simon vs.
the Homo Sapiens Agenda*

I don't think this is my bed.

It's hard to know for sure, as my head is in excruciating pain, but there's something about this bed that doesn't feel like me. It's got extra fluff.

This is disappointing. I had a very clear vision for how the day of my funeral would start, and it involved waking up in my own bed. I would yawn and stretch like a well-rested comic strip character as the smell of bacon wafted up from downstairs. *There's so much bacon down here!* my stepmom would shout.

But instead, I'm swiping at my skull to make sure there aren't any knives sticking out of it as I listen to the voice of some lady who's not my stepmom talking about something that is not bacon. "Nothing yet," she says, from out in the hallway. "Yes, trust me, I know this is important."

Ow. Something's lumped up under my back. Possibly

my old faithful companion, Blue Bronto. Maybe this *is* my bed after all!

Nope.

It's a pink koala.

I have never owned a pink koala.

"Well, I'm doing everything I can," the woman in the hallway says.

Of course. It's Paolo's mom. I'm in Paolo's house.

I make a halfhearted attempt at sitting up, and as the room slowly spins, I look around. My eye lands on a poster for the National Sarcasm Society. LIKE WE NEED YOUR SUPPORT, it reads under the logo.

This is not Paolo's room.

It's a room I've been in approximately three times before, the room of Paolo's older-but-not-by-much sister, Veronica. So: I just woke up on the day of my funeral in my best friend's sister's bed. This was never part of my plan.

"Denton . . . Are you awake in there?" Paolo's mom says from just outside the door.

I shoot back down and pull the blanket up over my head. She doesn't seem to care that I'm in her daughter's room, but I'd prefer to hide.

"No, he's still out cold," she says as she walks away.

I shrug the blanket off, noticing a Band-Aid on my right index finger. I have no idea why it's there. I must have hurt my finger.

At least my critical thinking skills are firing on all cylinders.

I need to mobilize. I turn onto my stomach, and my face mashes deep into the pillow, getting a full-on blast of girl smell. The scent—a mysterious amalgam of soap, peaches, and . . . mint?—travels up my nasal passages and slams into my brain.

Wait.

Veronica's face appears in my mind, speaking as she gets within kissing distance: "It's just because I feel bad for you."

I remember. I made out with my best friend's sister in my best friend's sister's bed last night. That's incredibly exciting.

But waitasecond. I have a girlfriend. A girlfriend who is not Veronica.

I lift up the covers and look down at myself. My plaid shirt is unbuttoned. Thankfully, I am still wearing jeans. But pants or not, I have completely betrayed my girlfriend, Taryn. Who I really like. Her face pops into my brain: "You're really cool and great and fun, but I don't think I can do this."

Hold on.

Did my girlfriend dump me last night? I put my hands on my face and joggle my head back and forth, hoping to ease my brain-pain and settle my thoughts into some logical arrangement.

She totally did.

I made out with Veronica and got dumped by Taryn last night. Hopefully not in that order.

My headache pulses. My mouth is sand.

"Don't be *ridiculous*," I hear Paolo's mom say in a sharp tone. "He's just gonna mess this up." Her intensity is sobering, but only for a fleeting second.

Time to go. I roll to the other side of the bed. A rotting-fruit smell collides with my nose, and I vomit. Right on Veronica's pillow.

Oh man. Through throw-up tears, I see an almost-empty bottle of peach schnapps on the carpet near the bed. Gross.

I hear a scary buzz from under the covers, and I spring into action, legs scrambling wildly as I propel myself back against the thin metal columns of Veronica's headboard. Approximately two seconds later, I realize the buzz was my phone, and not some sort of hostile bug.

I am a cool, manly dude.

Hey you awake yet? Paolo has texted.

Yes. You in your room? I text back, wondering if he's writing to me from across the hall. As I wait for a response, I push the vomit-pillow onto the floor, where it lands amongst a tiny village of bags and crates, detritus from Veronica's first year at college. She just got home a few days ago.

Ha no we got school today bro, Paolo texts. *Well you don't haha.*

Right. Of course I don't.

Because my funeral is at 2 p.m. this afternoon.

For the first time since opening my eyes, I don't think about what I'm doing in this room, what happened last night, or when the construction crew in my brain is going to let up.

What I think is: *Tomorrow is the day I'm going to die.*